D0949582

Field of Honor

American Indian Literature and Critical Studies Series
Gerald Vizenor, General Editor

Field of Honor

A Novel

D. L. Birchfield

University of Oklahoma Press : Norman

Also by D. L. Birchfield

The Oklahoma Basic Intelligence Test: New and Collected Elementary, Epistolary, Autobiographical, and Oratorical Choctologies (Greenfield Center, N.Y., 1997)

This book is a work of fiction. Names, characters, places, and incidents are either the product of the author's imagination or are used fictitiously, and any resemblance to actual events, locales, or persons, living or dead, is entirely coincidental.

Library of Congress Cataloging-in-Publication Data

Birchfield, D. L., 1948–
Field of honor : a novel / D.L. Birchfield.
p. cm. — (American Indian literature and critical studies series ; v. 48)
ISBN 0-8061-3608-1 (alk. paper)
1. Choctaw Indians—Fiction. 2. Technology and civilization—Fiction. I. Title. II. Series.

PS3602.I725F54 2004
813'.6—dc22

2003063448

Field of Honor: A Novel is Volume 48 in the American Indian Literature and Critical Studies Series.

The paper in this book meets the guidelines for permanence and durability of the Committee on Production Guidelines for Book Longevity of the Council on Library Resources, Inc. ∞

1 2 3 4 5 6 7 8 9 10

Contents

Part 1. Stockholm Cowardice Syndrome Dysfunction 1

Part 2. The Children of the Sun 95

Part 3. The Secret of Bugaboo Canyon 217

PART 1

Stockholm Cowardice Syndrome Dysfunction

CHAPTER 1

15 October 1976
Valley of the McGee
Ouachita Mountains
Southeastern Oklahoma

The squirrel did not know it was a sentinel. It had no idea it was standing guard for a nearly invisible half-blood Choctaw Indian who knew a thing or two about disappearing in the woods.

All morning long, Lance Corporal Patrick Pushmataha McDaniel had watched the squirrel's every move as it buried acorns in the clearing. The squirrel, much like McDaniel, was an extremely cautious individual. Whenever the squirrel showed alarm, there was always a reason for it. Not even a deer could approach the clearing without the squirrel taking notice.

Already lying dead in the clearing was a big doe that had come up the trail shortly after daylight. She had walked so close to McDaniel that he had decided upon a neck shot. His arrow had severed her spinal cord, dropping her instantly.

An hour later a yearling buck had been gingerly sniffing at the dead doe when McDaniel's arrow flew completely through his body, piercing the lungs. The buck had wheeled and run away, but McDaniel knew he would find him lying dead no more than a few hundred yards away.

He'd get one or two more, then work like the dickens making jerky, butchering and cutting and salting and hanging the strips in the sun to cure. Then, once again, as so often for more than a decade, he'd not have to worry about food for quite some time.

He had very little need of money. For what little he did need, he traded finely tanned deer hides to an old moonshiner named Zeb Calloway, who lived downriver at the jumping-off point to the McGee Creek wilderness.

The Valley of the McGee was a nearly forgotten place in 1976, much as McDaniel was a nearly forgotten man. No roads penetrated the rugged, isolated valley, except a few old logging roads dating from the Great Depression, long ago abandoned and overgrown with vegetation, leaving hardly more than a trace of them anywhere. Only someone very good at reading the woods, someone like McDaniel, would even know the roads had been there. Eventually, the pristine valley would not be able to escape its fate of being the perfect place for a lake. Today nearly all of it is buried beneath McGee Creek Reservoir.

But in 1976 it was still a place where Lance Corporal McDaniel could nourish his hope that he might be able to redeem himself. That hope had grown dim down through the years, but McDaniel still clung to it.

Patrick Pushmataha McDaniel did not look like a lance corporal in the United States Marine Corps. For that matter, he did not look much like a Marine Corps deserter, or a man who had spent the last eleven and one-half years waiting for the Marine Corps to track him down. In fact, he didn't look like a man at all. He looked remarkably like a young, green bush.

From head to toe he was perfectly camouflaged. His body bristled with leafy twigs and dense foliage, sprouting out from his legs and hips and shoulders, completely breaking up his silhouette.

Beneath the foliage, his shirt and pants were United States Army camouflage combat fatigues, taken in a burglary of the National Guard Armory in Atoka, along with his camouflage combat hat. He had stolen his United States Navy camouflage combat boots from the Naval Ammunition Depot in McAlester. His hands and face were smeared with green and brown streaks of camouflage cream, but he could no longer remember which burglary had produced it.

He held a camouflage compound bow in his left hand, with an arrow nocked lightly on the string. A small backpack made of camouflage cloth held the few things he would ever need in the woods.

He stood in the shadow of a tall boulder. To even the most careful, practiced eye, he was just one of a number of bushes at the foot of a steep, brushy hillside that had been swept by fire and now supported seedlings not even waist-high, a relatively open spot among the pine-studded, rocky ridges. Not even the squirrel knew he was there.

Down through the years, McDaniel had become the most cautious, suspicious, alert, most invisible living thing in the McGee Valley. He was its sole human inhabitant. He made very few mistakes. On this October morning, however, he made a big one.

Out of the corner of his eye, McDaniel saw the flash of a bluejay as it came soaring into the clearing. The bluejay glided along silently, skimming across the ground, on a collision course with the squirrel.

The squirrel pretended not to notice. An instant before impact, it turned and charged the bird. With effortless ease, the bluejay dodged to one side. It swooped up to a low branch on a nearby oak tree and began scolding the squirrel unmercifully.

The squirrel ignored it. Not to be ignored, the bluejay practiced divebombing the squirrel, forcing it to interrupt its work. The first several times the bird attacked it, the squirrel reacted violently, once jumping high in the air to swat at it. Then it ignored the bird entirely.

Finally the bird swept over close enough to take a nip out of the fur on the squirrel's backside.

The squirrel screamed its outrage and set up a constant spitting fuss at the bluejay. McDaniel expected the squirrel to give up and leave, and be pestered and taunted all the way to its den tree, a stout old storm-damaged sycamore down in the hardwood river bottom. But it was the bluejay that suddenly darted away through the underbrush.

The squirrel didn't question its good fortune. It went back to digging. McDaniel, however, went on full alert.

He couldn't see anything out of the ordinary. But, after a moment or two, it was what he wasn't hearing that began to bother him.

Before the bluejay showed up, there had been a chorus of background noise all around him, the intermittent territorial talk of half a dozen different species of birds, the cry of a passing crow, the scampering of small things through the leaves—the kind of sounds that normally did not penetrate his consciousness. But it was now so quiet he could not hear the buzzing of a single insect.

He had a sudden desire to be somewhere else, maybe down by the shoals below the mouth of Crooked Creek, where the McGee River emptied out from one of its deep holes of water into a babbling, rocky run of sparkling mountain water, or maybe up among the windswept pines on the big ridge overlooking the upper valley, where he could see the twisting belt of hardwoods down by the river, still bursting with autumn leaves turning gold and red and purple, and a sparkle of river visible here and there as the McGee snaked away into the distance.

The squirrel suddenly stopped digging. It stood upright on its hind legs, twitching its ears nervously.

Beyond the squirrel, McDaniel saw a flicker of movement in the underbrush, enough to tell him that a deer was coming up the trail.

But the squirrel didn't look in the direction of the deer. It turned and looked directly at McDaniel.

Its ears stopped twitching. It lowered its head almost imperceptibly and froze in the unmistakable posture of a wild thing fearful for its life.

The deer stopped, too, beside a charred stump, just a few feet short of stepping into the clearing, its body only half-hidden by the underbrush.

The squirrel suddenly panicked, scrambling madly up a nearby oak tree. Within a few moments it had jumped from the branches of one tree to another until it was out of sight. The deer snorted and stamped the ground with a hoof.

It was then that a sudden breeze kicked up the leaves at McDaniel's feet and carried to his ears the distorted throbs of a distant, barely perceptible, machine-made sound.

McDaniel's eyes narrowed down. He forgot the deer, the clearing, everything but that faintly reminiscent, low-pitched, throbbing sound, almost, but not quite, like the distant sound of some farmer's wood-cutting chain saw. His brow wrinkled and he frowned as he strained to make out the muffled, staccato rhythm.

The sound seemed to hang in the air. It seemed to be coming from everywhere at once. As it grew louder and louder, McDaniel's heart rate shot upward.

The deer at the edge of the clearing bolted off through the underbrush.

McDaniel neither saw it nor heard it. He was straining every muscle, frantically trying to get a bearing on the sound, his nerves tensing with an anxiety he had not known for many years, when a low-flying helicopter suddenly burst over the top of the hill behind him, and, with a tremendous thundering roar, plunged straight at him.

McDaniel was so startled he dove headlong and face-first into the clearing.

The chopper thundered overhead, barely clearing the top of the boulder, kicking up a wild storm of dust. It banked sharply and began to climb.

McDaniel lay sprawled in the clearing. As the dust cleared away he looked for the chopper, but it was gone.

He had just about decided to pick himself up off the ground when a low-flying jet fighter plane came shrieking overhead, barely above the treetops, bursting out of nowhere so suddenly, and then so suddenly gone, that only the frightful sound marked its passing.

McDaniel struggled to his feet, searching the sky for the jet, for the chopper, but they were gone. He had hit the ground hard enough to tear loose his camouflage outfit, leaving him looking like a new species of droopy bush. He tore away the remaining branches and twigs.

He searched the sky again, growing more nervous by the second, trying to figure out if they could have spotted him from the air. He didn't think so, but if they'd seen him it would make a big difference in what he would have to do next. He could hardly think straight. He was nearly paralyzed with uncertainty at the thought that the

Marine Corps might finally have tracked him down. He wished he had gotten a better look at the chopper. He wanted desperately to believe that after all those years they had finally come to try to kill him, but he didn't dare allow himself to believe that his day of glory had dawned at last. There had been just too many frustrating years of waiting.

Quickly, he picked up his bow, but the arrow was no longer nocked on the string. He was looking for it frantically when, for the briefest moment, he thought a wasp or a bee was trying to fly into his right ear. He would have flinched and swatted the air, if there had been time to flinch, if the vicious buzzing had not been followed in a split instant by the deep booming of a high-powered rifle.

For the second time in as many minutes, McDaniel dove head-first into the dirt.

As he hit the ground, a second shot rang out. The bullet grazed the skin on the back of his neck. It touched only skin, not even drawing blood, but at three thousand feet per second the impact sent shock waves through his spine.

On the ground he rose to his hands and knees but got no farther. His body began jerking with involuntary spasms so violent he feared he was going into a convulsion.

A bullet slammed into the ground near his right hand. Another bullet kicked dirt into his face. In rapid succession, bullet after bullet tore up the ground all around him.

McDaniel could not make his body move. He could not stop the spasms, the nausea, the certain knowledge that he was about to pass out. He dropped to his elbows and clamped his hands to his head, trying to stop the shaking.

He tasted blood—warm, salty, sticky. His blood.

Out of nowhere a thought flooded his mind. Because it explained to him why he was now going to die, it got his full attention.

He had misread the bluejay and the squirrel and the deer. He would die in one of the next few moments because he, a Choctaw Indian, had misread the woods.

Three living creatures had screamed at him that something was wrong directly behind him, within their field of vision. They had been his eyes, and they had seen, but he had failed to see.

McDaniel didn't need anyone now to tell him what he had failed to see. It sounded like at least half a platoon from some crack rifle company, at last avenging the shame and degradation he had brought upon the Corps, and all because he had misread the woods.

He could imagine the glee on their faces and their utter contempt for how easily they had walked right up on him. Deep in his heart, he had always known that when the Corps finally tracked him down they would hit him hard. But he had never dreamed they would take him by surprise. In that moment, McDaniel saw the full depth of his failure, that there was nothing left for him to do but die.

But he would not die like a dog on his hands and knees in full view of United States Marines.

With all the will power he could muster, he hurled his body sideways, rolling over and over as bullet after bullet chased him across the ground, the last two slamming into the side of the boulder, sending a shower of fragments into the air.

Behind the boulder, McDaniel staggered to his feet and fell against the rock. His knees trembled. He felt the nausea welling up again. With his eyes closed and his mouth open, he leaned against the rock, breathing hard, until his head began to clear.

Without knowing why, he looked at his left hand. It was covered with blood. He turned it palm up and blood spurted everywhere.

Good God! An artery!

He jerked off his hat and tried wrapping it around his wrist. Blood poured around the hat in a bright red stream.

He threw down the hat and clamped his wrist against his stomach. He bent over nearly double, trying to stem the flow. He felt blood running down his legs.

Furiously, he grabbed for his handkerchief and tried wrapping it around his wrist. That wasn't right. He unwound the handkerchief and tried tying it into a tourniquet around his left biceps. All that did was get blood spurted all over his face. He threw down the handkerchief and got out his pocket knife and fumbled with the blade.

He forced himself to calm down.

He took a deep breath. He wanted desperately to look around the boulder to see where they were now and what they were doing. But it wouldn't make a whole lot of difference if he bled to death.

He got the blade open and cut away the left sleeve of his camouflage shirt at the shoulder. By holding one end of the sleeve with his teeth, he managed to tie a tourniquet on the biceps.

The blood stopped spurting.

He picked up his handkerchief and started to wrap it around his wrist, but stopped when he saw the wound. It was a deep slash. He stared at it for a moment, then looked at the ground in front of the boulder.

A big puddle of blood marked the spot where he'd hit the dirt. At the edge of the puddle he saw the razor-sharp blade of his broadhead arrow.

He finished wrapping the handkerchief around his wrist, eased up to the edge of the boulder, listened for a moment, then looked quickly around it, jerking his head back as bullet after bullet slammed into the edge of the rock.

He had gotten a quick glimpse of half a dozen men—not United States Marines, but men dressed in hunting clothes—crouched at the top of the hill. Halfway in between, two men had been heading toward him at a dead run. They all had rifles.

In the very next instant, McDaniel fell victim to a force of nature that was beyond his control, even though it sprang from some deep recess in his central nervous system. It sprang, in fact, from a physiological dysfunction. It could be described as an inability to do anything other than what he did.

If McDaniel had known that he suffered from a rare and extraordinary neurological disorder, then his life undoubtedly would have been greatly different. If he had understood that his central nervous system was hot-wired in such a way as to pre-program him for a particular kind of response to certain kinds of stimuli, then he might have made peace with himself and with the world around him long ago, and he would not have been in his present circumstance, and none of the things that were about to happen to him would have happened.

But McDaniel had no idea that he did indeed have the great misfortune to suffer from a condition that was first described to science in 1917 as "Stockholm Cowardice Syndrome Dysfunction," by a rather blunt and plain-spoken researcher whose choice of terminology for the disability was intended mostly to honor the location of the clinic where it was diagnosed.

A few decades later, a much more thorough and somewhat more sensitive team of researchers in Vienna diagnosed and documented the only other person ever known to suffer from the disability, a condition which those researchers described as "Involuntary Instantaneous Overriding Psychomotor Overdrive Dysfunction."

Whatever the condition should be called, the researchers in Stockholm and Vienna both documented a curious by-product of the dysfunction, that it rendered its sufferers capable, briefly, of nearly superhuman feats of athleticism.

And so it happened that, even though just moments earlier McDaniel had been on the verge of collapsing, when he peeked around the boulder the sudden intake of Stockholm Cowardice Syndrome sensory stimuli triggered his Involuntary Instantaneous Overriding Psychomotor Overdrive Dysfunction, rotating his body 180 degrees in a lightning-quick hop, while activating the muscles in his legs in conjunction with a massive discharge of adrenaline into his bloodstream, and he shot across the clearing as if he had been spring-loaded and trip-released.

In that instant, setting aside Western medical science for a moment, there might be a hint of revelation to a discerning Choctaw eye that McDaniel might possibly be what Choctaws call—in their fullest and oldest and most reverent sense of the word—*chukfi* (Rabbit), who has become partly known to non-Choctaws as ole Br'er Rabbit, a trickster as old as the ole mighty *misha sipokni* (Mississippi)—with both the ole trickster and the ole river being as Choctaw as Choctaw can be.

No one, least of all the one telling the story, could ever really know something like that. The very nature of that mystery precludes that kind of knowledge. But some things can be known, and they can be told, and one of them is that McDaniel wasn't even aware that the tall boulder was squarely between him and the men on the hillside, screening from their view the streaking blur of his exit. He was well across the clearing and into the brush before he even knew what had happened.

When he hit the brush on the far side of the clearing, he didn't slow down or stop but went rocketing straight through it—until reason finally caught up with him. He remembered the deer run and veered off sharply to his left. Another fifty yards brought him to the trail. He stopped then, to catch his breath and listen.

From back near the boulder he heard a voice, a man's voice, a voice full of Texas: "God almighty! Lookee here, Jimmy Joe. One of us did some good. It looks like somebody stuck a hog!"

And a moment later another voice with that same rich Texas drawl: "Come on, boys! We got him bad wounded. The double-crossin' son of a bitch can't go far!"

The hell he couldn't.

For three hundred yards down the deer run not even Crazy Hop, himself, the ancient Okla Hannali Choctaw messenger, could have matched McDaniel stride for stride.

When he stopped it was only because he tripped over a root and went sprawling on his face down an embankment. He landed in grass and sand beside water. Crooked Creek.

He tried to get up, fell back on his face, and just lay there, breathing hard.

From straight across the creek he heard bushes rattle and swish. McDaniel looked up as a man stepped out of the brush.

The first thing he saw was his weapon. An M-16. He was wearing regulation camouflage combat fatigues, just like McDaniel's, with a breast patch proclaiming U.S. ARMY. But the thing that held McDaniel's eyes was his hat, not a camouflage hat but a beret, a black beret, worn at a rakish angle, held tightly in place by a black chin strap.

The man dropped to one knee, raised his weapon, glanced at the brush all around and said, "Denton! Are you hurt?"

McDaniel just stared at him.

The man scrambled down the embankment and came splashing across the creek. Even at a distance McDaniel recognized the short, barrel-chested, incredibly nimble-footed physique of an Okla Hannali Choctaw.

McDaniel himself was of the Okla Hannali (Sixtown People) tribal division, but not of the classic physique. McDaniel was of medium height, with wiry strength.

The man approaching him was of a type that had made the Okla Hannali the most feared hand-to-hand combatants of all the southern Indians, their weapon of preference being a lightweight war axe. A dozen stout, barrel-chested Okla Hannali, shoulder to shoulder, leading a Choctaw charge, had been a mainstay of Choctaw military prowess for centuries unknown.

And this was Okla Hannali country; it was the portion of present-day southeastern Oklahoma where the Okla Hannali division of the Choctaws relocated after they were forced to move west of the Mississippi River a century and a half ago. It occurred to McDaniel that whoever was responsible for putting this soldier on the ground in this place might know something about what he was doing.

The man knelt beside McDaniel and looked at his wrist. The handkerchief had come off somewhere in the brush, and McDaniel's wrist was a bloody mess.

The man was bristling with AN-PRC UHF, VHF and FM radios, microphones, and antennas. McDaniel could hear what sounded like a whole war taking place from the man's body—air-to-air transmissions, overlaid with air-to-ground transmissions, ground-to-air, ground-to-ground.

He guessed he must be listening to at least half a dozen different radio nets. In all the noise and static he heard pilots asking for vectors, someone calling for a medic, Red Leaders talking to Blue Leaders, Kilo calling Lima, Apple One telling Cherry One there was smoke streaming out of his number two engine—and someone describing a tall pine tree, bent nearly double and tied to the ground with a dozen heavy ropes.

The man reached for his AN-PRC-88 "Handy Talkie." Instantly, the radios fell silent.

"Zebra Two. Contact. On the creek." He said it again and replaced the mike.

McDaniel finally found his voice. "What in the hell is going on?"

For an answer, the man looked quickly up and down the creek. "How many of them did you see?" he asked McDaniel.

"Seven or eight."

"How far behind you?" He was watching the brush McDaniel had just crashed through.

"Pretty close. Couple hundred yards, maybe."

"Can you walk?"

"I think so."

The man reached for his AN-PRC-41. "Kilo Two—Zebra Two. Plan Green." He said it again and replaced the mike.

Without preamble, he grabbed McDaniel's shoulder with one hand, and, with one strong jerk, flipped McDaniel flat on his back on the ground. He placed his right boot between McDaniel's feet and kicked them apart. He laid his weapon across McDaniel's ankles, pressed down on it hard to make sure it wouldn't roll off in the dirt, straddled McDaniel like a horse, sat down on his stomach, and took another look at his wrist.

He pulled out a length of elastic cloth and wrapped it tightly around the wound. Field snaps secured the cloth. He threw away the tourniquet, which McDaniel had tied much too tight. McDaniel's whole arm had turned blue. He extended the injured arm straight out from McDaniel's body, horizontal to the ground, and slapped the underside of the elbow joint with rapid, powerful wrist snaps. In a few moments McDaniel saw his blood veins begin popping up all along his arm. The man pulled out a thin length of rubber tubing and knotted it in a loose tourniquet at the biceps.

He picked up his weapon as a man came splashing up the creek, followed by three others running toward them from up the creek. They all carried M-16s. They all wore camouflage fatigues and black berets.

When they were in close, the man pointed with his weapon and gave half a dozen hand signals.

Without a word the other four men fanned out about ten yards apart and disappeared into the brush in the direction from which McDaniel had come.

McDaniel took a good, close look at the man sitting on top of him. His facial features were blurred by smears of brown and green camouflage face cream, making his solid black hat all the more incongruous, but on his collar, barely visible, were the miniature black chevrons of a sergeant major, combat insignia undetectable by the enemy at a distance. McDaniel's brow wrinkled. A sergeant major commanding a five-man squad?

The sergeant stood up, pulling McDaniel to a sitting position. Suddenly, McDaniel felt dizzy.

Gunfire erupted behind them, first the sharp pinging of M-16s, and then the deep booming of thirty-caliber rifles. It was not far off.

The sergeant helped McDaniel to his feet, but McDaniel's knees buckled. The sergeant supported him as they scrambled across the creek and into the brush away from the gunfire.

The sergeant stopped just inside the foliage and pointed downstream. "The rest of the platoon is on its way up here now. If anything happens to me, try to keep going downstream until you meet them."

McDaniel nodded and they took off downstream. The farther they went, the more he leaned on the sergeant. His knees were weak, he felt nauseous, a sharp pain began digging a hole in his liver. He knew he had lost a lot of blood.

They had gone a few hundred yards when the sergeant suddenly stopped and pulled McDaniel down beside him. He gave a strange whistle. An even stranger whistle answered. The sergeant stood up as men appeared all around them. They were dressed like the sergeant.

One of them came forward and took a mike from the sergeant's back. Cold, calm eyes swept over McDaniel once as the man spoke into the mike. "Fall back, Zebra." He did not repeat it.

The man held the mike and stared upstream, listening to the distant gunfire. On his collar, McDaniel could barely make out the miniature oak cluster of a major.

McDaniel looked around at the other men. The only other officer he could see was a captain. Most of the men were first sergeants or master sergeants. A few were sergeant majors. McDaniel could see no one below the rank of first sergeant.

He looked at the shoulder patch of the nearest man. It read: AIRBORNE RANGERS, 1st Bn. 75th Inf.

One man had a small insignia pinned to the edge of his black beret, just above his right ear. It didn't look like regulation equipment. McDaniel strained to read the writing on it: THE REALLY GOOD GUYS.

From far up the creek a new sound was added to the M-16s and thirty-caliber rifles. Hand grenades. McDaniel counted four hand grenades.

The major grunted his satisfaction and replaced the mike. He waved a hand and a squad of men, two of them carrying M-79 grenade launchers with curious-looking grenades, detached itself and moved off upstream.

McDaniel started to speak, but the major waved him silent. "Everybody quiet till we get out of here."

The major turned on his heel and started downstream. Two men reached down and lifted McDaniel to his feet. They fairly carried him down the hill. The sergeant who had found him on the creek stepped in behind the major and walked in front of McDaniel. Men dropped off on each flank.

Over his shoulder, the major said to the sergeant, "Kelley, if we run into trouble, stay close to Denton, no matter what."

A little farther on, McDaniel heard the major talking softly into the mike in a language he thought he recognized as Vietnamese.

Farther downstream they veered off to the right and plunged through the woods. After awhile they came to a clearing. The old Standridge meadow. By then McDaniel had gotten pretty woozy. They'd gone farther than he thought. There were at least a dozen men in the meadow, folding and stacking parachutes.

As they walked into the meadow, the drone of a helicopter grew louder from the west. It burst over the treetops and sat down in front of them. McDaniel and the sergeant followed the major aboard.

The chopper dropped them down six miles to the west at the old abandoned Katie Lake Lodge. The pilot killed the engine. They got out as a group of men in regular U.S. Army uniforms came out of one of the buildings.

McDaniel turned to the major and said, "Would you please tell me what is going on?"

No response.

McDaniel tried a different tack. "Well, you could at least tell me one thing—who in the hell is Denton?"

The major and the sergeant exchanged quick glances, then turned to McDaniel. There was panic in the major's eyes as a bulldog-faced bird colonel walked up to greet them.

CHAPTER 2

Of all the things vying for Patrick McDaniel's attention—a fifteen-gauge needle delivering a cold, dark mixture of type O plasma, red cells, and saline solution into an arterial vein in his right arm; an Army doctor stitching up the gash in his left wrist; the sergeant and the major standing at rigid attention in the middle of the room; the first lieutenant seated against the far wall; the quiet beauty of a grand old room with a high vaulted ceiling; the plate-glass window view of a lovely five-acre lake, ringed with lily pads and sporting a fresh-lumber swimming platform—of all these things and more, none could compete with Colonel Abbot Fay.

The blood vessels in Colonel Fay's neck bulged nearly to the point of bursting. His face was flushed to a deep, rich crimson, with eyes that snapped and popped as he stormed back and forth across the room in explosive bursts of energy that released just enough tension to keep the man from detonating into a million tiny pieces and leveling not only the lodge but twenty-five acres of surrounding timber as well.

McDaniel lay on a stiff canvas cot, his mouth hanging open, straining to catch every word as the colonel pursued an impassioned and startlingly coherent inquiry into the ancestral lineage and cerebral inheritance of one Major Mark Jameson.

Having begun his genealogical inquiry with a hound in heat—a blind, lice-ridden, diarrhea-plagued, mongrel, toothless bitch infested with every known parasite and suffering through the last dreadful state of a foul-smelling strain of the mange—Colonel Fay had progressed steadily backward through evolutionary and geologic time to a point where only slimy, slippery things inhabited an earth covered entirely by water, leading McDaniel to speculate, in holy wonder, just how far back the colonel intended to go.

For his part, the major had held up remarkably well, the only indication that his entire body had not been fresh-hewn from a block of granite being the irregular twitching of a small nerve on the right side of his neck.

McDaniel might have been more comfortable, might even have been able to relax and enjoy the spectacle, but for an unsettling feeling, a feeling that had begun with the slow realization that Colonel Fay, for all his rage, was nonetheless keeping himself well abreast of the doctor's progress by occasional side glances.

McDaniel could not imagine what had brought the United States Army to the McGee Valley, but of one thing he was now certain—it wasn't him. Hurriedly, he'd told Colonel Fay a story, had given him a name, the best he could come up with on short notice. He had not yet been questioned by the colonel, who had exploded on finding his men had brought a civilian to the lodge.

McDaniel did not want to try to imagine what might happen if they found out who he really was. It would be a hell of an ending for him after all he had been through.

McDaniel wasn't real sure *who* he was anymore. There had been a time when he had known, when he had staked out his place in history, his destiny, but if that McDaniel were to walk into the room and sit down on the edge of the cot beside him, he doubted he would recognize him.

That McDaniel had been worn down by years of frustration, dating from the dark days of his first arrival in the McGee Valley, when he had been in a nearly complete state of physical and mental collapse.

He had nearly died of starvation and nervous exhaustion as a stowaway on one freighter after another, zigzagging his way across the Pacific, until he had finally made it from southeast Asia all the way back to the states.

The odyssey wouldn't have been nearly so hard on him if he had been in good shape at the beginning, instead of physically emaciated and mentally exhausted.

He had expected to be executed shortly after his return to American soil. Within forty-five days of his arrest there would be a court-martial, and then the firing squad, and then his Choctaw relatives would speak his name no more. It was an end he had sought like a salve. It was all that had kept him alive, all the way across the Pacific. Shame had driven him to desert the Corps, a shame so great he had sought his death as a blessed relief.

For an Indian, he had done the unspeakable. He had gotten lost in the woods. He didn't know how it had happened. He didn't even remember it happening. But it happened. He, Patrick Pushmataha McDaniel, a Choctaw, got lost in the woods.

His rifle company had barely landed at Da Nang, in the spring of 1965, when it went out on patrol. McDaniel, being an Indian, was given the point. "Chief," the men had called him. His chest had swelled with pride at the thought of two hundred United States Marines following him.

That was the last thing he remembered. In his next conscious thought he'd been running so far and so fast that he collapsed from exhaustion. He'd heard of people getting lost, getting disoriented, and running until they collapsed, but he never imagined such a thing could happen to him. He'd run so far his clothes were in tatters. Somehow he'd lost his weapon, his pack, his hat. He had no idea where he was, no idea how to get back to his unit, no idea how to explain the loss of his equipment, the condition of his clothes.

At first he tried desperately to find his men. They were depending on him. He was supposed to be out front, looking out for them. The worst thing a Marine could do was let down his buddies.

But he couldn't find them. He couldn't even find Da Nang. Panic drove him forward. For two or three days he climbed trees, he climbed hills, he tried everything he could think of, until he had to admit to himself that he was utterly and hopelessly lost.

Then shame set in. He became acutely aware of his Choctaw military heritage, of how his people, generations ago, under the leadership of his namesake—the great Okla Hannali war chief, Pushmataha—had set their feet firmly on the course that had made them the most loyal military allies the Americans had ever had.

McDaniel couldn't bear to think of what he had done, and of what he had failed to do. Suddenly, he couldn't bear to think about things that had once been a source of great pride, that had given him a feeling, as a Choctaw United States Marine, of being truly special—of how Choctaws had served as scouts in the American Revolution for General Washington, General Morgan, General Sullivan, and General Wayne; of how the Choctaws, under Pushmataha's leadership, had saved hundreds, perhaps thousands, of American lives throughout the South by defeating Tecumseh's vision for bringing all the southern Indians into Tecumseh's pan-Indian military alliance; of how Pushmataha had then led eight hundred Choctaw warriors against Tecumseh's allied Indians, and against the British at the Battle of New Orleans, shedding Choctaw blood on the battlefields in behalf of the Americans, in support of General Andrew Jackson's U. S. Army in the War of 1812; of how Choctaws had been the first Indian code talkers for the Americans in World War I, a service they had performed again in World War II; of how his own father had been a Marine Corps hero in World War II and had died fighting for the Americans in Korea—and now, when his turn had come to show what he could do, he had proven himself unworthy—unworthy of the Marine Corps, unworthy of his own family, unworthy even of his own people.

Suddenly, he didn't want to find his unit anymore. He didn't want to live anymore. He just wanted to go home and die. That was the one thing left that he could do like a man.

But once arrived in the states, to his utter astonishment, in a depth of shame his mind could not deal with, he found that he was now afraid to die, that he was afraid of everything. Somewhere in those dark days something happened to his mind, and whatever it was, it happened in the midst of terror.

He had cringed in holy terror at every sound, at every movement in the woods. He had slept in a different place every night.

Everything he did, every breath of air, every hot meal he ate, when he could mount the courage to build a fire, he savored to the fullest, knowing he might be doing it for the very last time. He knew to a moral certainty that sometime soon the sky would suddenly darken as squadron after squadron of Marine Corps choppers descended upon his refuge to drop an entire battalion of outraged Leathernecks who would come storming across the creeks and canyons in a devil-may-care footrace to claim the honor of stringing his guts from tree to tree from the mouth of Bugaboo Canyon all the way downriver to the mouth of Dog Dead Bayou.

It had been a horrible year, but even though he did everything for the very last time, the choppers never came.

At the end of that first year McDaniel began to take a certain pride in his accomplishment. He knew, of course, that he must surely be an embarrassment to the Corps, and he had no doubt that the Corps eventually would track him down, that no man could long evade the relentless, sleepless quest of the entire Marine Corps to find his hiding place; and yet, surely he had held out longer than any deserter in the history of the Corps.

That sort of thing just didn't happen by accident. Increasingly, McDaniel became more and more convinced that he must be some kind of evil genius.

It was that line of reasoning—the pride in his achievement mixed with the guilt of knowing that with each passing day he became a greater embarrassment to the Corps—that caused him to begin thinking there might yet be a way to redeem himself. After all, if he held out much longer the very reputation of the Marine Corps would be at stake.

Already it would be a thing Marines would be talking about. He started hearing voices, whispers at first, and then louder and louder, until, finally, at the Marine Corps recruit depots he could hear the drill instructors shouting at the raw recruits: "Even though it took the Marine Corps more than a year to track down P. P. McDaniel, the Marine Corps *did* track him down!"

As the second year went by and still the choppers didn't come, McDaniel's pride began to be overshadowed by his guilt. No matter how he looked at it, no matter how he tried to figure out why the choppers didn't come, the cold, hard truth remained—he had held out far too long.

It had reached a point where it would not be enough for the Corps merely to track him down, not two whole years just to track down one lousy deserter. That would be just the sort of thing the bums in the United States Army would love to hear about. The mighty Marine Corps, outsmarted for over two years by a lance corporal!

For weeks he couldn't sleep. He hadn't intended for something like this to happen. As the days went by, his stomach churned with anxiety.

He knew he had to find some way to salvage the reputation of the Corps, some way to justify a quest that should have taken no more than two months but that had already consumed more than two years.

But the only answer, the only way out that he could see, was for him to become something more than an ordinary deserter, something more than an evil genius at the art of hiding in the woods. He would have to become a man worthy of holding the Corps at bay for so long, a man who would make the United States Marine Corps pay a frightful toll in human life to track him down, a man of legend, a man to match the Corps!

It would not be easy. If he were to perform a true service to the Corps, if he were to take an embarrassing situation and turn it into a thing of pride, if he were to become the arch example to raw recruits that the Corps would pay any price, bear any burden, to track down any Marine who spat upon the honor and tradition of the finest fighting force the world had ever known, he knew he would have to bring to the task all the evil cunning he could muster.

But already he could hear them talking. He could hear the drill instructors strike terror into the hearts of raw recruits when they shouted: "Even though the dreaded deserter, P. P. McDaniel, killed half the battalion that finally tracked him down, the Marine Corps *did* track him down!"

McDaniel set to work at a feverish pace. From one end of McGee Valley to the other, he surveyed the most strategic locations for entrenched positions. He knew, of course, that the Marine Corps would overrun even the most heavily entrenched position, just like in World War II, as though it were another Japanese machine-gun nest, so he selected places that offered ingenious methods of escape.

His problem, he understood full well, was that if he were going to kill at least half a battalion he had to lead them from one entrenched position to another. Half a battalion is a lot of men.

With shovel and axe and muscle and sweat, from before daylight until after dark, he constructed one death trap after another. As month after month of increasingly daring visions materialized to transform the Valley of the McGee into a place where he was lord and master, he became increasingly bold.

He burglarized every National Guard armory in southeastern Oklahoma. He soon had a fifty-caliber machine gun mounted in each entrenched position.

Quickly growing bored with burglary, and having encountered needs beyond the capacities of the armories to fill, he hitchhiked to Lawton, coldcocked a military truck driver, stole his clothes, his papers, his truck, and drove right into the big middle of Fort Sill. He soon had more hand grenades, bazookas, flame throwers, and explosives than he knew what to do with.

Of all the feats of military engineering he accomplished with the explosives, he was most proud of the precise calculations required to booby trap the south slope of Chimney Ridge. It was a difficult problem, the major complication being that his machine gun nest was situated directly beneath the towering mass of rock.

For weeks he studied the fissures in the rock, plotting the course of each crack, expostulating the lines of continuation, estimating the tonnage of each block. He used sixteen-inch stick powder with electrically timed, battery-powered, multicolored detonating wire, with each blast timed to follow one upon the other, removing first a block here, and then a block there, until the entire chimney should be cut in half, leaving the last series of detonations to topple the twin spires on a charging Marine Corps rifle company and miss his machine-gun nest, on either side, by a matter of inches. When he had finished, he wished he had some way to test his calculations, but the nature of the thing precluded any kind of test.

Some of his entrenched positions he learned to escape by rappelling down the faces of sheer cliffs. At others, he learned how to float underwater while breathing through a reed. At some, he devised ingenious human catapults constructed of bent green pine trees. He gathered flour sacks and sewed parachutes and placed them near the straining living energy of the flesh of the bent trees.

His crowning achievement was to have been the installation of a 210 mm Naval cannon overlooking the upper valley. He discovered it one night in a warehouse while prowling through the back areas of the McAlester Naval Ammunition Depot. The papers in the box told him that it was an experimental prototype of which only three had ever been manufactured, a thing no one would ever miss. The sheer size of the cannon, weighing several tons, was a challenge. Though it occupied him for nearly a year, he did manage to completely disassemble the cannon, right down to its tiniest component part, and to pack it piece-by-piece to its emplacement position, the barrel section requiring the use of the warehouse crane and a flatbed tractor-trailer truck stolen from the depot and a clever travois pulled by thirty mules, the mules stolen painstakingly, one or two at a time, from farms as far away as Arkansas and Missouri, with the travois leaving a trail through the woods that took him a month to eradicate. But once he had poured the concrete for the emplacement, and mounted the reassembled cannon, he discovered he had a bucket filled with thirty-seven leftover parts. Again and again he tore apart and reassembled the inner workings of that cannon, but every time he ended up with that bucket of leftover parts until, finally, he gave up.

Undaunted by his one failure, he sweated and planned and plotted. For fourteen, sixteen, sometimes eighteen hours a day he worked at a feverish pace. He managed, finally, by the most ingenious series of sympathetic fulcrums and counterweights and levers and pulleys, to bend a ninety-foot pine tree that he was confident could catapult him all the way into Pushmataha County.

But even though the months rolled by, and he faithfully slept in a different place each night and did everything he did for the very last time, the choppers never came.

McDaniel wondered very little about this, especially after visiting Zeb Calloway one day and overhearing on the radio that there was a war going on somewhere. He couldn't make much sense of what he was hearing and didn't catch who we were fighting this time. It mattered very little. The Marine Corps was always being sent in somewhere. He knew it couldn't still be Vietnam, as little more than a couple months would have been required for the Corps to mop up that ragtag bunch of pajama-clad peasants, but whoever it was had stirred the nation to the heights of patriotism, that much he learned from hearing a report of a student riot. The students, he gathered, were fighting with one another to be first in line to enlist.

Another whole year went by before McDaniel began to grow weary of building entrenched positions and doing everything he did for the very last time. Once, he grew careless and slept in the same place two nights in a row. After that he gave himself a talking to. He asked himself what good would he be to the Corps if they caught him napping? How could he possibly risk the reputation that for two hundred years Marines had unhesitatingly stepped forth to uphold? After his little talk, he felt better, but he began to wonder why it was taking so long.

Gradually, his curiosity turned to concern. He began to wonder if maybe something might be wrong at Headquarters Marine Corps. Finally, he broke down and wrote his first letter to the commandant. He asked the man, pointblank, why it was taking more than five years to track down one lousy deserter?

He didn't dare sign the letter. And after he had written it, he didn't have any idea how to go about mailing it. He couldn't just drop it in a local mailbox. It would be too easy to trace the postmark. It just wouldn't look very good if people found out that the Corps hadn't been able to track him down without his help.

Finally, he walked down to Highway 3 and flagged down seven truckers until he found one bound for Los Angeles. For a pint of Zeb Calloway's moonshine whiskey, the trucker agreed to carry the letter to Los Angeles and drop it in a mailbox. McDaniel carefully explained that, for the trucker's own protection, he'd better not leave any fingerprints on the envelope.

After he mailed the letter, McDaniel still had a nagging feeling that something was wrong. He regretted that he hadn't signed it. A man of his position should taunt the enemy, laugh at them, dare them to come and get him. But still, he couldn't find much fault in his own actions.

Then one morning McDaniel had a frightening thought. Maybe there had been another deserter and the Corps had already tracked him down and was this very minute holding him up as their arch example to raw recruits. The thought troubled McDaniel. It might explain why he had remained free for so long. If the Corps already had an arch example maybe they didn't have any use for him at all. Maybe he was just too embarrassing. Maybe the Corps had changed commandants and some of the big shots at Headquarters Marine Corps had decided P. P. McDaniel was something the new commandant shouldn't know anything about.

Then a terrible thought struck McDaniel. "My God! Maybe the Marine Corps isn't even *trying* to track me down!"

For days and nights he couldn't sleep. He had to find some way to reassure himself that the Corps hadn't gone soft, that it just wasn't possible to compromise honor and tradition. Finally, he hit upon a bold plan, an elaborate scheme. It would require the cooperation of an old childhood friend who now lived in western Colorado, but he was certain the plan would work.

This time he wrote two letters and addressed two envelopes, placing one inside the other. The inside envelope he addressed to the Commandant, Headquarters Marine Corps, Eighth and I, Washington, D.C. The note was short and to the point. It read: "I'm alive and well and waiting right here in the good old U. S. of A. Come and get me, you gutless bastards!" He signed it, "Patrick P. McDaniel, Lance Corporal, USMC, c/o Billy's Gas 'em Up, Whitewater, Colorado."

The outside envelope he addressed to Billy. It had no return address. The only clue Billy would have as to his whereabouts would be the bogus postmark, and that was the evil genius of McDaniel's scheme, as the Corps, and Billy, would soon discover. A brief note asked good old Billy to drop the inside envelope in his local mailbox.

Again, McDaniel walked down to Highway 3 and flagged down truckers until he found one bound for Los Angeles. Another pint of Zeb's moonshine whiskey did the trick. He settled back to wait.

That night, and each night for about two weeks, McDaniel had trouble sleeping. Every time he dropped off to sleep he was awakened by poor old Billy's hideous screams.

McDaniel would wake up in a feverish sweat with a vivid picture still fresh in his mind: poor old Billy, his body strapped to the rack, with one hulking gunnery sergeant twisting a thumb screw while another one carved his body to shreds with a bayonet. But good old Billy, he always hung in there to the very last minute, taunting his tormentors, laughing in the face of death until, with his dying breath, he gasped, "Los Angeles."

So vivid were the dreams that McDaniel had to get up and go for long walks on the moonlit trails. But no matter how far he walked, nothing could overcome the depression of knowing that, in the end, even his old childhood buddy would betray him.

He knew the Corps would somehow make it all look like an accident, maybe a car wreck or a fire. But McDaniel would know the truth. By killing Billy, they would have tipped their hand, and all they would have learned for their trouble would be a phony postmark.

He figured, in a couple of months, he'd hitchhike somewhere far away to a pay phone and call Billy's mom to express his condolences. The thought of poor old Billy's grief-stricken mom gave McDaniel a new-found resolve. He vowed that his friend should not have died in vain.

Nearly a month went by, and then one day McDaniel was practicing rappelling down the face of the cliff at the mouth of Wildcat Canyon. When he got to the bottom of the rope, Sheriff Grady, sitting on a horse, was waiting for him.

"McDaniel," the sheriff let fly with a long brown stream of tobacco juice that splattered against the canyon wall, "I wish you goddamn Indians would figure out why everybody else in the whole damn county has a mailbox in front of their house."

"Huh?" said McDaniel.

"Here." The sheriff threw a package at him. "This is the last time I'm gonna saddle a horse and ride all the way up here just because some jackass thinks I took you to raise."

With that, Sheriff Grady wheeled his horse and started back down the trail.

CHAPTER 3

McDaniel looked at the package. It was addressed to him, in care of Sheriff's Office, Atoka County, Oklahoma. He tore it open.

Inside were two items. The first was a note from Billy. It read: "Injun, this looks important, so I thought I'd better send it to you."

The second item was a bulky envelope with a return address from Headquarters Marine Corps.

It took McDaniel a long time to work his way past the other part of the address. It was the first word that hung him up: "Major Patrick P. McDaniel, USMC, % Billy's Gas 'em Up, Whitewater, Colorado."

For a long time he stared at his own name, his mind completely blank. And then he began to wonder, first of all, if there could possibly be another Patrick P. McDaniel in the United States Marine Corps, and secondly, what the hell the man was doing taking his mail at Billy's Gas 'em Up.

Finally, he tore open the envelope, and a piece of paper fluttered to the ground. He reached down to pick it up but froze when he saw what it was.

It was a government check drawn on the United States Treasury. It was made out to Patrick P. McDaniel, and the amount was $327,464.35.

McDaniel nearly fainted.

Quickly, he dumped out the rest of the contents of the envelope. Among the materials he found a personal letter from the commandant of the Marine Corps. The very first sentence addressed itself to the foremost question on McDaniel's mind.

"I suppose you are somewhat surprised to learn that you have been promoted to major." The second sentence, however, threw McDaniel's head into a spin.

"But, since you were awarded a battlefield commission in 1965, and since you have already received two normal promotions in grade to 1st lieutenant and captain during your period of captivity, and, in view of your unprecedented escape from incarceration by the enemy, and, by the powers vested in me by the Congress of the United States, I hereby award you a merit promotion to the rank of major, USMC, effective immediately; furthermore, by the express orders of the Commander In Chief, you are to be compensated for your years of captivity retroactively at the temporary grade of full colonel, USMC, thirty years in grade, plus accrued benefits, bonuses, and perquisites. Welcome back to the Corps, Major! The whole world is waiting to hear your story."

There was more, much more. With a numb brain McDaniel read of an invitation to dinner with the commandant at Eighth and I, of an invitation to dinner with the commander in chief at the White House, of plans for a ticker-tape parade down Madison Avenue in New York City.

There was one delicately-worded paragraph advising him to report to the nearest Naval hospital for immediate psychiatric examination.

Officially, he was ordered to take six months' accrued annual leave and report for active duty, in 180 days, on 3 October 1971, at Marine Corps Barracks, Twentynine Palms, California.

There were two other items: an official notification that his status had been changed from prisoner of war to active duty; and a computer printout sheet of the names and addresses of the 10,431 American citizens who had been wearing copper bracelets with his name engraved upon them. He was advised that a thank-you note to each one would be in order.

McDaniel began unraveling the computer printout sheet, but it was too much for him. His mind was numb. He reread everything, and then he read it all again, trying to make some sense of it. It had to be a mistake. But how could anyone make such a mistake?

He didn't know what to do. He thought of all the years he had wasted building entrenched positions and rappelling down cliffs and floating underwater while breathing through a reed and constructing ingenious human catapults; of all the years of never sleeping in the same place twice, of all the years of doing everything he did for the very last time.

In a blind rage he stomped all the way to Zeb Calloway's. He bought a quart of moonshine whiskey, drank every last drop of it, and for the first time in years slept two nights in the same place.

When he woke up, he knew what he had to do. He spent three days writing the letter.

First, he vented his rage at the stupidity of whoever had messed up his files. Then he set the record straight: he was not only a bona fide deserter, but a battlefield deserter in a theater of war. Not only did he expect to be tracked down, but tracked down pronto.

His greatest fear was that too many people might already have learned about the foul-up. It just wouldn't look very good if too many people found out that the Marine Corps had a deserter it didn't even know about. He promised faithfully never to breathe a word about it to anyone.

Then he got to thinking about that and he scratched out his faithful promise. He told the commandant that if the Corps didn't track him down without delay he'd tell the whole world what idiots they were.

When he finished, he stuffed the letter and the check into an envelope, addressed it to the commandant, and headed for the highway. He'd flagged down three truckers, trying to find one bound for Los Angeles, before he realized what the Corps was up to.

Instantly, he saw all the way through their plan of attack. The beauty and simplicity of it all stunned him.

He sat down beside the highway and reread the letter he had written, marveling at how much concrete information he'd given away. He had even complained about wasting more than five years of his life hiding in McGee Valley!

McDaniel could not believe his own stupidity. But his respect for the Corps was complete. Whoever had thought up this scheme was a military genius.

They had him whichever way he turned. If he did nothing more than report for active duty in six months at Twentynine Palms,

California, they had him. If he checked into a Naval hospital for psychiatric examination, they had him. If he sent thank-you notes to the people they said had worn the copper bracelets, the Corps would end up with thousands of valuable clues about his whereabouts.

Or, if he simply became outraged at the injustice of it all, well, look what he had nearly done. They had gotten to him emotionally, that's what the conniving bastards had done. And in a fit of passion, he'd come within one or two truckers of playing right into their hands.

But the clincher was the government check. Here the bastards had underestimated him. They probably figured the check was their surest bet.

He took it out of the envelope and examined it closely. He couldn't find anything funny about it, but that wasn't necessary. It was for more than a quarter of a million dollars. Anybody who walked into a bank and tried to cash a check for that amount of money would get nowhere until a few phone calls had verified it as good.

And that would be it. As soon as that banker's call came through, the Corps would fly into action. By scattering troops all across the country they could have a battalion anywhere, by choppers, in a matter of minutes.

The simple genius of the scheme was sobering. With genuine humility, McDaniel stood in awe of the elite group of men he was stacked up against. There was no way he could ever win against such men. His eyes misted over, and he knew as he had never known before that it was only a matter of time before they tracked him down.

But they'd have to come up with something better than this. Two could play at this sort of game. If they wanted to match wits, by God, they'd come to the right place!

For days McDaniel wrestled with the problem of how to turn the tables on the Corps. He wanted to come up with a plan that would make them show their hand, that would expose their foolish trick. He wanted to send them a message that it would take more than a clever ruse to track down the most dreaded deserter in the history of the Marine Corps.

The plan he came up with was bold; it was also devilishly clever. If the Corps thought they could find him the easy way, they were in for a big surprise.

To kick things off, he wrote a letter to Billy telling him that from now on he was to forward all of his mail in care of Zeb Calloway, Farris, Oklahoma. Of course, the Corps would have no trouble finding old Zeb, and he would be more than happy to tell them where they could find McDaniel, but first—and here was the linchpin of McDaniel's scheme—they'd have to sober up old Zeb. And if the Corps could do that, without killing him in the process, nobody would ever say they'd found McDaniel the easy way.

Next, McDaniel endorsed his name on the back of the government check. He put it in an envelope and headed off through the woods to Zeb's house.

As he slipped up on Zeb's place he saw a pickup truck parked outside. He eased in through the trees to see who the visitors were. As he got in close he saw two fellas from town, talking and laughing with old Zeb. Each one bought a pint of moonshine whiskey, and they both slipped another couple pints in their hip pockets when Zeb wasn't looking. In a few minutes they were gone.

McDaniel stepped out in the open.

"Mornin' Zeb," he said.

Zeb wheeled around. He put a hand on a big sycamore tree to steady himself, waited until he stopped swaying back and forth, then squinted his eyes and said, "Well, hullo, McDan'l."

McDaniel bought a pint of whiskey and worked around to telling Zeb what he had in mind, that he was having a little problem with his mail delivery and would it be all right if he took his mail at Zeb's for awhile?

"Why hell yes," said Zeb. "No trouble a-tall."

McDaniel handed Zeb the envelope. "Zeb," he said, "It's liable to be a spell between the times I come to get my mail, so I want you to have this little government check I got to pay you for your trouble in looking after the mail for me."

McDaniel nearly had to fight him to get him to take the envelope, but finally Zeb gave in. "You can force me to take it, McDan'l, but by God you can't force me to cash it!"

When McDaniel left, Zeb went back in the house. He was inside about ten minutes, just long enough for McDaniel to touch up his camouflage face cream and climb to the top of a tall, thickly branched tree.

McDaniel barely had time to get comfortable when he saw Zeb Calloway come flying out his backdoor, slapping the screen nearly off its hinges. He ran all the way across the lot to the barn, grabbed a bridle and took off across the pasture trying to catch Miss Becky, his nineteen-year-old mule, stopping every now and then to look at a piece of paper and click his heels in the air.

When he finally got the bridle on Miss Becky, Zeb climbed aboard and coaxed the old mule out of the pasture. By cussing and kicking, he finally got her up to a trot, and off they went, down the road toward Farris.

McDaniel settled in for a good long wait. It was four miles to Farris. From there Zeb would thumb a ride into either Atoka or Antlers. If they didn't nab him at the bank, they'd surely get him before he made it back home. But either way, they'd probably bring him back home for the interrogation. That's what McDaniel wanted to watch.

It was nearly sundown before McDaniel saw the cloud of dust coming down the road. He couldn't tell from the distance, but it looked like a convoy, at least a dozen vehicles. Instinctively, he drew himself down closer to the tree.

CHAPTER 4

It wasn't until the lead car turned up the lane to Zeb's house that McDaniel knew for sure it wasn't a military vehicle. It was a brand-spanking-new Cadillac sedan, and it was pulling the gaudiest-looking horse trailer McDaniel had ever laid eyes on.

Behind it were three or four delivery vans, and behind them, in a wide assortment of battered-up old pickup trucks, were half the Calloways in the county.

When they all pulled to a halt, somebody opened the backdoor of the Cadillac sedan and Zeb Calloway fell out. He was laughing and singing all at once and trying his best not to drop three half gallon bottles of Chevis Regal.

Everyone pitched in and helped unload the delivery vans. Lawn chairs, picnic tables, case after case of liquor, beer, and wine, box after box of groceries, several big wall tents, cots, blankets—McDaniel soon lost track of it all.

They unloaded a big galvanized water trough and filled it up with ice and beer. They built a big bonfire, pitched the tents and started cooking supper. By the time the delivery vans left, several more had arrived, along with half a dozen more truckloads of Calloways. Calloways were still arriving after midnight, when McDaniel finally curled up among the limbs as best he could and fell asleep.

The next morning men from the Rural Electric Co-op came out with backhoes and poles and started running electricity to Zeb's house. The phone company followed right behind them. Electricians arrived and began wiring the house. After that, the familiar glow of Zeb's kerosene lantern disappeared.

Plumbers arrived and began installing an indoor toilet, hot and cold running water, a big septic tank, and half a dozen portable outdoor toilets. Delivery vans brought two big refrigerators, a big freezer, and—McDaniel could hardly believe his eyes—enough air conditioners to cool not only the house, but every tent as well.

It wasn't long before Calloways began arriving from as far away as Arkansas and Tennessee. They tore down Zeb's old barn and outbuildings and used the planks to keep the bonfire going.

And every day, like clockwork, the delivery vans arrived from the liquor stores and the grocery stores. One day a big tractor-trailer pulled in and unloaded a whole truckload of Lazy-Boy reclining chairs.

It was a family reunion the likes of which McDaniel had never seen before. When the men finally tired of pitching horseshoes and holding turkey shoots and sitting around telling stories, they got an earth-tamping machine from town, dug up Zeb's vegetable garden, tamped the earth down hard and flat as a rock, and constructed the finest croquet grounds in the county. They hunted and fished. They strung trotlines up and down the McGee and the Muddy Boggy River, competing to see who could catch the biggest catfish.

The women knitted and cooked and gossiped. Three of them delivered babies in camp. One night two of them got into a cat fight and scratched and clawed and screamed and cussed for a solid hour, while the men gathered round in a big circle laying wagers on the outcome.

Late at night McDaniel would climb down from his tree and sneak around the tents, careful to stay in the shadows away from the bonfire, until he had found himself something to eat. Sometimes he would follow the men down to one of the rivers to watch them run the trotlines. After awhile, he got bored. He took to climbing back up the tree each morning with a bottle of whiskey. He soon lost all track of time.

And then late one morning McDaniel woke up and looked down to find that all the tents were gone. Everybody was gone. The fences were torn down, the outbuildings demolished. Litter was piled hip-high everywhere. He kept a sharp vigil all day long, but not a soul was to be seen.

The next morning the men from the Rural Electric Co-op came out and cut off the electricity. That afternoon a man from the phone company came out and took away the phone. McDaniel noticed that somebody had run into the septic tank, rupturing it, but nobody came out to fix it.

Late that afternoon, just before sundown, McDaniel saw Sheriff Grady's jeep coming down the road. The sheriff and a man in a fancy suit got out and pounded on Zeb's door for a long time. Finally, Sheriff Grady stood on the porch and read a notice about a levy of execution and a court judgment in favor of Harold's Retail Liquor Store in Atoka. He tacked some papers on the door, and then the man in the fancy suit got behind the wheel of Zeb's new Cadillac sedan, and, towing the gaudy-looking horse trailer, they went back down the road.

It was another two days before McDaniel saw any sign of Zeb Calloway, or anyone else for that matter.

Early on the morning of the fourth day, McDaniel was awakened, up in his tree, by the smell of woodsmoke. He looked down to see smoke coming out of the kitchen stovepipe. In the kitchen window he saw the faint glow of Zeb's old kerosene lantern.

About two hours later old Zeb came out the back door, scratching and yawning and rubbing his face. He had the worst set of bloodshot eyes McDaniel had ever seen, set way back in dark smudgy sockets, while the rest of his face was a bright pink cheery glow. He looked as if he had lost fifty pounds.

He fell down twice trying to walk across the lot, and when he got to the place where his barn used to be, he seemed confused. After half an hour of searching, he finally found a bridle and a packsaddle, and after half a morning of hollering and hunting, he finally found Miss Becky.

He brought the old mule to the backdoor of his house and loaded her up with a fifty-pound sack of sugar. Then, walking along in front of her, he led the mule across the pasture and disappeared into the woods toward his still.

McDaniel sat in the tree for a long time, just staring at the place where they'd disappeared into the woods. Finally, he climbed down and walked over to Zeb's house. He went inside and looked around to see if he had gotten any mail.

There was only one item, a letter addressed to Major Patrick P. McDaniel, from Headquarters Marine Corps, which Billy had faithfully forwarded to Zeb Calloway.

McDaniel tore it open. It was a short letter: "You were ordered to report to active duty at Twentynine Palms, California, ten days ago. As of that date you are officially listed as ABSENT WITHOUT LEAVE. Report to your duty station immediately."

McDaniel stared at the letter. AWOL! He looked around the room in stunned disbelief. He felt demoted.

And then the realization hit him. Nobody, not even the United States Marine Corps, would go to all the bother of tracking down somebody who was merely absent without leave.

He set to work immediately, trying to straighten out the mess the Marine Corps had made of his files. He realized he would have to start all over again from scratch. Only after he succeeded in convincing the Corps that there had been some kind of terrible mistake, that he really was a bona fide deserter, only then would the search for him begin in earnest. And after that he'd still have to elude them for a full year to reach the point where his evasion could properly become a thing of legend.

It was too frustrating, too infuriating, to think about all the years he had wasted. For a time, he toyed with the idea of killing the whole goddamn battalion when it tracked him down, threrby forcing the Marine Corps to track him down twice, just to make up for all the lost years. But he had to abandon that idea when he realized it just wouldn't look very good for the Corps if one lousy deserter wiped out a whole battalion.

McDaniel then entered into a hopelessly frustrating, infuriating line of correspondence with Headquarters Marine Corps. The only progress he made after twelve months of nonstop letter writing was that Zeb eventually stopped asking him if he'd gotten any more government checks.

Finally, McDaniel walked down to the highway and hitched a ride with a trucker to Kansas City. There, from a pay phone, he put through a person-to-person call, collect, to the commandant of the Marine Corps.

He talked to five different liaison officers before his call was finally routed to a Major Crenshaw, who said he was some kind of a doctor. Crenshaw proved more than willing to listen to his problem.

When McDaniel had finally finished venting his frustration, Major Crenshaw told him he was pretty sure he could help him. He said there were so many men in the military that a few files were bound to get mixed up now and then and there was no need for McDaniel to be offended just because the Marine Corps had made a mistake. If McDaniel wanted to be listed as a deserter, he was certain something could be done about it, but it really would be a lot simpler for everyone concerned if McDaniel would just check into a Naval hospital for a little rest. And, if McDaniel felt compelled to redeem himself, to repay the Corps, Crenshaw was convinced that some way could be found for him to do so without killing half a battalion of Marines.

McDaniel hung up in disgust. He fired off letters to everyone he could think of—to congressmen, to chambers of commerce, to the House Un-American Activities Committee, to the Daughters of the American Revolution—telling all of them that he had discovered a goddamn Communist at Marine Corps Headquarters.

Somehow, all his efforts seemed in vain. When someone at Eighth and I finally took it upon himself to look into the business of whether McDaniel's status could be changed, the result was a letter reassuring McDaniel that, even though he had been AWOL for quite some time, out of deference to his extraordinary military service he would not be listed as a deserter.

McDaniel read that letter amid tears of frustration. He bombarded Marine Corps Headquarters with letter after letter, until, finally, the Marine Corps responded that, out of deference to his extraordinary military service, and in view of his peculiar circumstances, he was being recommended for a special amnesty that would carry with it an honorable discharge from the United States Marine Corps.

McDaniel read that letter and nearly fainted. He fired off letters to everyone he could think of. He told them that an amnesty, any amnesty, for any United States Marine, was unthinkable. He told them that it would not only undermine the entire structure of Marine Corps discipline, but that it would defeat the very purpose of the Marine Corps—that it might not make much difference for the tank-tracking draftees in the United States Army, but that it made one hell of a difference for United States Marines. He told them "My name is Patrick!" not because of some frivolous whim at his birth but because it honored Patrick Henry—told them that "Give me liberty or give me death!" still rang in his ears as though the words had been spoken only yesterday, that death for some people was sometimes the necessary price so all the people might have liberty, that United States Marines were the ones who knowingly and voluntarily and unhesitatingly stepped forth to be those necessary people, and that every genuine American patriot had to know, deep in his heart, that the only reward for battlefield desertion by a United States Marine had to be a bloody, violent death!

He received two replies to his letters: one, from the John Birch Society, offering him a four-year scholarship to the college of his choice; and the second one, from the White House, reassuring him that the commander-in-chief's position was firm—there would be no amnesties.

After that, McDaniel recovered from his panic that he might soon find himself drummed out of the Corps and settled into a long series of writing unanswered letters to the commandant, pleading with the man, threatening, daring, challenging him to do his duty.

His last remaining hope was that the Marine Corps was engaging in some new kind of psychological warfare, that there was a method at work and a purpose to their actions only time would reveal. Eventually, the frustration took its toll and he stopped bothering to write any letters.

By then, his entrenched positions had, through neglect, fallen into disrepair. He couldn't find the energy to maintain them. Inexorably, the forest reclaimed them. Bushes sprouted up amid the breastworks. Pine seedlings took firm root and shot steadily higher with each passing season. Erosion and the burrowing of animals undermined substantial earthen and log fortifications to a point where floods and rock slides simply carried them away. Machine guns that had once commanded a clear field of fire rusted unseen amid the tangles of bushes and briars and storm-toppled trees and limbs.

McDaniel became a shadowy, wispy presence in the valley, at times a creature of the night, silently padding the moonlit trails—at all times and in all seasons, day or night, nearly invisible, almost a ghost.

He thought about many things, but rarely about himself. He thought about the creatures with whom he shared the valley. He thought about its special places. If it was winter, he might think about the many fine blackberry thickets where, in June, he would pick berries as big as his thumb. If it was spring, he might think about the scattered persimmon trees where, in November, he would gorge himself on the delicate ripe fruit.

His thoughts of the future consisted of such things as imagining that somewhere up on Potapo Creek, along the divide between it and its confluence with the McGee, there was likely a wet place among the pines and boulders, which, with a little digging and shaping, might become a small, clear pool of spring water, and wondering why he hadn't already searched for that place, and when might be a good time to go looking for it.

The one thing he never imagined was that he might find himself captured by the United States Army.

As the blood bag drained into his arm, as the Army doctor stitched up the gash in his wrist, as Colonel Fay stormed back and forth across the room, something nagged at the back of McDaniel's mind, something that had bothered him from the moment he first saw it, something that was not quite right. He found his eyes wandering toward the plate-glass window.

Everyone in the county knew that Katie Lake had long ago become a dumping ground for the most hazardous kinds of toxic chemical waste. No one had been allowed within a half-mile of the old lodge compound for many years.

And yet, there was the lake, lovely in the midday sun, and there was the brand new swimming platform. Maybe it wasn't a swimming platform at all. Who would swim in a cesspool of toxic waste?

As he watched, a dragonfly came buzzing out from the lily pads, flying quite some distance out over the pond. It touched down on the water, flew, touched down again. Suddenly there was a great splash of water where the dragonfly had been, as a largemouth bass weighing at least five pounds exploded into the air, turned a complete somersault, and plunged beneath the surface in another splash that sent a second big ring of ripples chasing after the waves of the first one, both rings growing larger, rushing out in all directions across the pond, not reaching even the nearest edge of the lily pads until long after the bass, and the dragonfly, had disappeared.

CHAPTER 5

McDaniel saw that Colonel Fay had been glancing out the window when the bass went airborne. The colonel immediately looked at McDaniel, noting that he had seen the leaping fish. From across the room their eyes met.

Colonel Fay stopped pacing in front of the major and the sergeant. In the middle of a thoroughly convincing oration on the utter mindlessness of cosmic dust, he broke off and came to stand directly beside McDaniel's cot. Colonel Fay said nothing. He merely stared at the doctor, but if the colonel had been an actor at a screen test, told to exude the very essence of impatience, he would have gotten the part.

It didn't look to McDaniel like the doctor was entirely finished with what he was doing, but he tied off the suture immediately and hastily wrapped a bandage around the wound. The blood bag hadn't entirely finished draining either, but he removed the needle and placed a small bandage over the needle puncture.

McDaniel took a good close look at Colonel Fay and was immediately struck by two things that he had not noticed earlier, probably because of the explosive vitality of the colonel's oratorical rampage. Colonel Fay was an old man, certainly at or beyond retirement age. And there was an unmistakable, advanced degree of exhaustion in his face. McDaniel knew that he was looking at a man who had slept very little for many days, a man now running on raw nerves.

"Sir."

McDaniel and Colonel Fay turned to look at the major. The nerve on the major's neck, McDaniel noticed, was still twitching.

"My men should be back at the meadow by now. If I use the radio I might find something out from them."

Colonel Fay said, "You damn sure better find something out."

The major turned to go, saying, over his shoulder, "Sergeant, come with me."

Sergeant Kelley's expression didn't change, but something in his eyes did.

"You stay here, Kelley," Colonel Fay said. "You found him first. I want you here in case he starts changing his story." Colonel Fay looked into McDaniel's eyes as he spoke. There was something odd about the colonel's eyes, something chilling. McDaniel felt a shiver run up his spine

In one smooth-flowing, graceful motion, the sergeant's posture changed from rigid attention to equally rigid parade rest, his feet spread precisely thirty inches, shoulders square, chest out, stomach in, his right wrist clamped tightly in the grip of his left hand behind his back, eyes gazing into the middle distance.

The major continued out the door, closing it behind him, it seemed to McDaniel, a little too softly. The doctor took a seat along the far wall, beside the first lieutenant, whose attention was entirely engaged with shuffling through papers in several file folders.

"So," Colonel Fay said, "they sneaked up behind you and shot you with an arrow, huh?"

"That's right," McDaniel said. "I guess they thought I was that guy Denton. If your men hadn't come along when they did, I'd likely have bled to death. What's it all about, anyway?"

McDaniel saw Colonel Fay wince on hearing the name Denton, and McDaniel had a delicious feeling of being in possession of knowledge that this bird colonel obviously wished he did not know. McDaniel had never particularly liked bird colonels.

"War games," Colonel Fay said. "A training exercise. These men," the colonel nodded toward Kelley, "are members of the Army's anti-terrorist tactical battalion, the Black Berets. Perhaps you've heard of them."

McDaniel shook his head.

"Do you feel well enough to sit up?" Colonel Fay asked, but he was motioning to the sergeant as he spoke, and before McDaniel could answer, Sergeant Kelley stepped behind his cot and helped him to a sitting position. McDaniel was a few moments realizing that the sergeant was not going to step back into his field of vision. There was just enough reflection in the plate-glass window for McDaniel to see an indistinct, almost ghostlike image of the sergeant, standing once more at parade rest, directly behind his cot.

"Actually," McDaniel said, "it was my arrow. I must have fallen on it when they shot at me, when I thought they were shooting at me."

"I see," Colonel Fay said.

"Were they actually shooting at me?"

"They were playing the part of the terrorists in this exercise," Colonel Fay said.

The colonel, for all his exhaustion, seemed to be running on automatic. He had a detached air about him now that made McDaniel distinctly uncomfortable. The colonel's demeanor had changed when his eyes met McDaniel's, the instant after both had seen the leaping fish. The faint image of the sergeant behind his cot hovered in the window and hovered at the back of McDaniel's mind.

Tell me . . . Mr. Calloway, is it?" Colonel Fay said.

McDaniel nodded, wishing he'd been able to think of a better name.

"Zeb Calloway, did you say?"

McDaniel nodded again. Maybe it wasn't such a bad choice.

"Who is he, Hornbostle?" Colonel Fay said, speaking to the first lieutenant.

The first lieutenant opened a file folder. "He's a moonshiner, Sir, an old hillbilly bachelor, lives alone at coordinates six and three, the nearest human inhabitant to the south end of the zone. His place is pretty isolated, last house on the road, but his moonshine customers account for most of the traffic along the southern periphery of the zone. And he is . . . " Lieutenant Hornbostle looked up from the folder, looked at McDaniel as he spoke, " . . . sixty-five years old, Sir."

Silence fell heavily upon the room as McDaniel sat staring at Lieutenant Hornbostle. As the seconds ticked away, McDaniel could feel Colonel Fay's eyes boring into him.

"That's my uncle Zeb," McDaniel said, glancing up at the colonel. "I'm named after him."

"I see," Colonel Fay said. He looked at Lieutenant Hornbostle.

"Nothing on any nephew," the lieutenant said, shuffling through the papers in the file.

"Nothing at all?" Colonel Fay said.

"Nothing, Sir."

"Tell me, Mr. Calloway," Colonel Fay said, "do you by any chance happen to have a government security clearance?"

McDaniel shook his head.

"Have you ever been in the military?"

McDaniel shook his head again.

"Do you have any identification on you?"

"No."

"Not even a driver's license?"

"I don't drive."

"This is unfortunate," Colonel Fay said, "and I don't quite know what to do about it."

"Do about what?" McDaniel said.

"What to do about you."

"I was just minding my own business," McDaniel said. "This is not the Army. This is Oklahoma. You don't have a right to do anything about me."

"Oh, but I do, " Colonel Fay said. "You see—." He moved closer to McDaniel and squatted down until they were eye to eye. The colonel smiled, but the smile lighted no part of his face and no warmth reached his eyes. McDaniel gazed into the depths of a wintry, steel-grey landscape. "You see, I am God. You had an accident today and you got killed. The Army was at fault, and the Army will be apologetic, and the Army will compensate your heirs. But you died. You're dead right now. Of course, being God, I can bring you back to life, if I choose."

Colonel Fay's eyes held McDaniel's, and the colonel's eyes spoke volumes. For the first time in his life, McDaniel was inches away from a man he knew to be insane.

"Who are you?" Colonel Fay said.

"I told you. I'm Zeb Calloway. I live with my uncle Zeb. Everybody knows Uncle Zeb. He—"

"What do you know about Denton?"

"I don't know anything."

"What does the name mean to you?"

"It's a town in Texas, down by Dallas. And it's what your men called me this morning, so I assumed—"

"Tell me your life history," Colonel Fay said, "quickly."

"I was born in California, then lived here with my grandmother for awhile when I was a little kid, but I was raised mostly in an orphanage out there. I moved back here when our family had a big reunion awhile back, a few years ago, at my uncle Zeb's house. I decided to stay, and since then I've been hunting and—"

"Give me the dates of those events," Colonel Fay said.

"I was born in 1946, dropped out of high school in the tenth grade, worked in California for awhile, then moved here in 1971, been here ever since." It sounded reasonable enough to McDaniel, and it was close to the truth.

"Why do you carry no identification?"

"Well, why does anybody need any ID around here?"

"You know the McGee Valley pretty well, I suppose."

"Just within a mile or two of Uncle Zeb's house."

"You know that area pretty well?"

"Pretty well."

Colonel Fay stood up. He looked at the first lieutenant seated against the wall. He said, "Hornbostle."

McDaniel felt himself relax, felt as though he had been pulled back from the edge of a cliff.

The first lieutenant brought the colonel a file folder. The colonel spent some minutes looking through it. He handed McDaniel an 8 x 10 black and white glossy photograph. He asked, "Have you ever seen anything in the valley like this?"

The photo was a close-up of a metal disk buried in the ground nearly flush with the surface. It reminded McDaniel immediately of the U.S. Geological Survey benchmarks, small metal disks that the USGS survey crews had placed at intervals throughout the valley, indeed, throughout the United States, with the elevation of each particular spot stamped on the disk.

But this disk had no elevation stamped on it, nor did it have any U.S. Geological Survey identification, or warning that it was a violation of law to tamper with it.

There was but a single item stamped into the surface of the disk, a finely etched engraving of a seagull in the last stage of flight, with wings spread wide and feet reaching down, in the final moment before landing.

As a matter of fact, McDaniel had seen a metal disk exactly like the one in the photograph, and he remembered his surprise when he had found it, and the extraordinary circumstances that had led him to its location.

He had been stalking a robin, one with a broken wing, the bird evading him for hours, leading him into, and then deeper and deeper into, a place he never ventured—the eerie, twisting, thicket-clogged, briar-tangled, boggy depths of Bugaboo Canyon, where some freak of nature sent a constant wind moaning through it, and where some combination of a high water table and a shallow bedrock had turned most of the ground into a sucking muck that grabbed at his legs, pulled him down, and did not want to let go.

McDaniel had floundered around, at times waist-deep in the muck, then swimming out of it to better footing, until finally he had caught the robin, trapping it in an almost completely hidden, narrow, twisting box canyon, an offshoot of the main canyon. It was there, at the head of that narrow little box canyon that he had seen the metal disk. The entrance to it had been so narrow and so clogged with brush that he knew he never would have found it, even if he had been looking for it, if the robin had not led him into it.

He had fixed a splint for the robin's wing and kept the bird captive in a small cage made of twigs until its wing seemed to be healed. After turning it loose in the upper valley, he had gone downriver for a long time, not wanting to know what had happened to it.

He handed the photo back to the colonel. He said, "No, I never saw anything like that anywhere. It looks a little like some of the USGS benchmarks, but they don't have anything like that on them, not the ones I've seen anyway."

If Colonel Fay was disappointed, he didn't show it. But McDaniel knew immediately he'd made a mistake when the colonel said, "You've found benchmarks?"

"Well, sure," McDaniel said, "one or two."

"You searched them out? Saw them on a 7 ½-minute quadrangle and then went out looking for them?"

The question gave McDaniel pause. He didn't want to admit to any knowledge of the USGS maps covering the McGee Valley, the most god-awful botched job of mapping he'd ever seen. The quadrangles bore so little relation to the actual terrain that entire canyons feeding into the McGee were missing, and Bugaboo Canyon and Wildcat Canyon were so misrepresented as to be laughable, almost as though the maps had been intentionally distorted—a thought that occurred to McDaniel now for the first time. Bad maps were one reason people stayed out of the valley.

He also didn't want to appear to know any more about the place than he'd already admitted to. Colonel Fay's intense interest told him instinctively that nothing good would come from letting him find out that he knew the valley better than any man alive.

"Well," McDaniel said, "I just sort of found one by accident is all."

"Show me which one," Colonel Fay said.

The colonel motioned to the first lieutenant, who rose immediately and went to a series of wide trays built into the wall, pulled one of them out, and removed a thick stack of 7 ½-minute quadrangles.

The lieutenant spread the maps out on the floor, and long before he had them all arranged McDaniel had seen that these were not the maps the USGS sold, though they looked in all respects exactly like them, except that, from what he could see, these maps were accurate right down to the smallest, most insignificant detail.

McDaniel wished fervently, at that moment, that he were somewhere else. His heart was darkened by the knowledge that he would never again roam wild and free in his beloved valley.

Colonel Fay was staring at him, waiting.

McDaniel pointed to a map in the lower valley, one showing Cat Hollow on Crooked Creek.

"Here, use this," Colonel Fay said. From a tabletop the colonel picked up a long metal pointer, one that telescoped. He extracted it to a length of about two yards and handed it to McDaniel.

McDaniel placed the tip of the pointer on a benchmark, one that he knew for certain was marked by a metal disk on the ground.

The colonel took the pointer from him and walked to the edge of the maps of the upper valley. He placed the tip of the pointer just inside the mouth of Wildcat Canyon, at about the exact spot where someone back in the 1930s had abandoned a dilapidated old logging truck. He said, "Are you sure it wasn't along in here somewhere?"

"It wasn't up there," McDaniel said. "I never get up into that part of the valley."

Colonel Fay extracted another photo from the file folder. "I suppose then you've never seen this."

The photo had obviously been greatly enlarged and was probably only a portion of the original frame. It was a fuzzy, grainy picture of the front end of that old broken-down logging truck, taken from above. A notation at the bottom of the photo read: "SR 71—71,000 ft.—12 December 1967."

"The SR 71 is a high-altitude reconnaissance plane," Colonel Fay said. "It was flying at 71,000 feet when it snapped that picture on the date you see there."

McDaniel was staring at the photo, at a place on the ground near the left front wheel of the truck, where, plainly visible, was a partially crumpled, empty pack of Camel cigarettes that some deer hunter had left there. Though nearly nine years had passed, McDaniel remembered that crumpled cigarette pack and group of hunters who had come in by jeep because they had left litter everywhere.

"I'm surprised you don't remember ever having been there," Colonel Fay said, handing McDaniel another photo.

The picture was nearly identical to the first one, taken a day later, except that in the lower left portion of the photo McDaniel was sitting on the left front wheel of the truck, looking up at the camera, looking directly into the lens. He was wearing a full set of buckskins, a garb he had abandoned after a deer poacher had taken a shot at him.

It had all been back about the time he had stopped hiding in the thickets during the daylight hours and had begun surveying the valley for the best places to build entrenched positions.

McDaniel sat staring at the photo, saying nothing.

"It's funny, isn't it?" Colonel Fay said. "There you are a full four years before you got here, and in the upper valley, where you never go."

A notation at the bottom of the photo gave McDaniel a bit of hope. It read: "Photo reconnaissance discontinued, 20 December 1967."

"Oh, yeah," McDaniel said. "Sure. That must have been that trip I made out here to visit Uncle Zeb. I'd forgotten all about that. I hiked all over the valley that time, but I didn't see any benchmarks anywhere."

He handed the photo back to the colonel, giving him his best "so what" shrug.

If Colonel Fay had any more surprises in the folder, McDaniel was never to learn of them, because a door opened and both men turned their heads toward the sound.

"Sir," said a second lieutenant standing in the doorway, "We found this in his backpack."

Dangling from the man's hand, on the thin little neck chain that had been issued with it, was McDaniel's United States Marine Corps penicillin medical alert tag.

CHAPTER 6

Colonel Fay took the tag and held it in his hand, reading it: "Patrick P. McDaniel, USMC, Penicillin." He glanced at McDaniel.

To the second lieutenant, the colonel said, "Did you talk to the Marine Corps about this?"

"Lieutenant Farnsdall is talking to them now, Sir."

"You tell Farnsdall to let me know the minute he finds out."

Colonel Fay walked to McDaniel as the second lieutenant left the room.

"I suppose you found this somewhere, huh, Calloway?"

"I found it in the woods," McDaniel said. "What is it?"

"Let's see if you know what it is." Colonel Fay turned to the doctor. "Give me a syringe filled with penicillin. Make it a big needle, a horse needle."

Cold sweat popped out on McDaniel's brow.

The needle the doctor pulled out of his bag nearly caused McDaniel to faint. He stood up. He looked at the door, at the plate-glass window, at another door along the far wall.

Colonel Fay said, "Kelley."

Before McDaniel could comprehend what had happened, he was immobilized, locked in the grip of a full nelson.

Colonel Fay grabbed the front of McDaniel's shirt with both hands and ripped it apart. The doctor handed the colonel the syringe.

"I saw a man once," Colonel Fay said, "who was allergic to penicillin. He got a dose of it by mistake at a field hospital. It wasn't pretty." He brought his face close to McDaniel's. "Who are you?"

"I told you who I am," McDaniel said. "I'm Zeb Calloway. I found that thing in the woods. I don't know anything about—"

Colonel Fay plunged the needle into McDaniel's stomach, burying it to the hilt.

McDaniel screamed.

Colonel Fay placed his thumb on the plunger. He said, "Who are you?"

"McDaniel, Patrick P., Lance Corporal, United States Marine Corps."

"When did you join the Marine Corps?"

"1963."

"Why did you lie to me?"

"I got shell-shocked. I have trouble remembering who I am."

"You don't seem to be having any trouble now."

"It comes and goes."

"I'll bet it does. What are you doing here?"

"I live here."

"Where?"

"In the valley."

"Where in the valley?"

"Everywhere. I never leave it."

"Never?"

"Never."

"Not even to visit a girlfriend?"

"I don't have a girlfriend."

"Why not?"

"You already know why not."

"And why is that?"

"I'm allergic to penicillin."

The door opened. A very young second lieutenant stuck his head around the doorframe. He said, "Sir."

Colonel Fay turned his head toward the doorway.

"That medical alert tag was issued to a major in the Marine Corps," said Farnsdall, the second lieutenant.

"A *major*?" Colonel Fay said. "This sniveling idiot says he was a lance corporal."

"He was, Sir, when he landed at Da Nang, 25 March 1965. Extraordinary combat service in 'Nam. Recommended for the CMH, but awarded a battlefield commission instead, one of the few since World War II. Hell of a deal. I talked to a lieutenant whose cousin knew a gunnery sergeant who was there. Rifle company got ambushed from behind. Their first engagement in 'Nam. They were about ready to take off for a treeline up ahead when this guy, who had been on the point, came flying out of the trees like a jackrabbit. Ran right through his own men. Charged the enemy. Nobody could stop him. Utter contempt for the enemy. Didn't even have a weapon. Rallied the whole company. Ran right through the gooks and kept going. Half the company followed him. The gunney said he'd never seen anything like it. Shocked hell out of the gooks, ran right through the middle of their command post, and they shot themselves to pieces trying to hit him, killing the NVA commander and half his staff. The Marines scattered the rest. Turned out the main force was in the treeline where this guy had come from and his charge was all that saved them. But the gooks captured him. Escaped POW, merit promotion for that. Nobody knows how or when he escaped, or how he got back to the states. The White House wanted to use him as a 'Nam hero, for PR, but he told them to go take a flying leap at the moon. It gets a bit complicated after that, but apparently he felt he'd rather be dead than see the sacrifices of his military service desecrated by some Madison Avenue advertising agency. A man of uncompromising principle. He threatened to kill half a battalion of Marines if they didn't call off the ticker tape parade they had planned, and then he went AWOL. He was never court-martialed. Special presidential amnesty and honorable discharge, 23 April 1973. He'd been AWOL for a long time by then. The honorable discharge was by the express orders of the commander in Chief."

Colonel Fay looked at McDaniel with different eyes.

McDaniel held his breath. He didn't know whose records had gotten mixed up with his, and at the moment he didn't care. Later, there would be time to try to adjust to the shock of learning that the mix-up had finally caused him to get drummed out of the Corps, that he had been a civilian for almost three and one-half years. But right now, he could concentrate on nothing but the needle stuck in his stomach and the intense scrutiny the colonel was giving his face.

McDaniel wished fervently that the second lieutenant would say something else, anything, to distract the colonel even more.

"Sir, there's something else," Lieutenant Farnsdall said. "It runs in the family. His father was a Marine. Killed in Korea. Fought in the Philippines in World War II. Heavily decorated. When the war broke out he was captured by the Japanese, but he escaped. Helped organize a guerrilla unit on Luzon made up of Army, Navy, and Marines who had evaded the Japanese. But it consisted mostly of Igorot headhunters. They—"

"God Almighty!" Colonel Fay said. "He was Breakneck McDaniel!"

Lieutenant Farnsdall looked surprised. He said, "That's right, Sir. That's what they called him. He—"

Colonel Fay threw his arms in the air and shouted to the heavens: "He was the only living, breathing bastard who ever scared the shit out of an Igorot! If they didn't shape up, he *gutted* the sons a bitches!" The colonel's face was beaming. "Craziest goddamn Indian that ever lived!"

"You knew him, Sir?" Lieutenant Farnsdall asked.

"Knew him? *Knew* him? He was the best damn first sergeant I ever had!"

Colonel Fay slapped McDaniel on the shoulder so hard that McDaniel nearly passed out when Sergeant Kelley, still applying a full nelson, strained to keep the two of them from toppling over sideways.

And then, suddenly, Colonel Fay was laughing hysterically, uncontrollably. He shouted, "Captured by the Japanese!" and laughed so hard he doubled up and nearly fell over. He shouted "Escaped!" and laughed until tears welled up in his eyes and rolled down his cheeks.

The colonel's men just stared at him.

Finally, McDaniel said, "What's so funny about that?"

"I'll tell you what's so funny about that," Colonel Fay said, struggling to regain his voice. "He was *drunk* when the Japanese invaded! He'd been AWOL for so long he didn't even know there was a war on, until the Japs blew up the Marine Corps brig. *That's* what he escaped from!"

Colonel Fay stood smiling at McDaniel as if he were looking at a long-lost son. And then, as though seeing McDaniel and Sergeant Kelley for the first time, he said, "Kelley, release that man!"

McDaniel found himself standing free. He pulled the needle out of his stomach. He was standing there holding it, not quite knowing what to do with it, when the colonel took it from him, tossed it casually into a far corner, put his arm around McDaniel's shoulders and walked him to the plate-glass window, away from the others, saying, "Major McDaniel, you're a godsend, sent to me in my hour of need."

CHAPTER 7

"You really knew my father?" McDaniel asked.

"Son," Colonel Fay said, "your father was the main reason I became the commander of that guerilla unit." The colonel's face glowed. Years seemed to melt away.

"What was he like?" McDaniel said.

"I'll not lie to you," Colonel Fay said. "He was seriously mentally unbalanced, as cuckoo as they come. A man for that time and place. He didn't think he could get killed, and he made the Igorots believe it. I owe him a lot. There were a lot of officers in that guerilla unit, from every branch of the service. When the war started, they all outranked me. But they kept getting killed, and I kept getting promoted. Your father and I were a team. By the end of the war, we'd made the Japanese regret they'd ever set foot on Luzon. We played a big role in paving the way for MacArthur's return to the Philippines. By the time the war ended, I was the youngest colonel in the United States Army."

"And you're still a colonel?" McDaniel asked.

Some of the glow left the colonel's face. He let out a deep sigh, and he took his arm from around McDaniel's shoulder. Weariness and frustration crept back into his face. He said, "I was given a special job, one that required that the man be a colonel. It was an honor, a position of great trust, and I figured it would last only a few years at the most. I thought it was a stepping stone."

"You were put in charge of this outfit?" McDaniel said.

"God no," Colonel Fay said. "I work at the Pentagon. These men were put under my command only a few days ago, because they're the best we've got. Some of them have worked with me before, like Sergeant Kelley. He used to be on my staff. But these men, they're our nation's premiere defense against terrorists. They're a shadow battalion of the Black Berets."

Colonel Fay paused. He studied McDaniel's face carefully and said, "What I am telling you, you understand, is strictly classified."

McDaniel nodded.

"I shouldn't be telling this to a civilian," Colonel Fay said, gazing into the distance for a moment. "But this is an emergency. I'm only telling you because I think you need to know who you'll be working with, to get some idea of what's at stake. You understand?"

McDaniel nodded again.

"The public," Colonel Fay said, "thinks that our military preparedness against terrorism consists of Black Berets, Airborne Rangers, one unit stationed at Fort Stevens, Washington, and one stationed at Fort Bragg, North Carolina. Hell, they're just kids. Eighteen, nineteen year-olds who spend half their time wading through swamps, climbing mountains, that sort of thing. But foreign intelligence tracks their every move. You see what I'm getting at?"

"They're decoys," McDaniel said.

"That's exactly right. These men are the real Black Berets, handpicked, seasoned veterans, all with combat experience, men who have proven themselves. They stay in the shadows. They're not quite as quick as a nineteen year-old, maybe a half-step slower, but when they get in position, when they get that one split-second chance, they kill without hesitation, with precision. You can't train that and you can't predict it in untested troops. You've got to go with a pro when the chips are down. You keep that in mind. The men you'll be working with are the best there is, bar none. They'll expect a lot from you, too. You just follow right along in your daddy's footsteps, and you'll fit right in, I have no doubt of that."

"Fit right in doing what?" McDaniel said.

"Son, you're going to find this man Denton for me, and it's got to be done quick."

"You mean," McDaniel said, "this is not a training exercise, like you said?"

"It's the real thing. As real as that blood you lost."

"This guy Denton, he's a terrorist?"

"Christ, no! The son of a bitch is a member of my staff. He's a cartographer, in charge of my maps. At least he was, until he took off like a jackrabbit."

"You mean. . . ," McDaniel swallowed hard, "he's a deserter?"

"A goddamn deserter," Colonel Fay said. "Scum of the earth, the kind of bug you step on and squash."

"When you catch him," McDaniel swallowed hard again, "are you going to have him court-martialed or are you going to kill him?"

"Oh," Colonel Fay said, glancing around the room and lowering his voice, "I'm going to kill the son of a bitch all right, make no mistake about that, but first I've got to make him talk. You understand?"

McDaniel nodded.

"To catch him, you're going to look at those maps and tell my men anything about them that you find the least bit funny, anything that the maps don't show, where a man might go to hide, where he couldn't be seen from the air."

And that's what McDaniel did, starting immediately. For hour after hour he pored over one map after another, with aerial photographs at his beck and call. Men streamed in and out of the room, waiting for McDaniel to show the slightest bit of hesitation about some feature of the terrain, and then off one of them would go, to take a chopper with a squad of men to go check it out on the ground. Or a radio call would go out to a unit already in the area, and men would be on the move.

Colonel Fay introduced McDaniel to the men, to the officers and noncommissioned officers of the Black Berets, as "Major McDaniel, retired Marine Corps, from my adjunct staff, who will be in charge of the search." McDaniel found himself in command of an army, an army with an air force. When he casually remarked that he didn't know but what there might be some cuts under the bank of the McGee up around the big dog's-head bend, he also found that he had a navy at his disposal, gunboats airlifted to the scene, with frogmen.

For three solid hours, working at a large map table, McDaniel did not have a single moment when he was not surrounded by anxious faces, when he was not being pressed to look at one map and then another, or to look at aerial photographs. At first he made suggestions about where to look. As time wore on and tension mounted, he found himself telling men where to look. Finally, he was barking commands.

Being in charge, McDaniel at first tried to steer the Army away from his entrenched positions, but they stumbled upon some of them anyway, which excited such a degree of consternation in Colonel Fay that McDaniel gleefully steered the Army to the rest of them, saying he'd not been to those places, just to see the mounting confusion on the colonel's face as the reports came in.

As the afternoon wore on, Colonel Fay's ability to maintain his composure deteriorated visibly. The man seemed shaken that so much had been going on in the valley that he hadn't been aware of.

The men were clearly frightened of the colonel, something that made McDaniel uneasy, but which also gave him an exhilarating feeling of power. It wasn't so bad, bumping into his father's old war buddy, and the fact that the man seemed to be somebody who was dangerous to be around made it a little bit exciting. McDaniel was kept too busy to think about his own situation, to ponder his new status as a civilian, or to wonder what he would now do with his life since the Marine Corps clearly had no further use for him. He had vague feelings of failure about that, but he was also relieved to have that part of his life behind him. He was a free man. He'd get through the day, get this brush with this colonel behind him, and then figure out what to do with himself.

For a time Colonel Fay was at his shoulder, lending the full weight of his impatience to the urgency in the room. Then McDaniel, though concentrating intensely on the maps, noticed that the colonel was gone. A little later the colonel was back again, and after that McDaniel never knew for sure whether the colonel was in the room or whether he had gone to one of the other buildings in the compound, unless McDaniel broke his concentration and looked around the room for the colonel, something the pressing intensity of the search rarely allowed him to do. McDaniel did notice that wherever the colonel went, Sergeant Kelley went with him. After awhile McDaniel forgot about the colonel and the sergeant and concentrated on commanding an army.

Early in the search, when he had been handed one of the maps of Bugaboo Canyon, he had told Colonel Fay that Bugaboo Canyon was one of the places in the valley where he had never been. The colonel immediately ordered the canyon sealed off and surrounded. "We'll deal with it," Colonel Fay said, "when we've eliminated every place else."

Late in the afternoon McDaniel ran out of maps to look at. He'd sent men to look beneath overhanging rock ledges, to search dense thickets along the river bottom, to check out a lot of places where he wasn't sure the map detail portrayed the exact terrain.

Colonel Fay was at McDaniel's side when the last map had been examined. "That leaves only Bugaboo Canyon," Colonel Fay said. "Denton's got to be in there."

The Bugaboo Canyon maps were brought out. The room fell quiet as a dozen men stood around the table staring at them.

The door opened. Lieutenant Farnsdall stood holding a sheet of paper. "I've got one, Sir," Farnsdall said. "They dictated it over the phone, and we typed it up."

"Well, it's about time," Colonel Fay said. "We should have attended to this a long time ago."

Colonel Fay took the paper and turned to McDaniel. He said, "Son, this is strictly a formality, but a necessary one. Since you're a civilian, and it's been necessary for me to confide official government secrets, I'm going to have to ask you to sign this loyalty oath."

"Loyalty oath!" McDaniel said.

"I'm sorry about this," Colonel Fay said. "But it's got to be done." He handed the paper to McDaniel, indicating where he should sign. Someone handed McDaniel an ink pen.

McDaniel composed himself. To show that what he was being asked to do was beneath his contempt, he took the pen and signed his name with an elaborate, exaggerated flourish.

"And right here, too," Colonel Fay said, pointing to another place on the page.

McDaniel signed the paper again.

"And here," Colonel Fay said, pointing to the bottom of the page.

McDaniel signed again.

The colonel took the ink pen and countersigned his name, then he handed the pen to Lieutenant Farnsdall, who witnessed the signings by adding his name to the paper.

Jesus, thought McDaniel, there's a lot of paperwork to these loyalty oaths.

"Now," Colonel Fay said, "raise your right hand and repeat after me. I do solemnly swear."

"I do solemnly swear," McDaniel said, raising his right hand. He repeated each clause after the colonel.

"That I will support and defend the Constitution of the United States of America.

"Against all enemies foreign and domestic.

"That I will bear true faith and allegiance to the same.

"That I take this obligation freely.

"Without any mental reservation or purpose of evasion.

"That I will faithfully discharge.

"The duties of the obligation on which I'm about to enter.

"So help me God."

Colonel Fay stepped close to McDaniel, eye to eye. "So help you God," Colonel Fay said. He held McDaniel's eyes. Time stood still as McDaniel gazed into a lifeless, frozen eternity, so cold that McDaniel's spine began tingling long before the colonel finally stepped away.

Jesus, thought McDaniel, feeling his knees turn to jelly, his pulse accelerate, his breath return with a rush, they take these loyalty oaths bloody damn serious around here.

"Kelley," Colonel Fay said. "Get Private McDaniel outfitted for the assault on Bugaboo Canyon. And stick to him like glue."

McDaniel, contemplating the coldness of winter, wondering how his breath could so suddenly be drawn from his body, was slow to register the colonel's words. But when he did, he exclaimed, "*Private* McDaniel!"

"By the terms of these enlistment papers," Colonel Fay said, "duly signed, sworn and witnessed, a private in the United States Army for a term of four years. In *my* United States Army. And we *shoot* deserters."

CHAPTER 8

Storm clouds were rolling in from the southwest, and very little daylight remained, when McDaniel followed Major Jameson's platoon aboard a large chopper. The wind was picking up, and McDaniel knew it was going to be a wet, cold night. They were airborne almost before they had time to get aboard.

For McDaniel, getting outfitted consisted of being issued a fresh set of camouflage fatigues. Hardly had he buttoned his blouse when someone strapped a parachute on him and someone else stuffed a flashlight in his pocket. That was the complete inventory of his gear. They didn't even give him a cover for his head. Sergeant Kelley told him, "I'm carrying a rain poncho for you, but you'll get it when we're on the ground."

The plan was to jump into the canyon near its head, bypassing the mucky stretch just inside its mouth, but they'd have to hurry to catch the last of the daylight. McDaniel had listened as Colonel Fay planned the assault, noting that the colonel seemed to be as familiar with the canyon as if it were his own backyard.

Every man but McDaniel was heavily armed. McDaniel sat between Sergeant Kelley and a large, unsmiling man who looked as if he could kill a steer with one blow of his enormous hands.

It wasn't long before one of the crew, wearing a headset, yelled, "We're approaching the drop zone!" He and another crewman threw a sliding door back on its track until it locked in place.

The chopper banked and McDaniel saw the big dog's-head bend of the McGee glistening below. Another man wearing a headset approached Major Jameson. Above the roar of the wind and the rotor blades McDaniel could barely hear what the man said.

"Sir, it's too windy for a drop. We're going to set down in the valley."

The major nodded. He stepped to Sergeant Kelley and said, "Packs and weapons. Too much wind."

Sergeant Kelley began passing the word down the line.

The man to McDaniel's left took off his chute. Then he took off his pack. He began rearranging its contents. McDaniel saw hand grenades. The soldier was interrupted by the man to his left, who was having trouble with his chute. He turned his back to McDaniel.

McDaniel looked around. Every man in the chopper had taken off his chute, except Sergeant Kelley and the major. The side door stood wide-open. The sergeant and the major were two long strides away. The chopper was approaching the mouth of Wildcat Canyon, an area of dense thickets along the hardwood river bottom, not far from Bugaboo Canyon.

McDaniel eased his hand into the man's pack. He slipped out a grenade and put it in his pocket. Nobody noticed. He bolted for the door—to everyone's surprise. In three quick steps, and a headlong dive, he was out the door. He heard a man yell, "Hey!"

As soon as he was clear of the chopper he pulled the cord, praying the chute would open. It did.

The wind caught him, threatening to spill the air out of the chute. For a moment he swayed wildly, twisting the shrouds, plummeting as much sideways as downward.

He got one good look at the chopper. Behind it and below it, he saw two parachutes pop open, billow out, and stand silhouetted against the darkening sky.

McDaniel came down through the tops of a tree, accompanied by the sound of branches cracking and popping. He came to rest three feet from the ground.

He hit the release and dropped to earth. He searched the sky. Lightning flashed, but he saw no sign of the parachutes. The chopper was swinging back toward him, but there was no place for it to put down, and in the failing light they would not be able to see him in the brush. It might hover, and the men disembark down a rope, but it didn't matter. He had all the head start he needed.

He knew exactly where he was. Two minutes at a fast trot along the deer runs brought him to the foot of a steep incline. The little hill at the top of the incline was itself nestled at the base of the canyon wall that towered above the entrance to Wildcat Canyon.

McDaniel arrived at the top of the incline badly winded, but immediately he set about checking his old tree. The soldiers had left footprints all around it, but the tree was just the way he had left it, years ago.

Three years it had taken. Three years of returning to the tree twice each week to tighten the levers and pulleys and ropes. More than three hundred times he had nudged it, inch by inch, into its present position, where it stood, bent nearly double, poised to catapult him over Wildcat Canyon, over the divide, out of McGee Valley. But now the timing was going to be tight. It needed to get a little bit darker, or else they might see him.

At the base of the canyon wall, completely hidden by an evergreen tree, was the mouth of a small cave. Here he used the flashlight. He had to get down on all fours to crawl into the cave, but once inside he could stand up. He had no use for any part of the cave except its entrance. There he retrieved a chopping axe, a motorcycle helmet, and his parachute and crawled back out of the cave.

He put on the helmet and strapped on the chute. He walked around the tree one more time, double-checking that everything was in order. It was almost too dark to see. He sat down in the catapult seat, made of laced, interwoven branches.

His greatest fear of miscalculation was in the amount of *G* force he would have to withstand when he chopped through the big thick rope that would release all the other ropes. If the *G* force proved to be too great, he might pass out and be unable to pull the ripcord. He imagined his unconscious body hurtling through the heavens, end over end, to land he knew not where. There was also the slight risk that he might have miscalculated the trajectory of flight, and that he would get splattered against the canyon wall rather than hurled through the heavens just above it. But those were risks he would just have to take.

Seated, ready, he raised the axe high overhead. With a powerful swing, he chopped through the rope.

CHAPTER 9

McDaniel sat for a long time before he fully realized that he had not gone anywhere. He tried shifting his weight. Nothing happened. He bounced up and down. Nothing. He climbed out of the seat. He checked the rope he had chopped through. He checked the other ropes. Finally, he took the axe and chopped away all the ropes.

Denuded of all restraint, the tree stood bent just the way he had left it. He pushed against it. He kicked it. He took off his helmet and parachute and threw them on the ground and cursed it. But the tree would not budge.

"He's up there!"

The voice cut through the gathering darkness and shook McDaniel to the bone. He dropped to the ground. He crawled to the crest of the hill. Dimly, he could make out the shape of a man standing at the foot of the incline.

A second voice broke through the dusk. "You take that side, I'll take this one. If he makes a run for it, shoot the son of a bitch!"

McDaniel clambered down from the crest of the hill. He backed all the way to the evergreen tree, dropped to all fours, and scurried into the cave.

He'd never been beyond the entrance, but now he played the beam of his flashlight into the dark hole that disappeared into deeper darkness. The dust of centuries lay thick on the ground, undisturbed. McDaniel hesitated. He didn't like caves.

The sound of a boot scuffing against rock made his decision for him. He hurried down the tunnel.

After forty or fifty yards it rounded a boulder and doubled back almost to the entrance of the cave. Rocks had dislodged from the wall, leaving a hole about the size of a fist. When he shined his flashlight through the hole he could see the area just inside the entrance, where he had been standing a few moments earlier. Clearly distinct in the dust were his footprints leading off down the tunnel.

Behind him, the cave continued on. McDaniel played his light down it, but he couldn't tell how far it went. He switched off his light and waited.

"McDaniel!" The voice was Sergeant Kelley's. "We know you're in there. Come out with your hands up!"

McDaniel did not say a word.

"This is your last chance!"

McDaniel expected to hear the sound of a grenade being tossed into the cave. It might blow out the rest of the wall between him and the entrance, or cause the roof to cave in, or burst his eardrums.

He sat down on the floor of the cave, put his head in his lap and pressed his hands tightly against his ears. But he kept his eyes open, staring at the darkness.

Minutes passed. Then he saw a brief flicker of light, enough to tell him that someone was inside the cave, playing a flashlight beam all around. He took his hands away from his ears and heard Sergeant Kelley say, "It's all clear, Major."

Cautiously, McDaniel eased himself up to where he could see through the hole. He saw Major Jameson crawl into the cave and stand up beside the sergeant.

Sergeant Kelley played his flashlight beam on McDaniel's tracks, showing where they disappeared down the tunnel.

The major grunted. He played his own flashlight all around the walls of the cave. "A natural cavern," he said. "Definitely not man-made. Any idea where it goes?"

"No, Sir."

"We'll need more than the two of us. God knows how many branches this thing might have or how deep it goes. Get outside where you can use the radio. I want choppers with thermal sensors overhead. Spread 'em out. If he comes out anywhere in this valley, I want them to know it. Down here I want K9 squads and tunnel rats. God knows what we'll run into, but he'll play merry hell getting away from the dogs. Get it organized. We'll find out where this hole leads if we have to go all the way to—"

The major's head suddenly jerked backward. He dropped his flashlight. It lodged between a rock and the wall of the cave, its beam pointing nearly straight up, illuminating the major's face. He began clawing frantically at his throat with both hands. His neck and face began to swell. His eyes began to bulge. And then, after a few moments, his hands dropped limply to his sides.

The major collapsed in a heap on the floor, leaving Sergeant Kelley standing over him, holding a piece of wire with little wooden handles at each end.

It was then that McDaniel realized he had been holding his breath ever since the major dropped his flashlight. His pulse was pounding so loudly in his ears that he was afraid the sergeant could hear it.

The sergeant dropped down to all fours and scurried out of the cave. McDaniel could hear him outside, could hear the crackle and pop of the radio and the sound of rain. He heard snatches of what Kelley said: " . . . pursuing him downriver. Repeat. Downriver."

Several minutes passed before the sergeant crawled back into the cave. He was covered with splatters of rain. Off to the side, he dumped McDaniel's helmet, axe, parachute, and all the pieces of rope. He went back out and came back in with his radio pack and the major's pack and dumped them with the other things. He stood for a long moment looking at McDaniel's tracks in the dust, grim determination on his face.

Then he began to undress, or rather, he dropped his pants and his skivvies. He bent over and extracted a small cylinder from his rectum. Then he stepped out of the light.

Long moments passed. McDaniel heard the sergeant moan. He heard him breathing rapidly, as though in great pain. And then silence.

When he finally stepped back into the light he was fully dressed. He was also blinking his eyes rapidly and groping around with his hands, as though blind. Then he clamped his eyes shut and felt around on the ground for the major's flashlight. When he found it, he switched it off, plunging the cavern into darkness.

Outside, a tremendous clap of thunder shook the night air. Flashes of lightning lit the ground at Sergeant Kelley's feet. The wind howled and moaned and the rain fell in torrents. Then the sergeant opened his eyes.

McDaniel could not keep from gasping. Floating in the darkness were two big green brightly glowing eyes.

The eyes not only glowed, they began emitting a light of their own, a faint green mist. McDaniel stared through the hole, his mouth agape. As he watched, the mist seemed to fill the chamber. But it was a strange light, not really a light at all. It had no brightness to it. It left things in darkness, yet McDaniel could see them. It was something like looking at an X-ray, but not quite, something like looking through a night scope, but not quite like that, either. It was like nothing from this world, like nothing from the planet Earth, and the thought struck McDaniel hard that what he was seeing was something from some other part of the universe.

The green misty illumination emanated from a man shape, but then it didn't. McDaniel rubbed his own eyes, trying to make sense of what he was seeing. He couldn't see the body the eyes were attached to, not the way you see something and know it's there because you *can* see it. But he *could* see the body, only it was a perception different from sight, different from any of the five senses. It wasn't sight that told him the glowing eyes were attached to a body, yet he could *see* the body, could see it by some means other than sight. All he could actually see, besides pitch-black darkness, were two big green glowing eyes. Murdering glowing eyes.

Another thought struck McDaniel hard: God only knows what *it* could see in the dark, or what it could hear, or how many other ways it might have to kill its victims, or what it did with the bodies, or how long it had been pretending to be a sergeant major in the United States Army, or how long the real Sergeant Kelley had been dead, his body serving as the lifeless host for some alien organism. Maybe when it killed a person, that person became like it. Maybe it was only a matter of time before everyone on earth became like it—a Glowing Eyes.

As he watched, the Glowing Eyes tossed away the major's flashlight, as though flashlights were for mere Earthlings. Then it bent down and picked up the major's body and slung it over its shoulder. Bent slightly from the weight, it began following the tracks in the dust.

McDaniel stopped fearing for the survival of his country and the human race and suddenly feared for himself.

Within about a hundred yards, down to the boulder and back, those tracks led straight to him! He switched on his flashlight and took off down the tunnel. He tried to be as quiet as possible, but he tried harder for speed.

The tunnel didn't remain much of a tunnel for long. Soon he was scrambling up an incline, then crawling through a hole barely big enough to squeeze through. It dropped him down into a big cavern. Stalactites and stalagmites gleamed in the beam of his light, but he didn't pause to admire them. He passed through a succession of small caverns, each connected by a passageway. One of the passages was so narrow he could barely squeeze through it.

Now he was being offered choices. Dark holes yawned to the left and right. In each case he chose the route that he thought would leave the least trace of his passing. Most of these choices took him downward, deeper and deeper into the earth.

He crawled through one low passage and came out on top of a huge pile of sand at the head of a large cavern. He slid down the sand. At the bottom, he frowned at the clear trail he had left. It couldn't be helped.

Deeper and deeper he traveled. He stepped around nearly vertical shafts, some that didn't appear to have any bottom. He encountered a few pools of water, but he found ways around them.

Hours passed, and he began to tire, but he didn't dare stop, not even for a few moments' rest. Twice he encountered dead ends. Both times he retraced his steps in a feverish panic. Not long after he had worked his way back from the second dead end, when he was forcing speed to make up for the detour, disaster struck. He dropped the flashlight.

He stopped dead still, listening to the flashlight clatter against the rocks on a fairly steep incline he had been descending. He stared at the place where the light had gone out on its second bounce. For a moment he held the scene in his mind, trying to memorize every detail of the terrain, but it faded quickly.

Never in his life had he known such darkness. A coalbin at midnight could not possibly be as dark. For a long time he did not move. He stood and stared until his mind went numb.

If he could find the flashlight there was a chance that the switch had merely turned off. If he could find the flashlight.

Slowly, deliberately, he eased himself down the incline. When he had gone about as far as he thought the flashlight had fallen, he stopped and began groping around in the dark. When nothing turned up he moved a little farther down and tried again.

He found it on the third try. But the sound of broken glass, washing around inside the cylinder, told him the truth.

He fought against an urge to sit down and stare at the darkness until it was over. But something inside him forced him on.

It wasn't quite as bad as he had feared. He had grown accustomed to the terrain, to the feel of it underfoot. By taking short, cautious steps he worked his way to the bottom of the incline. He knew he was in a fairly large cavern. He'd seen enough of it from the top of the incline to know that it stretched away in front of him for quite some distance.

But when he tried to walk through the cavern, he stumbled and fell. He fell down twice before he decided the best thing to do was not to get up. He stayed on his hands and knees, feeling ahead with his hands. He didn't like putting his hands in front of him, feeling things on the ground that he couldn't see, but he didn't like the thought of stepping into a vertical shaft, either.

His pace was agonizingly slow. He crawled into places he had difficulty getting out of. He crawled into blind alleys and had to backtrack. How long he crawled, he had no idea, but it seemed as if he had been crawling for hours when he gradually realized that he was crawling through a fairly level passage about as wide as a hallway. He could touch the walls on either side. Standing up, he could touch the ceiling.

He decided to try to make some time by walking through the passage, touching one wall to keep his bearings, feeling ahead with one foot before placing his weight on it.

He had proceeded for quite some distance down the passage when, sniffing the air, he smelled gas. He stopped. It was definitely the odor of natural gas. Then he thought he heard, faintly, the sound of running water.

He dropped to his hands and knees and crawled forward. He had gone no more than three or four yards when the floor disappeared beneath his hand. He eased forward to where the floor fell away to nothingness.

Far below, and to the left, he could barely hear running water. He felt around for a pebble, finding one about as big as a golf ball. He dropped it over the edge and listened. Nothing. He felt around for a larger rock. He gathered several rocks, the smallest about as big as his hand, the largest about as big as a basketball. He dropped the smaller rocks over the edge, one at a time, and listened. Nothing. Then he tossed the big rock. He listened hard, counting the seconds as he listened. One thousand one, one thousand two, one thousand three, one thousand four, one thousand five, one thousand six—and then came the sound of a faint ker-splash.

Six seconds of free fall. He was standing on the side of a cliff. He gathered more rocks, throwing them out as far as he could to see if they hit anything anywhere nearby. But they sailed away into nothingness.

He turned to retrace his route back through the passage, but he stopped. In the distance, down the passage, he saw a green misty glow.

CHAPTER 10

There was nowhere to go. McDaniel froze, daring not even to breathe, as the green mist crept closer and closer until two bright green glowing orbs hovered in the darkness, only a few yards from him.

McDaniel inched backward until his feet were on the edge of the cliff. He reached inside his pocket and withdrew the grenade. Behind his back, he withdrew the pin, holding the clasp tightly in his hand. He yelled, "Halt!"

The Glowing Eyes halted. "Son," the Glowing Eyes said. "I've got to talk to you."

"You," McDaniel said, "are an alien invader come to enslave a liberty-loving people! If you want to talk to me, there is one thing you must do."

"What is that?" the Glowing Eyes said.

McDaniel pulled the pin and tossed the grenade lightly toward the Glowing Eyes, saying, "Hold on to that until I get back!" He turned and launched himself feetfirst into the darkness, over the edge of the cliff.

As he plunged downward, he looked up. In the bright orange flash of the explosion, he had a momentary glimpse of the Glowing Eyes, right above him, silhouetted against the flash, hurtling through the air.

An instant after the grenade exploded, the air high above McDaniel leaped alive in a tremendous explosion that lifted him upward and then hurled him sideways.

The next thing he knew, he was underwater, plunging downward. His feet touched bottom with such force that his knees were doubled up all the way to his chin. He pushed off, floating upward, needing desperately to breathe.

He broke the surface only to be faced immediately with a wall of fire so hot he could do nothing but gasp a lungful of sulfurous, pungent air and go back under. He swam underwater away from the fire. But when he came back up, it was still too hot. He swam underwater again, staying under longer, swimming farther. Finally, when he broke the surface, he could stand the heat.

All around him was a solid wall of flames. The water was on fire. He treaded water near the center of a large pool, looking for a way through the flames. There was none.

From high overhead a huge block of rock dislodged itself and came crashing down into the flames at some distance from him. But with the roar of the fire all around him, he could not hear it splash.

He could see that he was in a tremendous cavern. High along one wall he could see a blazing, spewing torch of flame, shooting upward. All along the bottom of the cavern was nothing but blazing, flaming water. He remembered the sound of running water that he had heard from the cliffside. From up there, the sound had been to his left. If water could find its way out of the cavern, maybe that would be a way out of the flames.

He searched the walls of the cliff, finally spotting the dark hole of a cave high up the cliffside. If that was where he had been, he had been hurtled through the air for a great distance when the gas exploded. He reoriented himself, getting his bearings. He figured out which way he needed to go to move toward the sound of the running water.

He swam as close to the wall of flames as he could, until he could not bear the heat any longer. He filled his lungs with air, dived under the flames and swam underwater as far as he could swim. He could see the light of the fire on the surface of the water above him. When he thought he had swum as far as he could, he saw the edge of the fire, and he was able to keep swimming until he was well beyond it.

He broke the surface near a sandbar on the shore, staggered out of the water, and collapsed on the sand.

His clothing was in tatters. He had lost his boots. He could not imagine how on earth his boots had come off, but they were gone. What was left of his pants hung in short strips from his waist. Very little of his blouse remained. His hair was singed, and he had burns here and there all over his body. He felt of his skin. It was coated with a light film that felt like oil. His self-inspection proceeded as far as discovering that his nose was bleeding and that there was blood in his left ear. Then he had to sleep. He couldn't fight it. He lay down and slept.

He had no idea how long he lay unconscious on the sand, but he woke up with a throbbing headache. The fire on the lake had nearly burned itself out, except for a solid wall of flame along the far shore. High on one wall the torch of flames was still spewing out of the rock, and the smell of burning gas was heavy in the air. Smoke was streaming through the air, near the ceiling, moving rapidly, disappearing somewhere in the distance, apparently following a strong air current.

He sat on the sand, staring all around him in awe. The fires had lit the cavern as bright as day.

"McDaniel! Are you all right?"

He jumped to his feet and looked all around.

"Over here!"

Across the lake, through the wall of flame, he saw the creature, now looking for all the world like Sergeant Kelley, standing on the shore, waving his arms. His clothing was as badly tattered as McDaniel's, but he appeared okay. In the bright light of the cavern, the eyes no longer glowed. "Wait right there!" Kelley yelled. "I'm coming over."

McDaniel watched as Kelley dove into the water and disappeared beneath the wall of flames. He watched for a long time, and was beginning to think the sergeant had drowned when he suddenly broke water not twenty yards in front of him.

McDaniel sprinted down the sandbar. Kelley yelled, "Wait!" But McDaniel didn't slow down, look back, or break stride until he came to the end of the sandbar. There he took a quick glance back and saw Kelley coming after him at a dead run.

Where the sandbar ended, the cavern narrowed, and the water plunged down a short steep drop and became a rushing river. The other side of the river was nothing but sheer rock wall, but there was a ledge on McDaniel's side, barely wide enough for walking, about ten yards above the water. The river, and the ledge, disappeared around a sharp bend to the right. The entire surface of the river was on fire.

The ledge was not level, and it was slippery. McDaniel had barely started down it when his feet almost slipped out from under him. He found he could only negotiate the ledge by moving very slowly. When he got to the bend, he looked back. Kelley was standing at the end of the sandbar, watching, frowning, but saying nothing.

McDaniel followed the ledge around the bend, but when he looked down at the river, his heart sank. The cavern, and the river, came to an abrupt end. The river ended in a giant swirling whirlpool. The blazing water simply disappeared in front of a solid wall of rock.

The ledge extended for another ten yards and then it, too, simply disappeared, becoming a sheer rock wall. McDaniel negotiated his way to the end of it, hoping to be able to see some way out from there, but there was nothing.

He stood at the end of the ledge and waited. Before long, Kelley came inching along the ledge, around the bend, and stopped, about ten yards from him. Kelly looked at the flaming whirlpool and looked at McDaniel.

"You're a hard man to catch up with," Kelley said.

"I saw what happened when you caught up with one," McDaniel said.

"I wish you hadn't seen that."

McDaniel just stared at him, marveling at how much the creature looked like a man again. McDaniel stared at his eyes, looking for a hint of anything odd about them, but now in the bright light from the flaming river, they revealed nothing.

"It had to be done," Kelley said. "You'll understand, if you'll come with me."

"I'm not going anywhere," McDaniel said.

"You've got no choice. There's no way out except back down this ledge."

McDaniel just stared at him.

"Here," Kelley said, extending his hand toward McDaniel, "take my hand."

McDaniel watched as Kelley inched his way toward him, until he was within reach.

"Take my hand," Kelley said.

"I'll take it when I'm ready to jump," McDaniel said. "And when I go, you go with me."

Kelley glanced at the water.

"You're mine, now," McDaniel said. "I just want to know where you come from."

Kelley stared at McDaniel. He said, "And if I tell you, will you go back with me, off this ledge?"

"We're going in the water," McDaniel said, "whether you tell me or not."

"Suppose I tell you something that makes you change your mind?"

McDaniel just stared at him.

Kelley let out a sigh. He said, "Just hear me out. I know things about you that you don't even know about yourself."

"Like what?"

"I know that you broke into a Naval ammunition depot and stole a Naval cannon, a big one."

"So what?"

"It was a prototype of an experimental cannon that was never put into production. Only a few test models were ever made. You dismantled it down to its smallest component part, hauled it away, and then reassembled it, didn't you?"

McDaniel said nothing.

"They found it up on that big ridge, heavily camouflaged, but there was something odd about its internal firing mechanism. Do you know what that was?"

"I couldn't get it put back together," McDaniel said. "So what?"

"Oh, no," Kelley said. "You put it back together all right. You just left out a lot of parts. Out of nearly three thousand component parts, you left out thirty-seven of them, left them sitting in a bucket beside that cannon. Do you know what you did? You left out the thirty-seven pieces of that firing mechanism that were not necessary to its operation. They were the *only* pieces of that mechanism not necessary to its operation. We got on the horn to the manufacturer, and their people studied the plans. They even disassembled one just like it in Maryland this afternoon, removed all of those parts that you left out, and fired the damn thing to prove that it would still work. They cannot calculate the level of IQ that it took to do what you did. Mechanical things aren't supposed to have unnecessary parts, and the engineers didn't think it had any. But you didn't have the drawings to work with. You just had to figure it out on your own. Son, they told us that you are some kind of extremely rare genius, something like—what did they call it—an autistic idiot savant."

Of the last three words, "idiot" was the only one McDaniel had ever heard before, and it brought a frown to his face.

"Don't get me wrong," Kelley said. "I'm being as honest with you as I know how to be. The Marine Corps psychiatrists say they had you pegged as a classic textbook paranoiac schizophrenic suffering severe alternating delusions of grandeur and persecution. But now they don't know what to think, with some kind of rare genius thrown into the mix. Their best guess is that someone like you would never be able to survive without medication, that you'd be a danger to yourself, that you'd lack any semblance of common sense and be completely unable to make any practical application of your abilities that wasn't in some way a serious threat to your own life. But what do they know? You've lived for years on your own. That proves them wrong on just about everything—except your being a genius, apparently a very rare kind. Do you hear what I'm telling you, Son?"

McDaniel said nothing.

"The thing is," Kelley said, "they say that your abilities for that kind of thought regarding mechanical relationships are probably nothing compared to your abilities for certain kinds of abstract thought, and for certain kinds of spatial relationships, and God only knows what else. Colonel Fay wants you for his own purposes, but if he gets you, you'll never be free again. There's a much better place for you, one that you never dreamed existed. Thank God you're a Choctaw. You'll fit right in. Come with me and I'll take you there. I'll take you to a world you will never want to leave. It's a place where you belong. It's where I come from."

Kelley extended his hand to McDaniel.

McDaniel grasped it tightly. He eased closer to Kelley until he got both hands on his arm. McDaniel said, "Nice try. But there's one thing you forgot, you murdering glowy-eyed bastard. I'm a United States Marine!"

McDaniel kicked backward with all his might, pulling Kelley with him off the ledge.

CHAPTER 11

The moment McDaniel hit the water he was out of control. The force of the current pulled him apart from Kelley. He barely had time to take a deep breath before the whirlpool sucked him under.

He took an awful beating. He was battered against rocks. He was bounced along the gravel bottom like a basketball. Then the current slowed. His feet touched bottom.

He had to breathe. He pushed off with both feet and struggled toward the surface. He broke water and drew in a great gasping breath, only to crack his skull on the rock overhead and go back under. He tried it again, more cautiously, with his hands held high overhead.

He floated along, touching the rock overhead. The current was slowing more and more. Apparently, the river had widened a lot. He felt one foot touch bottom, then the other one. By pushing against the rock overhead, he found that he could hold his position against the current. He rested there, catching his breath, regaining his strength, staring into the pitch-black darkness.

After awhile he began wading through the water, moving at right angles to the current. Soon he felt the gravel beneath his feet turn to sand. As the water became more shallow, the ceiling became lower and lower. By the time he came out of the water he was on his hands and knees. He found himself on a sandbar.

He crawled around, surveying the terrain, but after groping around for only a few minutes he discovered that the sandbar was only about three yards wide and no more than ten yards long.

He was so cold he was shivering. And he was exhausted. He curled up in the sand, against the rock wall, and fell asleep.

When he awoke, every joint in his body was stiff and every muscle ached. He lay curled in the fetal position, not wanting to move, not wanting to go back into the water, not even wanting to think about it. As he lay there, he slowly became aware that a current of air was hitting him in the face. It seemed to be coming from the rocks.

He felt around on the wall and found a crack where the air was coming from. The crack was no more than an inch wide, down at the base of the rock. He began scooping away the sand.

He worked for a long time, digging a deeper and deeper hole. The farther down he went, the wider the crack became. The crack never did widen enough for him to crawl through it, but finally he hit gravel, and the layer of gravel extended beneath the rock. He began tunneling beneath the rock.

It was slow work. He had to do the digging in two phases, slithering down into the hole and digging out fresh gravel from straight ahead, and then retreating from the hole to lay flat on his stomach on the sandbar, where he could reach down and remove the gravel, one handful at a time.

He had extended the tunnel far enough that he could stretch out in it for his entire length when the roof caved in, burying his head and chest and arms. He had to wriggle backwards to get himself out. But when he cleared away the debris from the cave-in, he found that it had opened up a passage, a shaft that went straight up.

Before leaving the sandbar, he washed himself in the river. He drank as much water as he could hold, saturating himself with it, not knowing how long he might have to go without it.

He began climbing the shaft. It was only about three feet wide, what mountain climbers would call a chimney. He had to brace his back against one wall and press against the other wall with his feet. After about twenty feet it began to slope and narrow. Soon he was crawling on his belly in a nearly horizontal position, barely able to squeeze through. Then suddenly he could stand upright. He had the feeling of being in a large chamber. He shouted, and listened to his voice echo into the distance.

It took him a long time to get out of the cavern. He made so many false starts, turned and twisted so many different ways, that he lost all sense of direction. He knew he would never be able to find his way back to the river.

How long he had crawled and climbed and twisted around in the darkness he had no idea, when the realization slowly dawned on him that he was in a different kind of passageway. For one thing, there was the wind, not a faint whisper against his face, but a steady, gentle breeze; and there was the floor, now fairly level and smooth.

He stood up. He felt around a bit, discovering that he was in a tunnel with walls about three yards apart. By walking beside one wall, touching it with one hand, he found that he could walk along at a normal gait.

He soon came to where another tunnel joined the first. After feeling around a bit, he stood at the juncture, debating which way to go. He decided on the direction he had been going, the direction the breeze was flowing from.

A little farther on, he found himself growing so tired he could hardly take another step. He eased himself down with his back against the wall and soon fell sound asleep.

When he awoke, he did so with a start. It took him a moment to get his bearings, to remember where he was. Then he heard what had awakened him.

"Clop, clop, clop."

He stood up. In the distance, in the direction he had been heading, he saw a light.

"Clop, clop, clop."

The sound, and the light, were getting closer. He eased back down the tunnel, away from the light. But the light kept coming.

When he came to the entrance to the tunnel he had bypassed, he entered it. He moved well up the new tunnel and waited.

"Clop, clop, clop." The light turned into the tunnel.

He tried to stay ahead of the light, but it slowly and steadily gained on him. Finally, he'd had enough. He stood his ground, waiting for the light. It came on so slowly that he had difficulty believing he had not been able to stay ahead of it.

When it was nearly upon him, he was able to make it out. It was an old kerosene lantern suspended on a pole about one yard in front of the most scraggly looking old mule he had ever seen. The mule was pulling a battered two-wheeled cart.

Seated on the driver's seat was an old Indian, a Choctaw from the looks of him, with a withered face and an old floppy felt hat pushed down on his head. Both the old man and the old mule were half asleep.

"Clop, clop, clop." With head down, the mule trudged along.

McDaniel stepped away from the wall, into the middle of the tunnel, directly in front of the old mule. He said, "Howdy!"

The mule's head flew up and his nostrils flared. He snorted. His eyes rolled and his lips quivered. The animal jumped backward and tried to turn around and climb into the cart. The lantern bobbed and shook and went out.

McDaniel stood in the darkness listening as the mule grunted and snorted and kicked at the ground, trying to fight the harness. For the longest time the mule thrashed and kicked and tried to climb into the cart. And then soon after quieting down, the mule would thrash around some more. Finally, the sounds of the creaking and straining slowly died away, leaving only the sound of the old mule's trembling.

McDaniel stood in the dark for a long time, waiting.

Finally, a match flared, and, a moment later a candle appeared. McDaniel could see the old man, in the back of the cart, peering around the mule. The mule was half in the cart and half on the ground, twisted completely around, tangled in the harness.

They stared at one another for several moments. The old man held out what appeared to be a pint bottle. He extended it toward McDaniel.

The old man said, "Hashninak aya tohwikeli?"

"Huh?" McDaniel said.

"Nitak omi," the old man said.

"What?" McDaniel said.

"Nahomi. Oka homi."

McDaniel just stared at him.

"Wishki," the old man said.

"Well," McDaniel said, "don't mind if I do." He eased up beside the cart, on the side away from the mule, and took the bottle. It was moonlight dew for certain. The real thing. It kept kicking and kicking all the way down.

The old man took a big swig himself. He took off his hat and wiped his brow. He grinned a big toothless grin and said something that McDaniel completely failed to comprehend.

The old man climbed down from the cart and helped McDaniel up into it. Then he set about calming down the mule and getting it back in harness. He relit the kerosene lantern, climbed back on the driver's seat, and they proceeded on their way.

The old man didn't have another thing to say, but he shared the bottle, and that was company enough to suit McDaniel.

"Clop, clop, clop." The old mule trudged on down the tunnel. The moonlight dew went straight to McDaniel's head. Soon he was mesmerized by the sound of the mule's hooves slapping against the ground.

Sitting in the gently rocking cart, watching the shadows cast by the lantern, listening to the hooves, McDaniel felt fine as down. He was warm and comfortable. He didn't think a thing about it when the old mule stopped and another man climbed into the cart beside him, and, a little farther on, another and another and another.

Someone produced another bottle and passed it around. They were babbling and chattering in that old Choctaw talk, laughing and drinking, having themselves a time.

Drowsily, McDaniel's mind drifted back to a warm, happy time, bouncing on an old woman's knee, listening to her laugh and hoot and talk that old Choctaw talk, a time so long ago he had not known until now that he could still remember the old woman.

A match flared, breaking McDaniel's reverie. A moment later the man sitting beside McDaniel handed him a large homemade, hand-rolled cigarette.

The man said something when he handed him the cigarette.

"What?" McDaniel asked.

The man repeated whatever it was he had said.

McDaniel just stared at him.

"Oh, I see," said the man, who grinned at his companions. "We have a virgin." There was laughter in the cart.

The man pointed to the cigarette. "Bali-spiced," he said.

McDaniel understood now. It was the brand of the tobacco. He took a long, deep drag.

The man leaned close to McDaniel, and said, "When you smoke Bali-spiced Indonesian Thai, hold on to the side of the cart."

CHAPTER 12

The knuckles of McDaniel's hands were white, so tight was his grip on the side of the cart.

"Cccccc-lllllllopity, c-l-o-p-i-t-y, cccc-l-l-l-l-lop."

The hooves of the old mule echoed down the corridor. Another bottle was being passed around, but McDaniel sat like a statue, his mind whirling as a kaleidoscope of colors formed and reformed in front of his face.

How long the old mule plodded along, he had no idea. His knees felt so light and tingly they hardly seemed to be a part of his body. He felt surely he must be lighter than air, that if he released his grip he would simply float away.

Absent-mindedly, he noticed that the tunnel was now dimly lighted. He saw that a horsedrawn wagon was traveling along behind them, it too filled with giggling, laughing voices. And behind it he saw another wagon, and another. He began seeing pedestrians, in groups of two and three and four, all walking along the corridor in the same direction he was traveling.

He heard someone say, "We don't have a prayer of winning this game." Someone else replied, "Yeah, but our defense is so good, they might not score, either."

Up ahead, he saw another wagon pull into the corridor and travel along in front of them. And then they rounded a curve and joined a long line of wagons and carts in a large corridor filled with pedestrians. The big corridor was also lit, at intervals, but still so dim that he could barely see what was happening. It appeared that the crowd was flowing into the mouth of a tunnel.

After awhile, he became aware that the cart had stopped. Strong, probing fingers were prying his hands loose from the side of the cart. He felt himself being lifted out of the cart and set on his feet. A hand on his elbow helped steady him until he found his legs, and then it fell away as he began to be swept along in the flow of the crowd.

Into the tunnel he went, in the midst of a stream of humanity. The tunnel was so dimly lit that he could not make out a single face, only shapes and silhouettes and faintly perceived shadows.

He heard a sound, a deep, throbbing, pulsating sound. It grew so loud that it overpowered every other perception. He saw, across the crowd, a door partially open. Two men stood in the doorway, talking. Through the door, he caught a glimpse of giant machinery and heard the whir of giant turbines. Then the crowd swept him along and the sound gradually faded behind him.

The sound was replaced, somewhere in the distance, by cheering. He worked his way through the crowd to the side of the tunnel. A little farther he saw a door. By standing with his back flush against the door, he was barely out of the flow of the crowd. He stood listening to the babble of voices passing in front of him, to the cheering in the distance.

He felt a doorknob behind him. The door opened when he turned the knob, and he stepped inside. The room was completely dark, but now the cheering was much louder. By feeling around in the darkness he discovered that he was on the top flight of a stairwell. He followed it downward. With each step, the cheering grew louder. Finally he found himself at the bottom of the stairs.

When he stepped through the door, he knew he had entered a cavern of immense proportions, even though it was pitch-black dark. Thousands of voices reverberated in the cavern, rocking the air with a mighty cheer.

"Ishtaboli!"

The crowd to McDaniel's left shouted out the cheer, and the crowd to his right shouted it back. It was a swelling, building, intoxicating chorus. The very power of it made the hairs on the back of McDaniel's neck stand on end.

He turned to go back through the door to the staircase, but there was no doorknob on that side of the door. He felt all along the door, and then along the wall all around it, but he found nothing. He stood gazing around, listening to the cheering, trying to figure out what to do. There had to be thousands of people in the cavern, but he couldn't figure out where they were, except that they were somewhere up above him.

The ground seemed strangely springy, almost spongy. He knelt down and touched it. It was level and smooth and covered with some kind of carpet that felt like thick, short-cropped grass. He looked all around, but it was so dark he could not even see his hand in front of his face.

He groped along the wall, trying to find another door. Finally, he decided that if he couldn't see anything, no one could see him either. He walked out onto the carpet, determined to find a way out.

He liked the springiness in the carpet. His step was light, almost bouncy. He had been walking along for quite some distance when the cheering suddenly died away. There was a moment of quiet, and then the sharp trill of a whistle, far away, and suddenly a small bright ball of light appeared, far in the distance, and seemed to bounce up and down. As soon as the ball of light appeared, the crowd roared back to life, but now the cheering was not organized but spontaneous in outbursts that rose and fell.

McDaniel had stopped, still in deep darkness where he stood, trying to figure out what he was seeing and hearing, when he felt something in the ground. The ground was vibrating. He could feel the tremor.

He got down on his hands and knees and felt of it. No doubt about it, the ground was shaking. He put his ear to the ground and listened. It sounded like a thundering herd pounding the ground. The sound was getting louder and the shaking more and more pronounced.

Then a very curious thing happened. A brightly glowing ball, no larger than a tennis ball, came bouncing down on the ground right beside him. It bounced high in the air and came down again on the other side of him.

It glowed a bright green color, and it illuminated a large area all around it, so bright it was like a spotlight.

McDaniel was mesmerized by the glowing ball. Still on his hands and knees, he was watching it bounce high into the air, reach the top of its arc, and begin its descent for its third bounce, when he became aware of the intensity of the ground vibrating beneath him.

He stood up and turned around just in time to be knocked completely off his feet, and then trampled, by a thundering herd of nearly naked men. In the bright light from the glowing ball he saw dozens and dozens of men, dressed only in loincloths, flaying the air with what appeared to be giant flyswatters.

As they tripped over McDaniel and piled up all around him, they continued to flay the air with their giant flyswatters, grunting and groaning as sweat glistened on their bodies. One of them made contact with the glowing ball, knocking it a great distance. A mighty roar went up from the crowd, a nearly deafening roar.

The men untangled themselves and took off in the direction the ball had gone, leaving McDaniel sprawled on the ground in the darkness, barely able to move. He pushed himself up to his hands and knees, and in that position rested a moment, trying to clear his head. He heard a man groan.

He cast around in the dark until he felt a foot, and then a leg, and then a broken bone poking out through the skin in the leg. The man writhed in pain when McDaniel touched the broken bone.

He quickly withdrew his hand, which then touched something else on the ground. He picked it up, feeling of it. It was a slim, yet stout piece of wood, about one yard long. At one end was a webbed pocket that felt like leather.

He sat on the ground, flaying the air a few times with the stick, marveling at the supple strength of it. He heard the crowd roar again.

He looked all around but could see nothing whatsoever in the darkness, no sign of the glowing ball or the herd of nearly naked men. He felt the ground begin trembling beneath him. Again, he got on his hands and knees and put his ear to the ground. The herd was definitely on the move and getting closer, but he could not tell which direction they were coming from. He heard the hard slap of many feet pounding the ground, until he was fairly bouncing up and down. Frantically, he turned in all directions, still on his hands and knees, trying to get his bearings. Not until they were nearly on top of him did he suddenly realize which direction they were coming from.

In a flash he was on his feet, streaking away into the darkness. From out of nowhere the glowing ball dropped down beside him. It bounced and bounced and matched McDaniel stride for stride. He tried to outrun the ball, but the ball kept pace beside him, bouncing high overhead, illuminating him, making him stand out for all to see.

He thought of veering to the left or the right, but on both sides he could hear the pounding thunder of many feet. They were closing in on him. The thundering herd was pounding louder and louder, about to converge on him, when McDaniel figured out what to do.

They wanted the ball! They wanted the goddam glowing ball! Without further thought, McDaniel timed his leap. With a mighty burst of adrenaline, he sprang from his left foot, high in the air, turning a hundred and eighty degrees. In one graceful smooth-flowing motion, he came up underneath the ball, caught it on its downward arc, and made solid contact with a powerful swing of his giant flyswatter. Without losing the rhythm of his stride, he continued his pivot, turned another hundred and eighty degrees on the follow-through, landed on his right foot, and continued running in the direction he had been going.

The ball sailed away far behind him, as though shot from a rocket launcher. He didn't see where it went and had no idea where it might have landed, but within a few moments the crowd burst forth in such a tremendous roar that McDaniel was swept along by the power of it.

Never had he heard such a sound. Never had he known the power of so many voices. The roar spoke a language all its own. It was a sudden, ecstatic, tumultuous disbelief. It was a bursting, overpowering joy that could not be constrained. It was a soaring, euphoric once-in-a-lifetime eyewitness to greatness that roared and roared and roared and scared the very bejesus out of McDaniel.

He accelerated through the darkness. He was a dark blur in a dark place. For a moment he had a sensation of actually outrunning the roaring, screaming cheers. He could run forever. He could run faster than the night. He could shift gears and achieve an even greater speed. With feet pounding and knees pumping and head held high, he ran headlong and face-first into a solid rock wall.

PART 2

The Children of the Sun

CHAPTER 13

McDaniel woke up in a hospital room. He woke up slowly, by gradual stages. He was aware that he was waking up from a very deep sleep, but he was also aware that he had not been fully asleep for the whole time.

Sometime recently he had been roused to a kind of half-sleep. He had talked to people. They had asked him questions. He hadn't known the answers. He hadn't known anything. They had been very puzzled. But they had treated him kindly, and had given him medicine. They had said, "Here is your medicine." And, oh, it was so good. It was so very good.

He remembered nothing of the questions he had been asked. He remembered nothing of the people he had talked to, except that they had brought him such good medicine.

These wispy half-memories brought a smile to his face. He felt warm and comfortable and completely content. Full consciousness gradually followed, and with it came a realization that he seemed to be having trouble breathing. He opened his eyes.

A young girl was sitting on his stomach. McDaniel stared at her. She stared at him.

She was sitting with her chin in her hands, with her elbows resting on her knees. Her feet were on the hospital bed on either side of McDaniel, and her bottom was planted squarely in the middle of his stomach. She had luxuriously silky, coal-black hair, shoulder length, with eyelashes and eyes to match, a pouty little turned-up nose, and a look of serene composure. She was ten or eleven years old, perhaps a little older.

"What are you doing?" McDaniel said.

"Watching you wake up."

"Why are you doing that?"

"Because I am a little Natchez girl, and I can do anything I want."

McDaniel didn't know what to say to that.

"I can also have anything I want," she said. "And I might want you."

McDaniel didn't know what to say to that, either. He stared at her, and she stared at him. Finally, he said, "Why aren't you in school?"

"Because I go to school at the Academy of the Little Choctaws," she said, "and right now they are taking instruction in how to be Choctaw." She tossed her head. "I don't have to learn that."

"You're not a Choctaw?" McDaniel said.

"I told you, I am a member of the Natchez tribe. We're not Choctaws, for heaven's sake! We are the Children of the Sun. We are a much older people than the Choctaws. We are the grandparents of all the Indians, though you had better put on a big pot of coffee and be patient if you expect to get any Choctaws to admit to that. I am a Stinkard, but my brother is a Sun. We have different mothers, but we're twins of sorts. We were born on the same day. His mother is a Sun, and my mother is a Stinkard. Our father is a Stinkard, too."

This meant nothing to McDaniel. But what she said next was plainly spoken. "When I am old enough to marry, will you marry me?"

He nearly laughed. But a caution based on many things gave McDaniel pause. Something about the girl's manner told him he had better not laugh. He wondered just how old you had to be in this place to get married. He said, "Do you go around asking everyone you meet to marry you?"

"Of course not," she said. She tossed her head again. "What sort of girl do you think I am?"

Before McDaniel could answer, a woman entered the room through a side door, a full-grown, completely and utterly nude woman, except for a white nurse's cap perched jauntily on her head. She had barely entered the room when she drew in her breath sharply, put her hands on her hips, and said, "Little Ejay! What do you think you are doing?"

McDaniel had never seen such a woman, had never imagined there could be such a woman. She didn't need to be nude to be breathtaking. She looked to be about thirty years old, with light brown hair and a body that could belong only to a dancer.

The little girl's eyes flashed. She put her hands on her hips and gave the nurse stare for stare. She said, "What does it look like I'm doing?"

The woman eyed her coolly. Then she laughed, soft laughter like music. She dropped one hand from her waist and stroked her pubic hair. She said, "You'd better grow something like this first, Miss Little Britches."

The girl gave a haughty "Ha!"

"I was supposed to wake him up," the woman said. "Now git! He's my patient."

"Want to bet?" The girl looked at McDaniel. "I don't believe we were properly introduced"—she glanced at the woman, looking for all the world as though she were admonishing a child—"before we were so rudely interrupted. My name is Little Ejay, and I have been assigned"—she turned her head slightly toward the woman—"by the Head Doctor"—she looked again at McDaniel—"to escort you to school. We're going to be classmates."

The woman walked across the room to stand beside McDaniel's bed. If she had been upset, she no longer showed it. She carried herself erect, divinely shaped breasts held high. Her pubic hair was thick and curly and golden brown. Her hips swayed gently as she walked. McDaniel nearly bit his tongue.

His bed was elevated so high off the floor that, when she stopped, her breasts were only inches from his face. He could feel a faint heat radiating from them.

She placed her hand on his arm. Her hand was warm and moist, the skin soft and smooth. As he watched, her nipples engorged and flared and reddened and strained toward him.

"Can you make yours do that, Miss Little Britches?"

"That," Little Ejay said, "is disgusting."

The woman laughed softly. She reached out and brushed the hair away from the girl's eyes. She said, "Your time will come, little one."

She looked at McDaniel. "My name is Elena. I'm your nurse." She glanced at Little Ejay. "This little brat is my niece. Be careful of her. She's out to get a husband."

Little Ejay looked away, up at the ceiling, a perfectly innocent look on her face.

"In Ishtaboli," Elena said, "only the foolish marry young." Then, she added, pausing for emphasis, "Our married women are chaste."

She leaned close to McDaniel. Her breasts disappeared, to be replaced by something infinitely more dangerous, her eyes. They were a brilliant, liquid, golden brown. Clear and expressive, full of life and promise, they beckoned to McDaniel as she spoke. She said, "I am not married." Her sweet breath was hot on his face.

Faintly, McDaniel heard Little Ejay give a slight "humph." But his heart was pounding in his ears so loudly he could barely hear anything else.

Elena said, "Your medication sometimes has the unpleasant side effect of rendering a patient immune to erotic stimulation. I'm to see to what extent that might be the case."

She stood up, and her breasts once again appeared only inches from his eyes. The feel of her hot breath lingered on his face. He stared at her breasts, at her nipples straining to reach him. She eased closer. He felt a bead of sweat trickle across his face. She eased still closer. He felt his veins begin popping up on his forehead. She eased even closer.

"My God, Elena," Little Ejay said, "he's going to burst a blood vessel."

"I hope not," Elena said, "but his pulse is already 112."

With an effort, McDaniel looked at the hand she had placed on his arm. Her thumb was on his wrist, her fingers on his pulse. Elena smiled. She said, "I didn't get your blood pumping just to take your pulse."

She held his eyes for a moment, then said, "Little Ejay, why don't you run along so I can care for my patient."

Little Ejay leaned down toward McDaniel. She had to tap him on the shoulder to get his attention.

"Is that what you want?" she said.

McDaniel, looking at Elena, was barely able to turn his head toward Little Ejay when he spoke. He said, "School can wait, can't it?"

Little Ejay stared at McDaniel. She put her hands on her hips and started to speak. She got as far as opening her mouth when temper spread across her face like a stain. She whirled off the bed and marched across the room. She said "Slut!" as she slammed the door behind her.

CHAPTER 14

McDaniel sat contemplating the unfairness of life. His posture matched his mood. He was propped up in bed, arms folded across his chest, glowering at the wall.

Beauty and grace and charm he had held in his arms. She had been warm and willing. Warm, hell, she had been hot. He had been willing, and she had been willing, and he had been . . . "dysfunctional," she had said, "temporarily medicinally dysfunctional."

It was the medicine. He learned that he was on "a twenty-four-hour cycle." His last dose had been at 5 P.M. yesterday. It would all be flushed from his system by 5 P.M. today. Then, "we can try again," she had said.

He closed his eyes, remembering her touch. He remembered the way she looked and the way she had looked at him. The very smell of her still lingered in the room. He was lost in a reverie of daydreaming when someone knocked on the door.

He opened his eyes. This was a change, someone knocking before entering. He said, "Come in."

The boy who entered the room was squatly built, barrel-chested, robust. If McDaniel had not seen him in motion, he would have guessed he played center on a football team. But having seen him move, he knew he would be a pulling guard. He had a gracefulness on his feet that belied the fireplug shape of his body.

He was dressed in black knee britches, and nothing else, but he carried a cloth garment, apparently silk, draped over his shoulder.

The boy had something else, too. He had a quality about him that McDaniel could only describe as command presence. It was a quality possessed by the very best officers and noncommissioned officers, those who had been born to command. Perhaps it was partly bearing, partly manner, partly a readily apparent intelligence. Whatever it was, the boy had it. McDaniel found himself unfolding his arms and sitting up straighter in bed.

"I understand," the boy said, "that you have already met my sister. I shudder to think of the handicaps I must now overcome in making your acquaintance."

McDaniel blinked at the boy. Whatever else the kid might have going for him, he understood something about his sister. McDaniel said, "Little Ejay?"

"That's right, Sir," the boy said. "I am Little Elroy, and may I say that I am deeply honored to have the privilege of bringing you your tunic."

The boy undraped the tunic, holding it toward McDaniel. Then something he could no longer contain overcame him. He began bubbling over with excitement. He said, "All of Ishtaboli is dying to meet you. We must have watched the replay a hundred million times!"

McDaniel made a polite frown of his puzzlement.

"You don't know, do you?" Little Elroy said. "You really don't know."

"Know what?" McDaniel said.

The boy waved his arms in the air, shrugged, and said, "Know anything."

"I know that I'm on some kind of timed medication," McDaniel said. "I know that I'm going to go to school at the Academy of the Little Choctaws, that I have a nurse—"

"Mother of the Sun!" Little Elroy said. "It's true! You don't have the faintest idea what's going on."

He hopped up on the hospital bed, dangling his legs over the side. In a conspiratorial voice, he said, "You are about the biggest thing that ever hit this place. I'm not just talking about the ball game. Mother of the Sun!" He slapped his palm against his forehead. "That alone would be enough. But I mean *you*. Do you know why you're being sent to school at the Academy of the Little Choctaws?"

McDaniel shook his head.

"Because they decided you must be mentally retarded."

"Retarded?" McDaniel said.

"Uh-huh," Little Elroy nodded his head. "Retarded. You don't speak Choctaw. I've never seen so many bleary-eyed Council doctors in all my life. They have no idea what to do with you. Do you know what this garment is?"

He held up the cloth he had carried in. McDaniel shook his head.

"It is the most sought after, most prized possession in all of Ishtaboli. It is the tunic of a Lighthorseman of Ball Play. It is yours. It has never been done before. There is no precedent for it. It is unheard of. But the crowd would have it no other way. They demanded it. They refused to leave the stadium until the tunic had been draped over your body. Mother of the Sun!" He slapped his forehead again. "They all thought you were dead."

McDaniel felt of the tunic. As he had thought, it was made of silk. He said, "A Lighthorseman of Ball Play?"

"Yes, a Lighthorseman is a varsity member of the Ishtaboli team. There is no higher honor to which one might aspire. A Lighthorseman is a man without restrictions. He has the run of the entire place. No doorway may be denied him. No secret of state may be kept from him. He lives by a code of honor as complicated as a Catawba divorce decree, but it is self-imposed and self-regulated. No one may discipline a Lighthorseman. Any Lighthorseman who commits a serious breach of the code of honor has always suffered some serious injury, or died in the dark, in the next ball game, but"—Little Elroy shrugged—"that's just a way the Lighthorsemen have of taking care of their own."

"The ball players run this place?" McDaniel said.

"No," Little Elroy shook his head. "This place is run by the Council of Doctors, men and women, every one of them a full-fledged *alikchi*, which is a doctor. The Council is run by the Head Doctor, who's an old man *alikchi* named Moshulatubbee, and by The-One-Next-In-Line, who's an old woman *alikchi* named Pelar. The *alikchi* doctors are games theory specialists. The religion down here is games theory. It is the foundation of this civilization, and it is the ancient religion of the Choctaws. The Lighthorsemen, and the Lighthorsewomen—the women have their own teams—serve as a check on the ambitions of the Council. In theory, a majority vote of all the Lighthorse can overturn any decision of the Council, though I'm not sure that has ever happened."

"And I am a Lighthorseman?" McDaniel said.

"Well," Little Elroy said, "you are and you aren't. You were when everyone thought you were dead. You were such a magnificent dead hero. But then you weren't dead. Then you weren't even from here. Mother of the Sun! Did the lamps stay lit then or what? Nobody knew who you were. Nobody knew where you came from. Nobody ever just walked into Ishtaboli before. The very fact that that could happen staggers the imagination. All they could get out of you, even under the strongest truth serum, was that you were being chased by some alien invader from outer space and that you swam here. Finally, it was decided that you must be suffering from a head concussion. My guess is they're going to study you for awhile, while they try to figure out what to do with you, maybe devise some kind of game to test you."

"What kind of game?" McDaniel said.

"Who knows?" Little Elroy shrugged. "You present them with so many potential problems that I am personally amazed they even let you wake up. But the power of the crowd was overwhelming. Even the *alikchi* were afraid to go against it. It's bought you some time. Meanwhile, they've given themselves a safeguard. They've hit you with a technicality. They can't take away your tunic—nobody can take away the tunic of a Lighthorseman, and nobody can keep you from exercising the rights and privileges of a Lighthorseman—so they've decided you are a Lighthorseman, A.B.E., meaning 'All But Examination.' You see, to become a Lighthorseman, you not only have to be a great ball player, you have to qualify first by passing a written examination. You've never taken the exam, so you're A.B.E., the first one ever. That's one of the reasons why you're being sent to school, to give you a chance to learn what you need to know to have a reasonable shot at the exam. There's an elemental sense of fairness in that, I think, but you would not believe how long the Council meeting took to decide all of this."

"A written examination?" McDaniel said.

"Yes, a tough one. In the natural order of things, that's the first step. You pass the exam, you become a Candidate Lighthorseman, or a Candidate Lighthorsewoman. Not many pass the exam because once you become a Lighthorse Candidate you're free to come and go from Ishtaboli. Of course, from among the Candidates only the greatest athletes become Lighthorse. But Candidate is a tremendously important rank. You can see why."

"Because you can come and go," McDaniel said.

"That's right. But so long as you are A.B.E., you can never leave Ishtaboli. That solves their greatest worry, that you might blow the whistle on this place. But, Mother of the Sun! You are a Lighthorseman! You don't even know Choctaw arithmetic, and you are a Lighthorseman!"

McDaniel looked thoughtful for a moment. He said, "I might not want to leave. My life wasn't working out so well. Maybe I ought to just try being an Indian down here and forget about my old life."

"Well," Little Elroy shrugged, "just because you're an outsider doesn't mean you're alone. My sister and I are Natchez. There's a lot about Choctaws that we'll never understand."

McDaniel looked a bit puzzled. He said, "Your sister told me that she is a Stinkard, and I think she said that you are a Sun? What did she mean by that?"

"That's Natchez social structure. You won't have to worry about that, unless you marry a Natchez. The Choctaws took us in a long time ago, and we are allowed our old customs. We Natchez have a very strict hierarchy. We have three classes of royalty—Suns, Nobles, and Honored People. Then we have the Stinkards, who are the common people. Everyone in our three classes of royalty must marry a Stinkard. The upward and downward social mobility is constant, in every generation. Everybody's children go either up or down. It's based on marriage, and it's all very complicated, but sooner or later everybody's children will be royalty, or will be Stinkard."

"Natchez?" McDaniel said. "Like the town of Natchez, in Mississippi, on the Mississippi River?"

"Yes. That's our home, our Great Mother Mound. We are the Children of the Sun. We invented civilization."

"Invented it?"

"Yes, at least on this continent. The Children of the Sun are the ancient Egyptians of this continent, so to speak."

"Egyptians? You mean like pyramid builders?"

"Mound builders," Little Elroy said. "Earthen mound builders, without all those enduring sharp edges. Our civilization is nearly completely biodegradable, and it is endlessly renewable. And we have some fairly impressive monuments. Our largest mound, up the Mississippi River at Cahokia, has a base larger than the Great Pyramid of Egypt. A few hundred years ago, Cahokia was a city larger than London or Paris at that time. It was one of the great cities of the world. A thousand years ago, two thousand years ago, three thousand years ago, we were building mounds, cultivating corn, inventing and refining and demonstrating what it means to be civilized. We were still demonstrating it, just a few generations ago, when the holocaust began. When the invaders began destroying our continent and our civilization. Our civilization is Mississippi's gift to the earth. All of the truly civilized people of this continent are descended from us, in one way or another."

"But," McDaniel said, frowning, "I thought Mississippi was the ancient, ancestral homeland of the Choctaws."

"The Choctaws," Little Elroy said, with an air of quiet dignity, "are the hillbilly people of Mississippi. You follow any stream in Mississippi to its headwaters, and there you find the Choctaws, or the Chickasaws, who were once Choctaws. Except that, nowadays, nearly all of them are either down here or up above us on the surface. Anciently, they were . . . ummm, how should I say this?—the barbarians at our gate, so to speak."

McDaniel sat lost in thought for a moment. He asked, "Can you tell me how this place down here got built?"

Little Elroy shrugged. "I don't know. The Choctaws say it's always been here."

"Always?"

"That's what they say. The Choctaw origin story tells of a time when most—but not all—of the Choctaws emerged from beneath the earth. They say they came from this place down here. The Choctaws living on the surface showed up at our doorstep in Mississippi about a thousand years ago, after the Fast-Dancing People drove them out of their homeland, the land above us. When they got to Mississippi, the Choctaws had been following a pole that they had planted in the ground each night. Each morning, they had traveled whichever direction the pole was leaning. They haven't changed a whole lot since then, I might add. Now, they say they've simply returned to the womb, to their place of origin, to join the old ones down here, until the danger passes."

"What danger?"

"Up on the surface. Surely you know that all the Indian cultures up there have had to go underground in order to survive the holocaust up there. It's just that the others, as far as I know, haven't done that quite as literally as the Choctaws."

"This whole place is underground?"

"Sure. They say it's the only place that's safe. The only place where Choctaws can still be Choctaws. It's huge, and it keeps getting bigger. It's all pretty much run by slave labor, mostly by unemployed Germans who get kidnapped and brought down here from the surface."

"Unemployed Germans?"

"Yes, lots of them. They make the best slaves. At least, they're by far the easiest to catch. And, whenever the Choctaws might need to know how to do something new, it's not much trouble for them to go up there and kidnap whatever particular kind of German scientist or engineer they might need, no matter how specialized that might be."

"How would they know they're getting the right kind of scientist or engineer?"

"Are you kidding? That's the easy part. They just put a job ad in the right publication. They specify exactly what they're looking for and, voila, their new slaves come to them. They can pick and choose which ones to take. And there's pretty much an unlimited supply of Germans. The Choctaws say that the Germans don't share with each other, that their economic system makes them hoard things from each other, that they compete with one another for everything, even for food, so nobody misses the unemployed ones. They tell me that the Germans try to avoid their unemployed ones, that they more or less just disappear anyway, that all the other Germans are afraid that they might ask them for some of what they've got. They tell me that a German who finds himself unemployed is something to behold, that he'll go into a panic and spend all his time answering job ads, that a German without a job, without work to be doing for nearly every waking moment, can never feel like his life is complete. It must be almost like heaven for them, to be slaves down here. At least, that's what the Choctaws say. We hardly ever see any of the slaves. But you would know all about Germans. Can you tell me what it's really like up on the surface?"

"You've never been there?" McDaniel asked.

"Oh, we've been up there, sure. To see the sun and the moon and the stars. But we never stay very long. There's too much risk of getting caught. We'll be taught how to blend in up there when we're older. Then, when I become a Candidate Lighthorseman, I'll be able to move up there."

"You don't like it down here?"

"I can't wait to leave."

"Why?"

Little Elroy let out a sigh. He said, "Did you ever live with Choctaws?"

"My father was full-blood Choctaw," McDaniel said. He saw no reason to mention that he had hardly known him.

"Well," Little Elroy said, "mine wasn't. I will always be Natchez. I cannot be a Choctaw. Don't get me wrong. The Choctaws are a generous people. We few Natchez are well treated, even privileged. We're allowed our ancient customs, even though the behavior of our unmarried females is a scandal among the Choctaws. Perhaps they feel guilty for helping the French nearly exterminate us in 1731. Perhaps not. The Choctaws also took in the Catawbas, and they are allowed their ancient customs, too. But everything down here is Choctaw this and Choctaw that. You spend any time at all down here in this Okla Hannali part of Ishtaboli and they'll have you believing that Pushmataha hung the moon. Don't get me wrong. He was a great one. But he was a Choctaw great one. See what I mean? And the Choctaws. . ." Little Elroy glanced around the room and lowered his voice. "Can you tell me any rhyme or reason why the sacred number should be four?"

"Four is a sacred number?"

"Four is *the* sacred number to the Choctaws. They have a million reasons why. Want to hear their oldest reason?"

"What's that?"

"Four is the sacred number because we have four hands: we have a left front catch hand, and a left hind hold hand, and we have a right front throw hand, and a right hind swing hand."

McDaniel had to think about that one.

"They never tire of explaining themselves to themselves," Little Elroy said. "Want to hear their explanation for the ultimate origin of what eventually evolved into their old taboo against speaking the names of the dead?"

"What's that?"

Little Elroy composed his face and said, with solemn dignity: "Who was the greatest ball player in all of Choctaw history? *We do not know.* How can it be that you do not know something like that? *He was so great, we retired his name.*"

Little Elroy shook his head. "You'll be learning a lot of that sort of thing in school. Right now, I am sick and tired of Choctaw sonnets. That's what we've been studying lately, the 'old year' sonnet form." He composed his face again, squared his shoulders, and said, reciting:

Year of Birth of Chahta Pushmataha
Ye Okla Hannali Chahta hear this old year!

If there be but *ONE* sun in our heaven
and
If meats in a turtle number *SEVEN*
and
If on the run he could throw, catch, and pitch
and
The number of towns is known to be *SIX*
and
The sacred number is *FOUR* and no more
The year was near *SEVENTEEN SIXTY-FOUR*

McDaniel had to think about that one, too.

"I guess I shouldn't complain about studying so much Pushmataha," Little Elroy said, "or his tribal division, the Okla Hannali—the Sixtown People. If it hadn't been for Pushmataha, the Choctaws might not have been in a position to return to their old homeland in the West, the land above us, or provide us Natchez with a home down here in Ishtaboli where we can still be Natchez. He's the one who swapped part of their Mississippi land with General Andrew Jackson for the land above us, in the Treaty of Doak's Stand in 1820, about ten years before all the Choctaws were forced to move out here to that land. Before that, they say that the land above us had been the home of the Fast-Dancing People for about a thousand years, ever since they had driven out the Choctaws. But then the Fast-Dancing People just sort of disappeared."

"Just disappeared?" McDaniel asked.

Little Elroy shrugged. "They say that smallpox and the Osages pretty much wiped them out. Before that happened, the Choctaws say that it was a dangerous journey to come out here from Mississippi to visit the Choctaws who still lived down here in Ishtaboli. They say that the Choctaws who still lived down here had to sneak around at night up on the surface to find something to eat. They say that they became so good at stealing things from the Fast-Dancing People that the Fast-Dancing People became afraid of the dark. They say that the Fast-Dancing People believed that their country was inhabited by strange creatures they called "the Little People" who stole from them at night. If only they'd known."

"This is only a part of Ishtaboli that we are in?" McDaniel said. "An Okla Hannali part?"

"Yes. Ishtaboli is huge. It includes a lot of ancient Choctaw tribes. The others down here are the Okla Acolapissa, the Okla Alabama, the Okla Bayogoula, the Okla Chakchiuma, the Okla Chickasaw, the Okla Chickasawhay, the Okla Chito, the Okla Falaya, the Okla Mabilla, the Okla Okelousa, the Okla Pascagoula, and the Okla Tannap. We don't see much of the others, except at the games and the festivals. Down here, the Okla Falaya, the Okla Hannali, and the Okla Tannap are by far the three largest divisions, because a lot of them moved down here after the Choctaws got removed from Mississippi."

"All of those other tribes are Choctaws, too?" McDaniel asked.

"Down here they are still Choctaws. Up on the surface, back in time, down through the centuries, a lot of the Choctaw tribes pretty much tried to stop being Choctaw. Choctaws have been deciding they didn't want to be Choctaws anymore for a long time. Some of them, like the Okla Chickasaw, became a separate tribe. A long time ago the Okla Alabama decided they wanted to join the Muskogee confederation, and they have more or less tried to become Creeks. All of the Okla Chito who were on the surface got exterminated in the Choctaw Civil War in 1750. Before that happened, they say that the Okla Chito had produced most of the great Choctaw leaders in the old times. The rest of the Choctaws never have been able to forgive themselves for what they did to the Okla Chito up there. Most of those other old tribes up there just wandered away at one time or another, most of them a long time ago, but a lot of their people ended up back down here with the old ones. By the time of Indian Removal, in the 1830s, only the Okla Falaya, the Okla Hannali, and the Okla Tannap, up on the surface, were still willing to admit that they were Choctaws. But, anciently, all of the others were Choctaws, and they all speak some dialect of Choctaw, and this place down here is an ancient place."

The mention of time reminded McDaniel of something. He said, "What time is it?"

"I don't know." Little Elroy shrugged. "About one o'clock, I guess. Why?"

"I'm supposed to see my nurse again this afternoon. I think you know her."

"Who?"

"Elena."

"Elena!"

McDaniel nodded.

"*My* aunt Elena? She's not a nurse! She's the girls' dance instructor at the Academy of the Little Choctaws."

"Well, she's my nurse," McDaniel said.

"Holy Catfish!" Little Elroy said. "You better watch your ass."

"Why?"

"Because she's got the hots for ball players, that's why. She's broken more hearts than all the women in Ishtaboli put together."

"Well," McDaniel said, "she's been taking good care of me, and I'm not heartbroken about it."

Little Elroy let out a low whistle. "She must have pulled some serious strings to get that job. I can see how it might happen, though. She's a favorite of old Moshulatubbee, the Head Doctor. And Elena is a Sun, one of our very few Suns, our highest Natchez royalty. And she's sort of Colonel McGee's girlfriend. And you're about the biggest thing to ever set foot on the Field of Honor. Elena would do anything for the team."

"Who's this Colonel McGee?" McDaniel said.

"You met him," Little Elroy said. "He splattered you out there on the Field of Honor, and then both squads went trampling by on top of you. He's the co-captain of the Okla Hannali Ishtaboli team. He was the talk of this place before you came along. He's about to become a candidate *alikchi* for the Council of Doctors. In fact, we form the experiment for his *alikchi* doctoral dissertation—the prodigies at the Academy of the Little Choctaws. The whole thing was his idea. That's why you'll be going to school with us, because we're

English-speaking. They started us out six years ago, teaching us English, and they set aside this whole part of Okla Hannali for us as English-speaking, to simulate the surface environment. We're going to finish our training up on the surface. I can hardly wait. But first, Colonel McGee is going to teach us Indian history. That will finally start tomorrow, some new kind of teaching method, and the experiment will either prove or disprove the gaming precepts of his doctoral dissertation. I sure hope the experiment is a success. Otherwise, we'll not get to go on up to the surface to finish the rest of our training. We're not supposed to have learned much Indian history yet, just enough to recite the famous speeches in the speech competitions. But old Moshulatubbee has been teaching it to me anyway. I'm his favorite. I know a lot of things that I'm not supposed to know."

"They spent six years getting you ready, and the experiment hasn't even started yet?" McDaniel said.

"An *alikchi* doctoral dissertation," Little Elroy said, "is a serious thing. It must present an original contribution to knowledge, something that was not known about gaming, or about how games theory can have some practical application. At the doctoral level, it's all mind games." Little Elroy gave McDaniel a look of frank curiosity. "How much do you like my aunt Elena?"

"I like her a lot."

"She's turned a few good men into turbine watchers."

"What's that?"

"Men who don't want to do much of anything anymore but sit down in the power plant and watch the turbines whirl."

"She does it on purpose?"

"Well," Little Elroy said, shrugging, "she's a Natchez girl. It comes natural to a Natchez girl, and nobody has ever come along who can match Elena stride for stride. She's a real thoroughbred."

"Do all the women in Ishtaboli go nude all the time, or just the Natchez women like Elena?"

"Nude! Elena was nude?"

"Well, she did wear a nurse's cap."

"Holy Catfish! No female of marriage age reveals herself to a man unless she means business. Was it sort of an accident that you saw her nude?"

"She was stark naked the whole time."

Little Elroy just stared at McDaniel, his mouth agape. "Stark naked. . . " He appeared awestruck. "A Natchez girl will not let a man see her naked until she's got him tied into so many knots he's helpless, not until she's ready to administer the coup de Natchez. It's an ancient game the unmarried Natchez girls play, one the French never did quite comprehend, one the Choctaws understand well enough, but are helpless to resist. The Choctaws are more interested in the gaming aspects of the coup de Natchez than anything else, but it's sad when one of them gets snared by a Natchez girl. There he is, knowing that he is seeing her like that for the only time, that the pleasure he will take will be the beginning and the end of it. I'll tell you, it just kills the Choctaws. But just coming right out and presenting herself to you stark naked, that's more than likely a declaration of intent to nail your butt. There's nothing very subtle about it."

"You mean marriage?"

"I do mean marriage. Did anyone else see her?"

"Only Little Ejay."

Little Elroy looked relieved.

"Well," McDaniel said, not quite knowing what to make of this information, but feeling an excitement he had never known before, "it may have been just part of her duties. She said it was her job to find out if my medication had affected my ability to respond to erotic stimulation."

Little Elroy looked doubtful. "We've got nurses specially trained for that, and there are procedures for it that don't require being naked."

"You know about things like that?" McDaniel said.

"Sure," Little Elroy said. "Sex is a natural biological function. We study all about it."

"Well," McDaniel said, "I don't know what Elena sees in me, especially if she had to pull a lot of strings, as you say, to be my nurse."

"Boy are you in deep water," Little Elroy said. "What she saw, she saw a million times. That's at least how many times she watched the replay. Talk about excited. She can't wait to see you play again. And she might not trust the Council of Doctors on what they're finally going to decide to do about you. I'll tell you flat-out, she thinks you're the greatest Ishtaboli player to ever come down the pike. Everybody else may think so too, but there's only one Elena, and if she thought they were going to dump on you, she'd darn sure put herself between you and them. She might be the best friend you've got down here. At least for another week."

"Why only a week?"

"That's about how long I figure you've got. See, you've got to understand something. I don't know how it is where you come from, but down here nothing is bigger than the national championship game. Okla Falaya—The Long People—and Okla Tannap—The People of the Opposite Side—have great Ishtaboli teams. In fact, it was universally acknowledged that the national championship next week would pit them as the two greatest Ishtaboli squads of modern times. That is, until the other day."

"What happened?" McDaniel said.

"*What happened?* We skunked Okla Tannap one to nothing, that's what happened. The goal you scored is being called the greatest play in the history of the game. With you on the team, we're now even money to beat Okla Falaya next week and take the title—the first title match that Okla Hannali has made it to in seventeen years. You never saw so much excitement around here in all your life. Everything of any value in all of Ishtaboli is riding on the game. You want my opinion on the matter, it's why you're still alive."

"You mean, they might kill me after the game?"

"It's hard to say what they might do, especially if you don't fit in down here very well. I'd darn sure win the game, if I were you. How much do you really know about Choctaws?"

"Well," McDaniel said, "you come right down to it, I guess maybe not as much as I thought. Most of what I know is Choctaw military history, from books. I was orphaned when I was a little kid and grew up mostly in California. I've never been around Choctaws all that much, not since I was a little kid, anyway. But I am a half-blood."

"Hmmmm." Little Elroy looked thoughtful for a moment. He said, "You know what, it just might be to your advantage that you don't know all that much about Choctaws. You see, even though quite a few Ishtaboli Choctaws—a lot of the Lighthorse Candidates—now live most of the time up on the surface, and they only come back down here for the games and the festivals, it's quite a struggle for them to try to blend in up there, even among all those other Choctaws. That's because the Ishtaboli Choctaws down here have evolved somewhat differently from the Choctaws up there, especially in the sort of games the ones down here are fond of inventing and playing—the truly dangerous kind being the mind games at the *alikchi* doctoral level. Those differences could get you into trouble, if you knew very much about the Choctaws up there. Down here the rules are different. I'll help you out as much as I can because, being a Natchez, I do sympathize with anybody who has to learn how to be Choctaw. But I'll tell you what, just because the ones down here in Ishtaboli might be a little different now from the ones up there, that doesn't mean they're not Choctaws. If you're still alive a week from now, I'll be impressed."

CHAPTER 15

McDaniel, accompanied by Little Elroy, left the hospital wearing the silk tunic of an Ishtaboli Lighthorseman of Ball Play.

Though the distance was not great, it took more than an hour to get from the hospital to the Academy of the Little Choctaws. Okla Hannali people lined every corridor they passed through. Everyone wanted to meet McDaniel. Small naked children scampered at his feet, clinging to his tunic, laughing and singing and scattering flower petals in front of him. It was a triumphal parade.

Men shook his hand and slapped him on the back. Married women hugged his neck. Unmarried women kissed his cheek. Some kissed him flush on the mouth and took their time about doing it.

Little Elroy introduced them all by name—men, women, and children—and by rank if they had any. McDaniel met what seemed like an endless stream of people, among them fellow Lighthorsemen and Lighthorsewomen, Candidate Lighthorsemen and Candidate Lighthorsewomen, old *alikchi* who were members of the Council of Doctors, and *alikchi*-hopefuls who had been admitted to formal *alikchi* candidacy for the Council of Doctors, and young apprentice-*alikchi* who hoped to become *alikchi* candidates for the Council of Doctors.

Old Moshulatubbee, the Head Doctor, came out of his office to greet him, shaking his hand with solemn gravity, saying he had just come from the Academy of the Little Choctaws, where he had lectured on the secret of a happy marriage.

Old Pelar, The-One-Next-In-Line, hugged him like a devoted grandmother, telling him, if she were fifty or even sixty years younger, she would court him herself and make every girl in Ishtaboli jealous. But she whispered in his ear, "Win the game."

Colonel McGee, tall, handsome, ruggedly built, stepped forward to shake his hand, telling him, "Our other co-captain cannot be here just now, so I am in charge of the team. I'm told it's highly unlikely you'll feel up to practicing before game time, that you need to regain your strength. But I've got you in the starting lineup nonetheless."

When they finally arrived at the Academy of the Little Choctaws, children were just beginning to come streaming out of a classroom. McDaniel saw Little Ejay in the middle of a group of girls and motioned to her. She came to greet him, followed by her friends.

She introduced them all around. Her manner was prim and proper, but she could not conceal her pride in the fact that McDaniel was already an acquaintance of hers, and that it was she who was making the introductions. There was no trace of the fury in which she had left his hospital room.

Each little girl curtsied as she was introduced. One girl blushed from unbearable shyness. Most, however, were eager to be introduced. They never took their eyes off McDaniel. Their faces glowed with a radiance, an eager curiosity they did nothing to conceal. All were naked above the waist, but none of them were the least bit shy about displaying their breasts, few of which were entirely childlike.

Two of the girls were identical twins. They were perfect mirror images of each other. They curtsied in unison, giggled, spoke, blushed, all in perfect synchronization.

Little Elroy, seeing the delight on McDaniel's face, whispered, "They intend to marry the same man."

One girl's curtsy exploded into a spontaneous display of gymnastic skill, including a backflip, during the middle of which she appeared to move in slow motion, walking upside down in the air, leaving McDaniel's mouth agape. Another girl sprang to her toes and pirouetted with such grace and poise that McDaniel was deeply charmed.

This was no ordinary collection of children, of that McDaniel was certain. For the first time in his life, he began to look forward to attending school.

When all the girls had been introduced, he turned to Little Ejay and said, "Did the Head Doctor tell you the secret of a happy marriage?"

Little Ejay nodded her head.

"What did he say?"

The other girls looked at Little Ejay expectantly. She stepped forward, curtsied, and fluttered her eyelashes. "He told every boy, 'Plan the kind of old man you want to be, then find a s-w-e-e-t little girl like me, and t-r-y to get there.'"

The girls all squealed and took off as a group, running down the corridor, giggling as they ran.

"I hope you are aware," Little Elroy said, "that Choctaw girls are chaste, though, once they are old enough to marry, a little sparking is not uncommon. My sister is the only Natchez girl in that group. There are only ten in the academy. They are different. Until they are married, they can have any man they want, and they decide at what age they are old enough to have one. It is our custom. One of them here at the academy is sixteen years old and quite striking. Her conduct is a scandal among the Choctaws. You'd better watch out for her. But with all the Natchez girls, you are on your own. Natchez girls are heartbreakers."

"Like Elena?"

"Yes, like Elena. The coup de Natchez is an old custom among our people, and our women take great pride in it."

"I'm supposed to see Elena for a checkup before five o'clock," McDaniel said. "Do you know what time it is?"

"We've got plenty of time," Little Elroy replied. "Do you want to look in on some classes?"

"I guess so. Are we supposed to go to class?"

"Not today. In a few days, when your head concussion is better, they'll give you a battery of diagnostic tests to determine which classes you should be in. In the meantime, you can go to class with me, if you want to. But we've got the afternoon off to get you settled in. That won't take long. All I have to do is show you to your quarters. We can do that later. We can just go around now and observe some classes, if you want to."

"We can do that? Just look in on them?"

"Sure. People do it all the time. Come on. I'll show you one class you'll probably be in."

McDaniel followed Little Elroy down the corridor.

"We'll go to an Elementary Choctology class," Little Elroy said. "This class is made up of some little bitty Okla Hannali kids, just beginning to learn Choctaw because they've been born into this English-speaking portion of Okla Hannali."

When they got to the classroom, Little Elroy pushed the door open a few inches, and they stood in the hallway, peering through the crack.

There were about two dozen very small boys and girls in the room, sitting at very small desks. The teacher, a young woman in her mid-twenties, had written on the blackboard, "*Chahta sai hoke.*" She was saying, "But there really is no way to say 'I am a Choctaw' in the Choctaw language. That kind of translation is called Missionary Choctaw, which we abbreviate MC."

She turned and wrote on the blackboard, "MC." She pointed to the abbreviation and asked, "And what does MC stand for?"

"Missionary Choctaw," the children said.

"*Hoke,*" the teacher said. "And how does Missionary Choctaw translate that sentence?"

"I am a Choctaw," the children said.

"*Hoke,*" the teacher said. She wrote on the board, "EMC." She said, "A somewhat more sophisticated understanding of what is being said is called Enlightened Missionary Choctaw, or EMC. Enlightened Missionary Choctaw translates that same sentence as: 'I'll *bet* you that I am a Choctaw.' And what does this abbreviation, EMC, stand for?"

"Enlightened Missionary Choctaw."

"*Hoke,*" the teacher said. "And how does Enlightened Missionary Choctaw translate that sentence?"

"I'll *bet* you that I am a Choctaw."

"*Hoke,*" the teacher said. She wrote on the board, "M*N*CC." She said, "However, the true level of understanding is something we call Missionary *No Clue* Choctaw, or MNCC. And what does MNCC stand for?"

"Missionary *No Clue* Choctaw."

"*Hoke*," the teacher said. "It is here that we find what is fully being said and how that sentence should be translated into English, which is: 'I'll *lay* you *four* to *one* that I am a Choctaw.'" How does Missionary *No Clue* Choctaw translate that sentence?"

"I'll *lay* you *four* to *one* that I am a Choctaw."

"*Hoke*." The teacher pointed to the MNCC abbreviation on the blackboard. "Always remember," she said, "in order to fulfill the requirements of Choctaw grammar, every sentence must contain the explicit offer of a bet and the explicit offer of odds. To offer a bet without offering odds is a terrible breach of Choctaw grammar, and to try to construct a Choctaw sentence without offering a bet is unthinkable."

Little Elroy closed the door. He said, "They'll spend a long time now learning to recognize the embedded odds in Choctaw inflections, and the embedded preverbal wagering referents. It can be a bit tricky at first. You can lose your shirt if you're not careful. It comes easy to a native Choctaw speaker, but it's hard to learn as an acquired language, especially for the Germans. They just don't have the ear for it."

"Germans again, huh?" McDaniel said.

"Yes. Up on the surface." Little Elroy looked across the corridor. He pointed in that direction. "There's a German History class in that room over there. Let's go listen in."

McDaniel followed Little Elroy to the door of the classroom, which Little Elroy pushed open a few inches.

McDaniel was beginning to feel a little woozy. He had to put his hand on the wall to steady himself. He wondered how long it would take for him to recover fully from his injuries. He had to shake his head and blink his eyes several times before his vision cleared enough to see a large room filled with several dozen boys and girls, who appeared to be a little younger than Little Elroy. The teacher was a middle-aged man, rather tall and awkward looking. He was writing on the blackboard: "449" and "1607."

The teacher turned to the class and said, "As you know, in 449 some of the European Germans began invading the English Islands and became the English-Island Germans. In 1607, some of the English-Island Germans began invading North America and became the North American Germans. Since that time, the civil wars among the Germans have had a great impact upon our Choctaw people. We are going to look at three of those civil wars that took place on the North American continent."

The teacher wrote on the blackboard: NAGCW I, 1776–1784. He said, "The First North American German Civil War took place between 1776 and 1784." He pointed to the blackboard. "That civil war is known as NAGCW I. It pitted the North American Germans against the English-Island Germans. Note that as a result of this civil war the North American German General George Washington later became president of the North American Germans."

The teacher wrote on the blackboard: NAGCW II, 1812–1815. He said, "The Second North American German Civil War took place between 1812 and 1815." He pointed to the blackboard. "That civil war is known as NAGCW II. It, too, pitted the North American Germans against the English-Island Germans. Note also that as a result of this civil war the North American German General Andrew Jackson later became president of the North American Germans."

The teacher wrote on the blackboard: NAGCW III, 1861–1865. He said, "The Third North American German Civil War took place between 1861 and 1865." He pointed to the blackboard. "It is known as NAGCW III. It pitted the North American Northern Germans against the North American Southern Germans. Note also that as a result of this civil war the North American Northern German General Ulysses S. Grant later became president of the North American Germans."

The teacher put down his piece of chalk and faced the class. He said, "The North American Germans place great stock in their victorious civil war military leaders. The surest method for becoming president of the North American Germans is to prove proficient in the slaughter of one's fellow Germans. You will also see this pattern repeated in the twentieth century, when the North American German General Dwight Eisenhower became president of the North American Germans after the Second German World Civil War. It is our misfortune that our continent is being invaded by such a barbarous, warlike people and that there is no way to escape their incessant and bloody civil wars, which now threaten all life on the planet."

Little Elroy closed the door. He said, "Surely all of that is old hat to somebody your age. You can probably test out of a lot of stuff."

McDaniel's brow wrinkled. He said, "That's not exactly what I was taught in school."

"What isn't?"

"About being a German country."

Little Elroy shrugged. "A German is a German. How else could it be taught?"

"Well," McDaniel said, "to begin with, Germany is in Europe."

"That's right," Little Elroy said. "If the Germans would just stay in Germany, we wouldn't have to be hiding out down here. But they don't stop being Germans just because they leave Germany."

McDaniel didn't know what to say to that. He didn't feel well at all. He was feeling more than just a little bit woozy and was having trouble concentrating. He began to think maybe he should lie down and rest for awhile.

"Are you any good at spelling?" Little Elroy asked.

"Why?"

"Because there's an English spelling class right down there. Surely spelling couldn't be taught much differently. Let's go listen in. You do know, I hope, that English is a Germanic language."

McDaniel followed Little Elroy to the classroom. Again, they stood in the hallway and watched through a partly opened door. With some difficulty, when he concentrated hard, McDaniel could see another large classroom with several dozen boys and girls. They, too, appeared to be a little younger than Little Elroy. There was no teacher in the room. The students were busy at their desks, all of them writing in their notebooks.

Presently a bell chimed faintly four times. The students stopped writing. They turned their notebooks to blank new pages and sat facing the front of the room, expectantly watching a doorway on the other side of the classroom.

The door opened and the teacher entered the room. She was a middle-aged, rather plump woman, carrying a stack of books and papers, and wearing very thick glasses. She put the books and papers on her desk and turned to face the class. She said, "Did you hear about the war between three and four?"

In unison, the students said, "Every time we heard the score, four had one more."

"Very good," the teacher said. "Today, we are going to examine another nonforthography. Enter it into your notebooks as I write it on the board."

She turned to the blackboard and began writing:

The Nonforthography Of English Nonfournicity
four
fourth
fourteen
fourteenth
twenty-four
twenty-fourth
thirty-four
thirty-fourth
forty
fortieth
forty-for
forty-forth
fity-for
fity-forth
sity-for
sity-forth
seenty-for
seenty-forth

eihty-for
eihty-forth
niety-for
niety-forth

When she had finished writing on the board, she stepped aside and waited until all the students had finished copying it into their notebooks. Then she asked, "What can we say about this nonforthography?"

All the students in the class raised their hands. The teacher pointed to a boy in the front row.

"They are disrespectful in their spelling," he said.

"Yes, very good," the teacher said. "What else?" She pointed to a girl behind the boy.

"They are disrespectful in their spelling for no logical reason," the girl said.

"Yes, very good," the teacher said. "What else?" She pointed to a girl in the middle of the room.

"They steal a letter from our sacred number," the girl said.

"Very good," the teacher said. "What else?"

A girl in the first row said, "They steal only the third letter."

"Very good," the teacher said.

A boy in the middle of the room said, "They steal the third letter three times in a row."

"Very good," the teacher said.

A girl in the back of the room said, "They are a three-people."

"*Hoke*," the teacher said. "They are a three-people." She turned and pointed to the blackboard. "From this pattern of disrespect, and also from the nonpatterns of noncontinuance, we can clearly see that their sacred number is three, and we can also clearly see that their sacred number is being employed only as a naked and aggressive attack upon four, upon our sacred number, not upon any other number. It is an attack upon the third letter of our sacred number, repeated three times in a row. It is an attack upon *u*. It is a spiteful and sacrilegious reduction of our sacred number to only three letters! What can we deduce from this about these people?"

The same girl in the back of the room said, "They are either an ancient Mediterranean three-people, or their culture has been conquered by the cult of the dead Jew."

"*Hoke*," the teacher said. "From some of the internal evidence in this nonforthography, they might merely be one of the ancient Mediterranean three-peoples. But, from all of the internal evidence, given the aggression apparent here in the employment of their sacred number, it is more likely that their culture has been conquered by the insatiable appetite of the Middle Eastern superstitions of the Mediterranean cult of the dead Jew."

The teacher put down her piece of chalk and perched on the front edge of her desk. "As it happens," she said, "we do know that these English-Island Germans came from somewhere besides the Mediterranean. And we do know that their culture has been conquered by the cult of the dead Jew, with its bizarre fusion of a father and a son and a ghost into a covetous, intolerant monotheistic tripartite that would be comical if they didn't endow it with such deadly seriousness, including having married virgins giving birth and other absurdities too tedious to hold the interest of any rational person. It is beyond comprehension why anyone but a German would willingly adopt such depraved superstitions. Their conception of their supreme imaginary being is a creature with such a severe personality disorder—angry, jealous, vengeful—as to be repulsive to decent people. Maybe that is why they must force it upon others—in the case of our people, under the pretext that they would merely be operating our schools for us. Notice how sneaky they are in how they go about waging their war of cultural genocide."

The teacher pointed to the blackboard. "At first, they appear to have no intention of doing us any harm, no intention of doing violence to our sacred number, until they have gained a good foothold, and then, too late, we learn their true intentions. It is a curse upon this continent that the dead Jew's mental illness, his delusions of grandeur, became a vicious proselytizing religion. If that poor man were alive today, he might have a chance at a normal life with proper medication—as long as he continued taking his meds. But his followers believe that his delusions were real, and that makes them dangerous. They will not tolerate the existence of people like us—people who do not believe that we exist for the benefit of any religious, political, military, or economic organization. Why *do* we exist?"

"To play ball!" the children excalimed in unison.

"Yes! But we must do that now in the dark, to keep you, our dear children, free of the brainwashing in their schools, because the Germans will not tolerate a civilization where anything is more important than their superstitions. When the Germans find a people who are free of the dead Jew Middle Eastern mysticisms, they turn loose the three-people missionaries upon them with ruthless cultural genocide, backed by the police power and military power of the state, until nothing, not even orthography, can withstand their onslaughts. If the Germans get you, they will steal you away from your families and make you prisoners in their Indian boarding schools, where they will force you to practice the cult of the dead Jew, force you to give up your language, your culture, your religion. Their single most distinguishing characteristic is the ruthlessness with which they suppress religious freedom on this continent. It is why we must hide until the threat is over, or they will do to us something similar to what they have done to English orthography. Some of us might still be here afterward, but we could forget about making any sense."

Little Elroy closed the door. He said, "Surely you haven't been taught that English spelling makes any sense."

McDaniel had difficulty hearing what Little Elroy said. He felt curiously strange. Little Elroy sounded far away, though he was standing right beside him. McDaniel blinked his eyes a few times and asked, "What time is it?"

"It isn't even four o'clock yet," Little Elroy said, eyeing McDaniel curiously, "but it must be getting close. Feel your forehead."

McDaniel did so. It was covered with light beads of perspiration. "That's strange," McDaniel said.

"It's the medicine," Little Elroy said. "By four o'clock you'll have the shakes."

"The shakes?"

"If you're on timed medication, the last hour can be a little unpleasant. That's when the medicine is being flushed from your system. If Elena will be there, she'll be able to help. Are you supposed to meet her back at the hospital?"

"No. She said she'll come to my quarters."

"Then I'd better take you there right now."

McDaniel, still feeling strange, barely able to concentrate on where they were going, followed Little Elroy through a series of corridors until they stopped at a door. Inside, McDaniel was shown a spartan two-room apartment, consisting of a combination bedroom/sitting room and a small bathroom. The larger room was furnished with a bed, two chairs, and a table suitable for writing. One wall had a clock. The time was 3:58.

Standing in the doorway, Little Elroy pointed down the hall. He said, "The boy's dormitory is at the end of the hallway. My bunk is the first one inside the door. After Elena leaves, come by if you want to go get some chow."

"Okay," McDaniel said. "But Elena might not leave."

Little Elroy grinned. He started to close the door behind him, then stopped. "Oh, I almost forgot. Tonight is the first dress rehearsal for our play during the Children's Pageant. You won't want to miss that. For us, it's the highlight of the whole national championship weekend celebration. We're going to perform *The Legend of the Little Bitty Bragger.* Little Ejay and I have the starring roles."

McDaniel was feeling even more strange. He couldn't seem to stand still. He felt hungry, empty, but he knew he did not want food. There was a feeling in his chest that frightened him. He liked Little Elroy but wished he would leave. He said, "Won't that spoil the pageant for me, if I see the rehearsal?"

"You're forgetting, aren't you," Little Elroy said, "that you're one of us now."

"That's right," McDaniel said. "I forgot." He tried to laugh, but the sound that came out didn't sound right.

"Are you all right?" Little Elroy asked.

"No," McDaniel said. "I'm not all right. I don't know what's happening to me." He had to sit down. He dropped into a chair.

Little Elroy was at his side. "You don't look well at all."

"Oh, God," groaned McDaniel.

"What does it feel like?"

McDaniel wiped his forehead. It was covered with sweat, but he felt cold. "It feels like I'm an inner tube and someone took an air hose and filled me way too full of air. I'm afraid my chest is going to explode."

Little Elroy took his pulse. "Fifty-eight," he said. "You're as calm as can be. Maybe a little high for an athlete of your caliber."

"My God," McDaniel said, through teeth beginning to chatter. "You mean this is all in my mind?"

"I better get Elena," Little Elroy said, turning toward the door.

McDaniel grabbed the boy's arm. "Don't leave me," he said. "I don't want to die alone."

"Mother of the Sun!" Little Elroy said, looking at the clock. "You've got the shakes."

CHAPTER 16

Elena arrived looking elegant in a white nurse's uniform, carrying a small plastic case. When she knocked on the door, Little Elroy yelled, "Come in!"

She entered to find McDaniel smothered beneath all the covers on the bed, and still he was freezing. His teeth chattered uncontrollably. Little Elroy lay on top the covers, trying to keep him warm.

Elena gasped at what she saw. She quickly closed the door behind her.

Little Elroy, plainly frightened, explained what had happened.

Elena placed the small plastic case on the table. She quickly undressed, peeling off dress, bra, panties, everything. She slipped under the covers and held McDaniel in her arms.

After awhile his teeth stopped chattering, but he was still shaking.

She said, "Thank you for helping, Little Elroy. I can take care of him now."

"Are you sure?" Little Elroy said. "Is he going to be all right?"

"He's just not used to our medicine. You run along now."

At the door Little Elroy said, "I'll be in the dorm if you need me." He had almost closed the door behind him when he popped his head back around the corner and said, "Except tonight. I have dress rehearsal."

"I know," Elena said, smiling at the boy. "Really, we'll be fine. And Elroy, forget you ever saw him like this. Remember, he is a Lighthorseman."

"Yes, ma'am," Little Elroy said, as he closed the door.

She peeled enough of the covers back to expose McDaniel's head. His hair was soaking wet, matted to his scalp. She pushed the hair out of his eyes. She stroked his face, wiping away the sweat.

She said, "Patrick. Patrick! Can you hear me?"

McDaniel moaned.

"Patrick, can you make it until five o'clock?"

McDaniel could only moan.

She slapped his face.

He moaned.

She slapped his face again, saying, "Patrick! I know you're in there somewhere!"

His eyes fluttered.

She slapped his face harder.

He opened his eyes. They were dull, glassy, unfocused.

She slapped him even harder.

He tried to raise a hand to his face. He said "What?" in a voice thick with tongue.

"Patrick, look at me," she said.

He looked at her and tried to smile.

She said, "Patrick, if you can go without the medicine, you'll be free of it. You want that, don't you—to be free of it?"

"Oh, God," he said. "I've got to have it."

"Can't you wait just a little longer? Maybe we can wait it out."

"What time is it?"

"Forget the time. Can you wait just a little longer? I'll help you. We'll make it through this together."

"Is it all in my mind?"

"Right now it is."

"What do you mean 'right now?'"

"At five o'clock the physical craving will begin."

"You mean it gets worse?"

"Patrick, at five o'clock it will all be flushed from your system. That's when you will think you must have it. But you can have *me* then. I'm hoping that at five o'clock you'll want me more than you want the medicine."

"How long will the physical craving last?"

"All night. Maybe ten or twelve hours. I've never seen a reaction this strong. I'm afraid it's going to be bad. But we can fight it." She stroked his face tenderly. "We can fight it all night long. We can do it. I know we can. If you can make it all night long, you'll be entirely free of it." She took his hand in her hands. She said, "Patrick, you can have me all night long."

"I don't know if I can make it. Oh, God, I don't know if I can make it even another minute."

She placed his hand on her breast and held it there tightly. She said, "We'll take it one minute at a time."

When the chills passed and he began burning up, they stood in the shower together, the water ice-cold. When the chills returned, she drew a hot tub of water. He sat in front of her in the tub and she wrapped her arms around him. She massaged his shoulders, his neck, his back, cooing to him softly, whispering in his ear, wrapping her body around him tightly, pulling his head back and kissing him until he forgot where he was, as one minute after another ticked away.

Five o'clock found them lying in one another's arms in bed. He didn't know when five o'clock came, but she knew it immediately by the tone of his voice.

"Get up."

"Can't we—"

"Get up." He pushed her away from him. He took hold of the tops of the covers, jerked them away, and pushed her to the edge of the bed. He said, "Get my medicine."

"Don't you want me?"

"No."

"Not even just once?"

"No."

"Hold me. Please hold me. We can—"

"Goddamn it, I'll get it myself." He got out of bed, took the plastic case off the table, fumbled with the lid. He said, "Don't try to stop me."

She started to speak, but the look in his eyes stopped her. She watched him fumbling with the plastic case. Finally, she said, "Here, let me do it. I know how to do it."

McDaniel sat in a chair, coldly watching her every move.

When the syringe was ready, when she had the needle poised at the vein, she looked at him, but the look in his eyes made her tremble.

She had to take a deep breath and steady herself before she could administer the injection.

She replaced the equipment in the plastic case and sat down wearily, shoulders hunched, dejected, eyes moistened, reddened. She looked at McDaniel, but he would not look at her.

"You wouldn't even try."

He said nothing.

"You wouldn't even try!"

He looked at her. "I would have killed you," he said, "if you had tried to stop me."

They sat staring at one another.

"It's not supposed to be that strong," she said. "Not that strong. Something is not right."

"Elena, you don't understand. I would have killed you. I'm scared. I would have killed you if you had tried to stop me."

"I almost did. I almost—"

"Oh, God," McDaniel said. He got out of his chair and got down on his knees in front of her. He took her hands. He squeezed them tightly. He said, "Listen to me. You've got to get away from me. You've got to let somebody else handle this. Let the people at the hospital do it. You've got no idea how close I came to hurting you. I don't want you around me if I ever get that way again. Do you hear me? I mean it."

"Who do you think is going to help you?"

"I don't know. But I'll work it out."

"The medicine is debilitating. It's habitual and debilitating. You've got to get off it as quickly as possible. It's not supposed to be so strong. A little unpleasant coming off it, but nothing like this. The only way is to go cold turkey."

"That's what I'll do."

"You'll need my help. You can't stop me from helping you."

Terror seized him. "No! You saw how I was."

"You would never have made it even until five o'clock without my help."

"No! I don't want your help!"

"You can't do it alone. Someone has got to help you."

"No!" He burst out in tears. "Not you! Please, God, not you! I would kill you. I know I would kill you."

"Then I would be dead." She stood up. She picked up the plastic case and walked to the door. "We all have to die sometime."

"I don't want you," McDaniel said. "I want you to leave and not come back. I'll get my medicine at the hospital."

At the door she turned. She said, "They won't have it. I'll have it. Look at me. Am I just a naked body you don't want?"

He looked at her naked body, but he fought bravely against looking into her eyes.

"Look at my eyes, damn it!"

He looked into her eyes.

She said, "I'll be back. I'll be back at 3:30 tomorrow, before you get the shakes. You can keep my clothes. They'll talk about us, but you know what, I don't care." With that she left the room, closing the door behind her.

CHAPTER 17

McDaniel was sitting with his head in his hands when Little Elroy burst into the room.

"Holy Catfish!" Little Elroy said. "She turned every head in the hall."

McDaniel looked at Elena's clothes, at her dress, bra, and panties.

"You've been disgraced!" Little Elroy said. "She has declared her shame."

"She what?"

"She has declared her shame. She will declare it all the way back to her quarters. By bedtime, everybody in Ishtaboli will know about it."

"Elroy, I'm new here. What are you talking about?"

Little Elroy closed the door. He sat beside McDaniel at the table. "You are a disgraced man," Little Elroy said. "How do you feel about getting married?"

"Married? Elroy, I've got other things to worry about right now."

"No, you don't. You've been disgraced. She offered herself to you, and you turned her down. She has declared her shame."

"There was more to it than that, Elroy."

"I'm just telling you how the thing works."

"You mean she's made some kind of public declaration about something?"

"She's making it right now! It's a long way to her quarters. Half of Okla Hannali will see her!"

"What does that have to do with getting married?" McDaniel said.

"She's gone public on you. She's forcing the issue, putting it to the whole community to decide. She's out to nail your butt."

"What? She goes traipsing off down the hallway naked, and because of that I've got to get married?"

"Oh, no. You might not be allowed to marry her. It's out of your hands."

"What do you mean?"

"She has declared her shame! It's out of her hands, too. It's up to the public to decide now."

"The public will decide whether I get married?"

"Oh, no," Little Elroy said. "The public might not allow her to get married. They might side with you and judge her a slut. In that case, she'll have to become a slut. She'll not be allowed to deny herself to any man, any time any man wants her. She'll be worse than a whore. I'll tell you, within a few months, you wouldn't even recognize her. A woman never lives very long, once she's been judged a slut."

McDaniel felt his blood running cold. "Is there any chance that might happen?"

"For a Natchez girl! Are you kidding? The Choctaws think Natchez girls are sluts anyway. It's stacked against her that she'll be judged a slut."

McDaniel just stared at Little Elroy.

"Declaring her shame is the most serious risk any woman can take," Little Elroy said. "For a Natchez girl to do it is unheard of. I doubt it's ever happened before."

"Why would she do it?" McDaniel said.

"I don't know." Little Elroy shrugged. "Why did you turn her down? Were you afraid she was just trying to turn you into a turbine watcher?"

McDaniel stood up. "It's more complicated than that, Elroy." He began pacing back and forth. "What can I do?"

"You're out of it. It's up to the public to decide whether she will be vindicated or judged a slut. If she is vindicated, the onus will fall on you. Actually, there's a presumption of onus anyway for both parties. That's why it's said that *you've* been disgraced and that the thing *she* has declared is shameful. To vindicate her, the Choctaws would have to decide that no unmarried man in his right mind would turn down what she offered you. They would be judging you a fool, and having judged you a fool, you'd be given an opportunity to act like one. You'd be allowed to make application to court her."

"Court her?"

"Oh, yeah. We're talking formal, chaperoned courting. If Elena would allow it. I'll tell you what, a woman who's had her reputation vindicated by the community can get some pretty high faluting notions about her wounded pride. You'd be the only man the community would ever allow to be her suitor, and she, along with the other women, would set the conditions for the courting. The thing might drag on for years, until she felt her pride had been restored. Or she might spurn your offers, thereby becoming an Honored Woman, never to marry, never to have relations with any man. Or you might decline to court her, in which case she would be forced to become an Honored Woman. I'll tell you what, some of the love stories down here are real tear-jerkers, and most of them have to do with Honored Women and how they got that way."

McDaniel put his hands to his face and rubbed his eyes. He groaned. He said, "Oh, God."

"I'll tell you something else," Little Elroy said. "You've got a real talent for grabbing center stage down here, and holding it."

McDaniel began pacing again.

"I'll tell you another thing, too. Your days of seeing Elena naked are over, unless you can ever get her to the marriage bed."

"How does this thing work?" McDaniel said. "I mean, what happens now?"

"Well, right now, anybody who knows anything about Elena will feel compelled to tell it. Anything she's ever done, anybody she's ever been with, it will all come out. Elena will be asked about things, too, and she'll have to answer truthfully. I tell you what, it's a real ordeal for a woman."

"She's going to be hurt, isn't she?" McDaniel said. "I mean, no matter how the thing comes out, she's going to get her feelings hurt."

"Yes. You'll have your work cut out for you, if you want to court her."

"Why would she do it?" McDaniel said. "I can't figure out why she would do it."

"I don't know. It's a big risk."

"But even if the community vindicates her, she's going to be hurt," McDaniel said.

Little Elroy shrugged. "Remember, if she's vindicated, she'll get to set the conditions for courting. Maybe she's just not sure about you. Maybe she knows that she loves you, but there's something she wants you to do, to prove to her that you love her."

McDaniel stopped pacing.

"Is there something she wants you to do, something that would prove to her that you love her?"

McDaniel stared at the floor.

"Something she asked you to do?"

McDaniel nodded his head.

"And you wouldn't do it?"

McDaniel looked at Little Elroy.

"There's your answer," Little Elroy said.

"I couldn't do it," McDaniel said.

"Well," said Little Elroy, looking uncomfortable. "I'm not sure it would be any of my business, anyway. Things between you and Elena. . ." His voice trailed off.

"It's very complicated, Elroy. I'm not sure I'll be able to do what she wants me to do."

"You mean, if she is vindicated, you might not court her?"

McDaniel ran his hand through his hair. He took a deep breath. "You saw me with the shakes, Elroy. They've given me medicine that's so strong I'm helpless. They've guaranteed that I'll not leave. I'm addicted to it. I have no will power against the physical craving. If I don't get it immediately, it turns me into a monster. And it's debilitating. I guess it'll eventually kill me if I keep taking it. Elena wants to get me off it without delay. She wants me to go cold turkey. She insists on trying to help. She doesn't think I can do it on my own, and I don't think I can, either. She doesn't understand the power of it. I'm afraid I'll hurt her. Elroy, I'm terrified of it. I'm scared to death I'll hurt her. I know I would, if she put herself between me and my medicine. So I told her to go away. I begged her not to have anything to do with me, until I can work this thing out. God, why couldn't she have done that?"

"You turned her down," Little Elroy said. "You rejected her, big time."

"I was trying to protect her, Elroy."

"The way I see it, she wants to share your life, with whatever risk that might entail. And she wants you to share her life. She wasn't offering sex. She was offering herself. Elena has never offered herself to anyone. I'll bet you've broken her heart."

McDaniel just stared at Little Elroy.

"I'm telling you, some of the romances down here can take a real tearful turn. I've got a feeling you two are going to be talked about for a long time."

"That's not very comforting, Elroy."

Little Elroy shrugged. "Comfort has its place. Truth is more important. Perception of situation is most important of all. If you are to work your way out of this thing, you don't need comforting, you need help in trying to figure out what to do. If Elena has got a broken heart, she might be better off dead. What she has done is not rational. It's dangerous. But she just might not care anymore. If they judge her a slut. . ." His voice trailed off.

McDaniel recalled her standing in the doorway, saw the look on her face, heard her words, "They'll talk about us, but you know what, I don't care." He shook his head violently. He heard her say, "Look at me. Am I just a naked body you don't want?" He shook his head again. He saw her sitting in the chair, dejected, eyes reddened. He saw her in the shower with him, in the tub, in the bed. He felt her in his arms again, saw her trembling as she tried to steady herself to give him his injection.

McDaniel put his hands to his face and rubbed his eyes. He said, "Elroy, I'll go insane trying to figure out what Elena wants, or why she is doing what she's doing."

McDaniel looked around the room. Little Elroy was gone.

CHAPTER 18

McDaniel was still standing in the middle of the room, still lost in thought, when he heard a noise at the door, as though someone were tapping the bottom of the door with a foot.

McDaniel opened the door. Little Elroy entered, carrying a large tray loaded with food.

"You were out of it," Little Elroy said. "So I went and got some chow. I didn't think you'd feel like going to the cafeteria."

Little Elroy placed the tray on the table. He had to move Elena's panties out of the way. He said, "Is my aunt Elena a piece of work, or what?" as he tossed the panties across the room. McDaniel couldn't argue with that.

McDaniel was not aware that he was hungry until he smelled the food. He found he had an enormous appetite, and he and Little Elroy ate nearly everything.

Little Elroy sat back with a glass of tea. He said, "I tried to see Moshulatubbee, but he had just gone into evening meditation. No one disturbs him there. I don't think he's heard about Elena. He may be one of the last ones to find out tonight. Boy would I like to see his face."

McDaniel sat back with a cup of coffee, listening intently.

"When I talk to him, I'll ask him about the medicine," Little Elroy said.

"You can find out about that?"

"I'm his favorite. Besides, I'm beginning to believe I finally might have met the man who will tie my aunt Elena's tail in a knot. I think you might become my uncle."

"You've heard something?"

"It's just a feeling I got listening to people at the cafeteria. The novelty of this thing has caught everyone's fancy. Elena not being

Choctaw seems to be making quite a difference. The Choctaws are going out of their way to make allowances for her being a Natchez girl. That could have gone against her; instead, it seems to be helping. The men, especially, are just in a daze. I'll tell you what, you've gone up a notch or two in the estimation of the men, if that's possible."

"How about the women?"

"That's another matter. You'd think they'd been personally insulted. I had heard that when Elena was little she was pretty much the darling of this place. I guess it must be true. The women I overheard talking seem to want blood."

McDaniel squirmed a bit in his seat. "What about Elena?"

"She's taking it pretty hard is what I heard. It's a bad time for her, and there's nothing much anybody can do about that. She's broken more than her share of hearts, and she's made enemies among the women. But she asked for it."

"Can I see her?"

"No way! You're persona non grata. She has declared her shame!"

Little Elroy looked at the clock. "I've got to get to rehearsal. I'd invite you to go with me, but it's not a good idea for you to be out in public tonight. You'd better stay in your quarters."

"Elroy, there's no way I can sit still right now. I'd go nuts. I can get out and walk around, can't I?"

"Well, yes. . ."

"Where can I go?"

"You're a Lighthorseman. You can go anywhere."

"Anywhere? No restrictions?"

"Well, there are the courtesy dictates of the code of honor, but, yes, anywhere, without restriction. But I'd be careful if I were you. You're at the center of a firestorm of gossip, and some of it is apt to be pretty mean-spirited. Now that you have been disgraced, people will feel free to say things in front of you that you might not want to hear. By tomorrow that phase of it will be over. But tonight, if someone were to say something to you about Elena, you'd be expected to defend her honor. Now that she has disgraced you, if she is vindicated, you'll be the only suitor that she will ever be allowed, and a suitor is expected to defend his lady's honor. It could lead to a duel."

"I'm not likely to get into a duel," McDaniel said.

"One thing can lead to another. It might get out of hand. The one thing you don't want to do down here is make an enemy. Choctaw duels are not like any other kind of duels."

"What do you mean?"

"Well, Choctaws don't like serious disharmony within the community. If two people cannot get along, the Choctaws say it's a lot better just to get rid of both of them, because everyone is affected when two people hate each other. In a Choctaw duel, both people die. Usually they stand facing each other. Each one appoints an assistant, called a second, usually his best friend, and, on signal, at the same time, each assistant chops his friend in the head with an axe. The whole thing is over and done with, and the community spares itself the grief of trying to live with two people who hate each other."

"This actually happens?" McDaniel said.

"Not very often. But it does happen. And there's no getting out of it, unless the other party doesn't show up for it. To not show up for a duel would be to have it converted into a death sentence that everyone in Ishtaboli would enforce. This place would come to a standstill until the culprit had been caught, whatever that might take, and regardless of how difficult it might prove to be, or wherever it might lead, even to the surface. That person would get tracked down. Dueling is the most serious thing down here, and simply because the custom does exist, people go out of their way to try to get along with one another, especially people of equal rank. It's probably not anything you'd have to worry about actually happening tonight, because you are A.B.E., the only person in all of Ishtaboli who is A.B.E. Only people of equal rank can challenge one another to a duel. But you might get out there tonight and make an enemy of a Lighthorseman, and then when you pass the written examination and are no longer A.B.E., that Lighthorseman might challenge you to a duel. I'm telling you, Elena has had the hots for ball players for a long time. I'll bet she's broken half of the hearts on the team. I'll bet some of those guys out there tonight are just itching to find you. I'll bet they're out there looking for you right now. I would not go out in public tonight if I were you. They'll not disturb you in your quarters."

"I'm just stuck here," McDaniel said, "for the rest of the night?"

"You are a person in transition, and that can be a dangerous thing to be. You are in the process of moving from Lighthorseman, A.B.E., to Lighthorseman. You must take care not to make an enemy within the rank you are moving to. Take Colonel McGee, for example. He is a Lighthorseman. For six years everyone has known that he is an *alikchi* candidate for the Council of Doctors, yet his candidacy has never been formally sanctioned by the Council. An artificial barrier was imposed that he could not be formally admitted to candidacy until he had made a demonstration of his new technique for teaching Indian history and the Council had reviewed the results and approved it. That will finally happen this week. But the only reason for the delay was that he had made two deadly enemies, old Yockenahoma, in Okla Falaya, on the Council of Doctors, who would surely challenge him to a duel if he were actually admitted to the Council, and Cshnaangehabba, in Okla Chickasaw, an *alikchi* candidate for the Council of Doctors, who was also a Lighthorseman, and who would surely challenge him to a duel if he were actually admitted to candidacy for the Council of Doctors. Old Yockenahoma finally died last year, and Cshnaangehabba got killed on the Field of Honor last month in the game against us. Everyone believes that Colonel McGee eventually will be Head Doctor."

Little Elroy drained his glass of tea and continued, "Everyone says he possesses the most brilliant mind in all of Ishtaboli. So his progress was slowed to allow him a chance to stay alive, for the good of everyone. Now there is nothing standing in his way, except possibly the Head Doctor, who has fought bitterly against the ideas in Colonel McGee's dissertation. But that is not life-threatening. The Head Doctor can challenge no one but The-One-Next-In-Line, and The-One-Next-In-Line, Old Pelar, is the only person who can challenge the Head Doctor. In fact, as it happens, she is the only woman in all of Ishtaboli who can challenge a man to a duel. Dueling is restricted by sex, even among the other members of the Council of Doctors."

"Do they get along all right?" McDaniel said. "The Head Doctor and Pelar?"

"They are inseparably close friends. They're quite a team, actually."

"If the Head Doctor were to die, would Pelar succeed him as Head Doctor? Can a woman be Head Doctor?"

"Yes. That's why she is The-One-Next-In-Line. Roughly half of the *alikchi* on the Council of Doctors are women. The Council of Doctors picks the Head Doctor and The-One-Next-In-Line for life from among their numbers, with the consent of all the Lighthorse."

"But the Head Doctor and Colonel McGee are enemies?" McDaniel said.

"No," Little Elroy said. "It is not personal. Intellectual disagreements are encouraged, are greatly relished. They say, when Colonel McGee was young, he was the Head Doctor's favorite. Old Moshulatubbee has been Head Doctor for many decades. They say that the Council entrusted this place to him when he was a young man, that he had the vision of transforming it into what it has become. Old Moshulatubbee has been a great one. They say, when he was a young man, he was a Lighthorseman to reckon with on the Field of Honor. They say he could put a spin on a pitch that only his teammates could catch. Okla Tannap was nearly unbeatable when he was in his prime."

"He is Okla Tannap?"

"Yes."

"He was born down here?"

"Yes. They say his ancestors were part of the big wave of Choctaws who went underground after the removal from Mississippi, when the German missionaries got control of the Choctaw schools up on the surface. They say that Old Moshulatubbee is descended from Aiahokatubbee, an Okla Tannap who everybody says was the greatest orator in all of Choctaw history, an even greater orator than Pushmataha himself. At the time of the Choctaw removal crisis in

Mississippi in the 1820s and 1830s, Aiahokatubbee was the *tichou mingo*, the spokesman, for a young Great Medal Mingo of Okla Tannap named Moshulatubbee. They say that whenever Aiahokatubbee was asked to speak against the ideas of the German missionaries, he could hold the Choctaws spellbound for hours."

"Does old Moshulatubbee live here, in Okla Hannali?"

"He does now. He moved his headquarters to Okla Hannali when the Council decided to build the Academy of the Little Choctaws over here. He has told me that he often feels out of place over here. The Okla Hannali have always been known as—ummm, how should I say this?—the most hillbilly of all the Choctaws."

"The Okla Tannap and the Okla Hannali don't get along?"

"Well, they get along better than the Okla Tannap and the Okla Falaya. The Okla Tannap are the ones who complain the loudest that the German missionaries are trying to standardize the Okla Falaya dialect as the definitive Choctaw language. But all the Choctaws, even the Okla Chickasaws, look down their noses at the Okla Hannali dialect. The problems between the Okla Tannap and the Okla Falaya go way back. The Okla Falaya were the ones who broke away from the French trade alliance in the middle of the eighteenth century and started trading with the Germans in the Carolinas. That started the Choctaw Civil War. In a lot of ways, the Choctaws are still fighting that civil war. They say it brought to a head a lot of things that had been stewing for generations, anyway. It pitted the Okla Falaya against the Okla Tannap. The Okla Hannali split about evenly between those two sides, causing the horror of Okla Hannali people butchering other Okla Hannali people. The Okla Chito got caught in the middle of everybody, and they got slaughtered from all directions. The carnage on both sides was unbelievable. The Choctaws were well on their way to exterminating themselves before they finally came to their senses. Ever since that time, the first law of Choctaw diplomacy has been never to have another Choctaw civil war, no matter what the provocation might be. They even suffered their forced removal by the Germans, from Mississippi in the 1830s, to avoid having a civil war over whether to submit to that—even though that removal turned into a horror that killed more than two thousand of them, maybe more than four thousand. It has not been easy for the Choctaws to avoid civil war. They have long memories, and there are many differences between them. They try to make sure that they thrash them out only on the Field of Honor. You want my opinion on the matter, it's why nothing is more important to them than the games, and why nothing is bigger than the national championship game."

McDaniel was thoughtful for a moment. He said, "If the Head Doctor is Okla Tannap, do you think he might have it in for me, for scoring that goal the other day that beat Okla Tannap?"

"Well, that probably didn't endear you to him any at that time. But I doubt that he wants to see Okla Falaya take the title, and the Lighthorse would not tolerate anyone interfering with the games. Okla Tannap and Okla Falaya have been roughing each other up on the Field of Honor for a long time. They've both got great teams, the two greatest modern dynasties. It's been so long since Okla Hannali even made it to the title game that all of Ishtaboli is still in shock about that. When you've been a doormat for a long time, it takes folks awhile to remember what all they might have against you. The Okla Hannali *alikchi* are saying that Okla Falaya might not have time before the game to shift gears from hating Okla Tannap to remembering that they hate Okla Hannali, too. And Okla Tannap has been gearing up all year to stick it to Okla Falaya. Now that they won't get the chance to do that, they'll surely be rooting for Okla Hannali to do it."

"How about old Pelar? Is she Okla Tannap, too?"

"No. Old Pelar is Okla Hannali."

"The dispute between Colonel McGee and the Head Doctor—what's it about?"

"I don't know." Little Elroy shrugged. "We've not been allowed to read Colonel McGee's *alikchi* dissertation, and the Council always goes into executive session whenever it discusses it."

"As a Lighthorseman, even a Lighthorseman, A.B.E., I could find out, couldn't I?" McDaniel said.

"Yes. No secret of state, no secret of any kind, really, may be kept from you. You have unrestricted access to anything and any place in all of Ishtaboli. But we'll all find out tomorrow anyway, when Colonel McGee gives us our first Indian history lesson."

Little Elroy looked at the clock again. He stood up. "Look," he said, "if you do go out, maybe you can just pretend like you don't hear things. If you take no notice of something, maybe you'll not be expected to act on it, though that might not be real easy to do if somebody were to splatter you with his fist to get your attention. There's a lot going on. The national championship week is a time of celebration for the Choctaws. There are lectures and speech contests and debates. And, here at the Academy, students will be rehearsing for the Children's Pageant. Drop by the theatre if you do go out. Drop backstage if you want. We'll be at it until late tonight. If the first act goes smoothly, they might decide to run through the whole thing."

Little Elroy left, leaving McDaniel in a restless state. He paced the floor. He wanted to see Elena, to talk to her. Twice he went to the door, opened it, and looked out into the hall, but each time he closed the door, undecided about what to do.

He picked up Elena's dress, folded it, and placed it on the table. He placed her bra on top of the dress. He looked around for her panties, saw that they had caught on the lever of an air vent along the wall when Little Elroy had tossed them across the room, and was reaching for them when the air came on, fluttering the panties in a light breeze.

McDaniel squatted down and examined the air vent. The grille plate was large, held in place by two screws, one on each side. He peered through the grille plate. The air vent tube sloped gradually upward. In the distance he could see a soft glow of subdued light.

From the tray of food on the table he got a small butter knife. The grille plate screws came out easily. He removed the grille plate, noting that it did not need the screws to remain solidly in place, and set it on the floor. He put his head and shoulders into the tube, feeling in front of him with his hands. The tube was solid enough to support his weight. It was just large enough to crawl into.

He crawled into it about ten feet, to a place of soft light emanating from no discernible source and to where the tube emptied into a slightly larger one, one large enough for him to move on his hands and knees. A plate on the larger tube read: K42. A plate on the tube leading to his room read: cc1282.

He turned around in the larger tube and crawled back down the tube to his room. He hid the two screws and the butter knife under his bed. He placed the grille plate within easy reach, crawled into the tube feetfirst, reached out, picked up the grille plate, and fitted it snugly into place behind him.

CHAPTER 19

McDaniel crawled to K42, debated which way to go, finally deciding it didn't make any difference. He went to the left, moving on his hands and knees. He soon came to a small side tube marked cc1283, on the opposite side of K42 from his room, the same size as the one leading there. When he stuck his head in the tube he could hear music, faintly, in the distance. He began crawling down the tube.

It was much longer than the one leading to his room. At intervals along both sides of the tube there were grille plates from side tubes that were too small to enter. As he crawled down the tube, the music gradually grew louder, and he anticipated that he would find children rehearsing for the Children's Pageant.

At the grille plate at the end of the tube, he could see a room that was all dance floor, with full-length mirrors along one wall. A troupe of boys were singing.

> Gonna swim a lake till it runs out of shore
> gonna follow a river till it ain't a river no more
> gonna climb a tall tree and shout at the sea
> you got it all, but you ain't gettin' me

All the while the boys were dancing, whirling, dividing into groups, reforming in various patterns.

But now the pace quickened, and they entered into a tap dance routine. They danced faster and faster, by turns taking center stage. McDaniel found himself keeping time with the music.

They finished the routine with a frenzied flurry and burst into song.

> Gonna shout at the sun
> go sleep in the sea

but come back tomorrow
and shine on me

When the music ended and the boys sat down to rest, it became quiet enough that McDaniel could hear clearly, through one of the adjoining small tubes, a plaintive female voice singing a slow-paced song with emotion and grace.

Sunshine, shine a smile at me
bounce it off a distant star
let it search the heavens far
prancing, dancing star to star
all the way from where you are
to where I wait to see
the smile you smile at me

A moment later, he heard music coming from another small tube behind him. He crawled backward to it, until he could hear a boy singing.

Upside down as it can be
there's a river in a tree!

Pulled by the sun
lifting water by the ton
from ground, to tree, to air
there's a river rushing there!

Rushing ever upward
upward does it run
The air will be its ocean
in the clutches of the sun

McDaniel crawled to a small tube a short distance away, where another boy was singing.

Going to school is a bore!
It's an utterly unnecessary
easily avoided chore

If a girl you can find
whose writing you can read
then going to school is a thing
for which you'll have no need

Let her take the notes
while you play ball
If you play it right
you can have it all

Picking the girl is the trickiest part
It's partly luck and partly art
If she's pretty as can be--that won't hurt
so pick what you like to see in a skirt

If it's left-over traces
of little girl faces
all lightly speckled about
do your looking at night
where you'll have to get close to find out

If it's legs on a lass you like
and it's swishing behinds all about you find
pick the girl blind
Chance a wish you'll draw the skirt
you'd love to try to flirt

But don't forget what you're looking to find
or what you must hope not to see
no matter how swishy that behind
or how pretty that girl might be

If between her *e* and her *l*
you cannot tell
her well
from her wlll
from her weee
And if where spaces there should be
you see wellwlllweee
Leave that one behind
and find a girl
who doesn't wlll
and doesn't need a weee

From another small tube nearby, McDaniel heard what sounded like a drummer begin striking a drumstick against something metallic, in a measured, even, fast pace that sounded for all the world like some rock 'n' roll band about to start up. He moved closer to the tube as someone shouted, "One, two, three, four!" and the band started up so loud it nearly blew McDaniel out of his skin. How many electric guitars it had, he could only guess, but it had at least one bass player, and a drummer, who knew how to lay down a back beat rhythm. The voice of a lead singer came blasting out of the tube.

I had one good crack at bat
and the ball it sailed away
but the ump he called me out
said I had to play his way
He said you got to run the bases
when you hit the ball
I said I hit the goddamn ball
I just don't run--that's all

A rock 'n' roll piano took over, and McDaniel felt as if he were being bounced up and down in the tube. The piano run lasted quite some time, before the lead singer took over again.

He said you got to run the bases
or else you cannot score
You touch all three out there
and then you touch one more
I said the way I touched that ball
ought to be enough
It ought to count a score
without all that other stuff

A rock ‘n' roll saxophone took over for a long, loud run, and, if anything, the saxophone outdid the piano.

He called me out then and there
denied me my just due
Said pard you didn't touch 'em all
your time at bat is through

A lead guitar took over, dueling with the piano and the saxophone, as the band went wild on a long instrumental run.

That one good crack at bat
was all I ever had
and though the ball it sailed away
they say that I was bad
They say I wouldn't touch 'em all
wouldn't touch a one
I say the way I touched that ball
there weren't no need to run

The guitars, and the piano, and the saxophone, and the drum were all cutting a rug when McDaniel crawled backward out of the tube, back to K42.

He went farther down K42 on his hands and knees, passing up a number of side tubes, noting that they were all in sequence—

cc1284, cc1285, cc1286, etc.—until he came to an unmarked tube that should have been cc1294.

Puzzled, and curious about the designation scheme of the tubes, he crawled into it. It, too, was a long tube, so long that he had just about decided to give up and crawl back out of it when, faintly, he heard the sound of applause.

By the time he had crawled the rest of the way to the grille plate, the applause had died down and a woman had begun speaking, ". . . our next oratorical contestant, representing Okla Mabilla in the Junior Boy's Speech Division. His talk is entitled 'The Athletic Aspect of Chess.'"

The grille plate was on the right side of the tube, and McDaniel could see nothing except what appeared to be the back side of a blackboard and a portion of the easel that held it up, only a few feet from the grille.

The voice of a young boy, poised and confident, came flooding through the grille. "Competitive chess is an athletic event. It is more than a game of thinking. It is a game of the body. It became an athletic event with the invention of the chess clock. The relentless ticking of that clock makes a tournament game a test of the speed and stamina of the electrical connectors in your brain. It is a test of your cardiovascular system that supports those electrical connectors. It is a test of the athleticism of your mind. It is no accident that world champions are young when they take the title. And though one might hold that title for a long time, it will almost always be surrendered to a younger person. Let's look at a spectacular burst of sustained athleticism by a young person, pitted against a formidable, much older opponent, with the youngster in severe time trouble in a tournament game that was played to checkmate. Let's consider Black's seventeenth move, by Robert Fischer of Brooklyn, New York, at the Lessing J. Rosenwald Tournament in 1957, when Fischer was fourteen years old, the year before he became chess champion of the North American Germans, thereby earning his Grandmaster title. Here is the position facing Fischer as he contemplated that seventeenth move, the shot heard 'round the world, as it has been called."

McDaniel moved farther down the tube. At some distance from the first grille plate, he came to another one, also on the right side of the tube.

Again, he could see nothing through the grille but the back side of a blackboard. A young girl was speaking. "But this Russian, Maizelles, has not demonstrated much practical application for his Theory of Coordinate Squares. In those end game positions where it is applicable, it is impressive. But there are many King and Pawn endings where it has no application at all."

McDaniel moved on. Finally, at the next grille plate, he could see into the room. There were only two people in the room, a young boy, perhaps four or five years old, and a woman. The boy was standing on a platform, holding up a chessboard, a strange-looking chessboard, one that had a hill in the center of the board. The woman was seated in a chair in front of the boy.

"Try it again," she said. "But don't raise the board so soon. You should use the board to drive home the point, not to make the point."

"Should I say 'Like this' when I raise the board?"

"Yes, try that."

The boy lowered the board. He composed his face and said, "When you take the high ground, you get—"

"No, no," the woman said. "Start further back. You've got to get the rhythm and pacing just right leading up to the visual. Start back at the Queen."

"*Hoke,*" the boy said, composing his face again. "The Queen, in her starting position, can command twenty-one squares. But put her on that mound in any one of those four center squares and she can command twenty-seven. Likewise, the power of the Bishop expands from seven to thirteen, and the Knight from four to eight. And a Knight in a corner of the board can command but two. Only the Rook and King gain nothing by being on that mound in the center of the board. Those four center squares are the high ground in chess. When you take the high ground, you get mathematics on your side, the power to threaten more ground and protect more ground. The chessboard should actually look like this." The boy raised the chessboard high overhead.

"That's better," the woman said, "but drop the word 'actually.' That's an adverb, and adverbs in English often weaken the verbs they modify, even when they are intended to strengthen them. Try it again."

McDaniel went on to the next grille plate. There, he could see nothing but the back of a chair. A woman was saying, ". . . representing Okla Tannap. He will recite the speech of Homasatubbee, Great Medal Mingo of Okla Tannap, at the treaty negotiations at Fort Adams, in 1801. He will recite the version recorded by the Germans in their State Department files."

A few moments later, McDaniel heard a boy's voice: "I understand our great father, General Washington, is dead, and that there is another beloved man appointed in his place, and that he is a well-wisher of us. Our old brothers, the Chickasaws, have granted a road from Cumberland as far south as our boundary. I grant a continuance of that road which may be straightened. But the old path is not to be thrown away entirely, and a new one made. We are informed by these three beloved men that our father, the president, has sent us a yearly present of which we know nothing. Another thing our father, the president, has promised, without our asking, is that he would send women among us to teach our women to spin and weave. These women may first go among our half-breeds. We wish the old boundary which separates us and the whites to be marked over. We came here sober, to do business, and wish to return sober, and request therefore that the liquor we are informed our friends have provided for us may remain in the store."

McDaniel moved farther down the tube as the sound of applause filled the room. At the next grille, he could see a boy, about Little Elroy's age, standing on a small podium, with a woman seated in a chair in front of him.

The boy was shouting: "We are honored to have this guest in our homeland. He has spoken with eloquence, and we have listened to all he has had to say. You have heard him ask, 'Where today are the Pequot? Where today are the Mohican? Where today are the Naragansett?' You have heard him tell of many wrongs our race has suffered at the hands of the *na hollo*. You have heard him speak many truths. But you have not heard him speak the most important truth of all. I will speak it to you! Ponder it with great care. The survival of our people depends upon it. That truth is this: The issue before us today is not what wrongs we may have suffered in the past. The issue before us today is what shall be the nature of our relations with the *na hollo* in the future! But whatever you decide, hear me now. Let there be no mistake about one thing. No matter what you decide to do, I will fight against him on the side of the *na hollo*! And I will kill any Choctaw who goes with him!"

The woman said, "There's no need to shout every word. Remember, you are Pushmataha. Everyone is listening closely. The people have been waiting all day, through all the other speeches, to hear what you have to say. You should speak loudly enough to make yourself heard, but without sounding desperate, even though you are desperate. You know that Tecumseh's words have made a strong appeal. You have heard the other speakers, and you can see that many Choctaws are ready to follow him. But you have been to Philadelphia. You have seen the industrial and military strength of the *na hollo*. You know that your people have no idea of the horrors that will befall them if they go to war against the *na hollo*. So you give them a horror to contemplate, one they can understand. You threaten civil war. You know that your words will bring this great meeting to a standstill, until the people can figure out what to do. But you mean the words you speak, and no one doubts for a moment that you mean them. You must convey all of that, not by shouting, but by your posture, your gesticulations, your facial expressions, and by the tone of your voice, as well as by modulating its volume. Reflect for a few moments how you are going to do that, and then try it again. Remember, also, that his manner of speaking was always nervous, always filled with tension."

"*Hoke*," the boy said.

McDaniel pulled away from the grille and lay in the tube, staring down it. There was no telling how far this tube continued, and he was tired of crawling on his belly. At least K42 was large enough to move through on his hands and knees. He began crawling backward toward it. Children were still speaking beyond the other grille plates, but he didn't pause to listen. He crawled backward all the way to K42.

At K42 he continued in the direction he had been going, but he encountered no more side tubes. Instead, he came to an arterial tube, big enough that he could stand up in it. It was marked MM.

The tube was well lighted and stretched away into the distance in both directions. There appeared to be no end to it. At intervals, he could see where smaller tubes the size of K42 fed into it, but only on one side.

He turned to the right and walked down MM, quite some distance to the next side tube. It was marked K41.

From there, he stood gazing down MM. Would the K side tubes keep descending in sequence all the way to K1? And then go through the other letters of the alphabet, all the way down to A? Was this designation scheme only for the Okla Hannali portion of Ishtaboli, or for all of Ishtaboli? Just how big was Ishtaboli?

As he kept looking down MM, first one way and then the other, he noticed in the distance on the other side of MM a large arterial tube feeding into it. It appeared to be the same size as MM. McDaniel walked to it.

It had an entirely different kind of designation. Its sign read: Theatre By-pass A. It sloped steeply upward for what appeared to be about twenty feet, and then apparently leveled off again.

Perhaps this theatre was the one where Little Elroy and Little Ejay were supposed to be. He climbed up the slope of the tube, to where it leveled off, and then walked down the tube. He tried the first small side tube he came to, on his right. It was unmarked, but was nearly as big as K42, and McDaniel was able to move through it on his hands and knees instead of on his belly. It led him to a grille plate near the center of a large theatre. The grille was high on the wall near the ceiling. He had a clear view of the stage.

The stage was dark, the theatre itself dim, with people scurrying about in the area in front of the stage. Presently, a loud voice shouted, "Places everyone! Let's try it again from the top, and this time let's have some fog!"

There was a drumroll, and a voice boomed, "Ladies and Gentlemen, the Theatre of the Little Choctaws presents *The Legend of the Little Bitty Bragger*."

Fog billowed across the stage, which was eerily and selectively lighted, showing a swamp. Wind howled and shrieked, dissipating the fog, revealing the outline of a large person sitting in shadows beneath a canopy of spider webs.

The voice of a narrator intoned: "There was an old woman who lived way back in what our people call the sticks. Everyone said she was a witch. Her sister said so, and the dying Head Doctor said so to The-One-Next-In-Line. How old the old woman was, nobody knows, but she was so old that the oldest old man could recall as a child being told not to go where the old woman was."

As the narrator launched into an explanation of how the old woman had become a witch, McDaniel pondered whether to leave immediately or wait until Little Elroy and Little Ejay had shown up on stage so he could be sure they were going to be occupied here for the evening. He decided to wait.

He looked all around the theatre, trying to see into the gloom, listening as the narrator explained that sometimes there was not enough food in the winter for everyone to survive, and at those times some of the old people would be asked to die so the little Choctaws might live. These old people did not want the little Choctaws to cry for them, so an elaborate ruse had been created in which the Head Doctor would accuse some old woman of being a witch, and the entire village would chase her down and kill her.

The narrator intoned: "Never in the history of our people was there an old woman so chosen whose eyes did not fill with tears, as her eyes spoke the words she knew she could not say: 'Oh, Head Doctor, you chose me to die for the little Choctaws! Please give me the strength to do what I know I now must do,' which was, before lighting out for the woods, to crouch down, and look all around, and cackle. They say that that old woman in the swamp outran everyone who chased her. They say that from then on they could hear her, that many were the times, on the darkest of nights, when the moon was gone and the wind was just right, from the depths of a swamp no eye ever saw, came the ear-piercing peal of her skin-crawling squall."

McDaniel was mildly startled when the stage lights came on full, but it was nothing compared to the way the hairs on the back of his neck stood straight up, as an incredibly fat, skinny-necked, tortoise-headed old woman, sitting at center stage, jumped up and screamed, "*Chahta sai hoke*!"

The narrator intoned: "The old woman lived fat and good, stealing from the snakes and the spiders. The spider webs were so tightly strung from cane to cane above her head that they were like a dinner bell telling her whenever a fat bug become entangled in them. And whenever the old woman heard that dinner bell ring. . ."

At center stage, the old woman jumped up and said, "You be as fat and juicy as me, and I'll be the very last thing you see!"

The narrator intoned: "Then one day the old woman heard something new, something she had not heard for a long, long time, the incredibly loud screaming and squalling of a baby newly born. It was so loud the old woman could barely believe it was a baby."

On stage, the old woman jumped up and said, "Wooooo Weeee! If there ain't a set of lungs on that honey, then I better go see what it is."

On stage, the lights dimmed away to darkness.

The narrator intoned: "The old woman found a little baby boy. She took him in and taught him what he needed to know, but she had a mean streak in the way she went about it. For pure spite, so he would grow up ugly, she did not force his head between the cradle boards, did not flatten his little skull, did not allow the top of his head to slope steeply downward to his little eyes. She made him a little hatchet and pretty much left him alone. The old woman raised him good, and then she died. He was still so little when the old woman died that for a long time he didn't know what to do. Somehow, he became a little dreamer, dreamed he was a great warrior. But he was bad to brag. Many were the times his mighty war cry burst across the canebrake."

On stage, the lights came up, and McDaniel saw Little Elroy standing there holding a little hatchet, naked as the day he was born. In a voice so loud and booming it took McDaniel by surprise, Little Elroy screamed: "I have no mother! I have no father! There was an old woman here, but she smelled so bad I ate her! By the bugs above, I am now the biggest, meanest warrior in this whole damn place!"

The narrator intoned: "The Choctaws, hearing this mighty war cry, called him Ishtilawata, the bragger. They were much afraid of this great menace in the swamp and knew not what to do."

As the narrator launched into a recitation of how the Choctaws cringed in their villages, fearing the great warrior who had eaten the old woman in the swamp, McDaniel scurried back into Theatre By-pass A. He followed it until it intersected another large arterial tube marked Theatre By-pass B. This he followed until it led him to Theatre By-pass C. At some distance down this tube, he crawled into a side tube. At the grille plate he found himself almost exactly across the theatre from where he had been, still high on the wall, near the ceiling.

The narrator intoned: "Of course, there were many such sweet little girls among the Choctaws, and they were prized for their beauty and charm and grace. At the flower festival each spring, the Head Doctor would honor the sweetest little girl of all by carrying her to the top of the mound, there to perform a clitoridectomy. Never in the history of our people was there a little girl so chosen whose eyes did not fill with tears as she said, 'Oh, Head Doctor, you chose me to be an Honored Woman among our people,' except for one little girl, who, when the Head Doctor leveled his finger squarely between her rapidly developing, naked little breasts, stamped her foot on the ground and said, 'Damn! If the witches don't get you, the Head Doctor does!' They say it was that little girl who was chosen to accompany the Head Doctor to confront the great menace in the swamp."

The stage, which had been dark, now brightened. And there, knee-deep in swamp water, apparently playing the role of the Head Doctor, was an old man. The old man, McDaniel noted, was not old Moshulatubbee. Holding the Head Doctor's hand with both of her hands was Little Ejay, wearing only a short skirt made of reeds.

The Head Doctor said, "Fear not, little one, for when you confront the great menace, I will be not far behind. Together, we will get rid of him."

Little Ejay said, "Oh, Head Doctor, it is not fear of the great menace in the swamp that causes my knees to knock, and my voice to quiver, and my body to be wet with sweat. I am afraid if I let go of your hand I will fall down and drown."

McDaniel backed out of the tube and continued around the theatre to Theatre By-pass D. There he negotiated his way to a grille plate, only to find himself on the wall of the backstage where curtains blocked his view.

He heard Little Elroy shout, "I have no mother! I have no father! There was an old woman here, but she smelled so bad I ate her! By the bugs above, are you an old woman, too?"

And he heard Little Ejay answer, "Oh no, great warrior, I am just a little girl."

McDaniel backed out of the tube, back to Theatre By-pass D. Confident now that both Little Elroy and Little Ejay would be occupied on stage for quite some time, he continued on down Theatre By-pass D. He knew that he had completely circumnavigated the rectangle of the theatre, going from A to B to C to D, but he didn't understand why he hadn't seen an entrance to By-pass D when he had been in By-pass A. Maybe By-pass D would slope downward and take him back to MM. But By-pass D began sloping upward, and it did not intersect with another arterial tube at the point where McDaniel estimated he should have encountered Theatre By-pass A. Instead, quite some distance ahead, he saw where By-pass D ended, where it joined an arterial tube running at right angles to it.

He decided he might as well find out about the new tube. Its sign read: Elevated Access Juncture C to Stadium. He stood debating what to do. It was a long way back around the theatre to K42 and his room. He certainly didn't want to go back to his room. He didn't want to get lost, either.

He decided he should backtrack to MM and get better acquainted with the tubes before he got too far away. He retraced his route around the theatre quickly, not stopping to hear any more of the play.

When he got back to MM, he saw something he hadn't noticed before. On the side of the tube, at intervals, were recessed ladders, built into the wall. He walked to one to take a closer look.

The ladder led to a hatch in the roof of the tube. Looking down, he saw that there was also a hatch in the floor at the bottom of the ladder. Cautiously, he climbed the ladder and raised the hatch. He peered into a small room filled with lighted dials, pressure gauges, switches.

He climbed down and carefully raised the hatch in the floor, lifting it only about an inch. He gazed down into one of the Ishtaboli pedestrian corridors and saw people moving along it. Looking to the side of the corridor, he recognized the Head Doctor's office, where the Head Doctor and Pelar had come out to greet him on his way from the hospital to the Academy of the Little Choctaws.

As he watched, a woman came out of the office. Farther down the corridor, he saw the old woman, Pelar, The-One-Next-In-Line, approaching the woman.

"Lorena, wait!" Pelar said. "I've got to see Moshulatubbee."

"He's in evening meditation," the woman said. "Can you come back in a couple of hours?"

Pelar took the woman by the elbow and led her back through the doorway, saying, "No. Announce me now. He'll not be angry with you, I promise."

The women disappeared through the office doorway.

McDaniel lowered the hatch. He looked quickly down MM in the direction the women had gone. The K40 side tube seemed to be just above their position. He hurried to it.

In K40, he gambled that the first small side tube would lead to an outer office, a reception area. He crawled down the second tube. As he neared the grille plate, he heard a voice.

"Have you heard the news about Lighthorseman McDaniel?" The voice was Pelar's. But at the grille plate, McDaniel could see nothing except what appeared to be the backside of a bookcase. Then he heard another voice that he recognized, the Head Doctor's.

"Forget Lighthorseman McDaniel. He lives on borrowed time. Besides, by morning, Elena will have his tail tied into so many knots he won't know his *isht halalli* from his *isht halupalli*."

"Perhaps. But not as you suppose. She has disgraced him."

"What?"

"She has declared her shame."

"*Elena*?"

"Yes, your precious pampered little pet, Elena. She is this minute bawling her eyes out in her quarters."

"My God!"

"A childlike idiot you called him, and he plucks the ripest plum in the place."

The voices trailed off as Pelar and the Head Doctor left the room.

McDaniel lay quietly in the tube, staring at the backs of books, contemplating what "borrowed time" might mean. He felt the strain of the ticking of his own medicine clock. He had to get out. He had to get out of Ishtaboli right now.

CHAPTER 20

McDaniel slithered backward out of the small side tube, to K40. He crawled on his hands and knees down it quickly to MM, where he could stand up.

One thing he was pretty sure about was that the stadium must be near the edge of Ishtaboli. That's where he had stumbled into the place. If he could get to the stadium, maybe he could find a way out.

He walked quickly down MM, back to Theatre By-Pass A, and then around the theatre again to Elevated Access Juncture C to Stadium. But when he got there, he didn't know whether to turn right or left. Which way led to the stadium? The sign didn't say.

He went to the left. It turned out to be a long tube, without side tubes, without intersecting any other arterial tubes, and without taking him to the stadium. After quite some distance the tube sloped downward and forked.

McDaniel stood at the fork, reading the signs. The tube that curved to the left was marked 2-2-10-10. The tube curving to the right was marked P8108.

Frowning, he went to the right, entering P8108, but the tube simply curved around and then straightened out, heading back in the direction he had just come from. He went back to the fork and entered 2-2-10-10. It snaked around in a short double curve and then straightened out in what he was pretty sure was the direction he had been going.

The tube stretched away into the distance, looking very much like MM. There appeared to be smaller tubes the size of K42 entering it from both sides. He walked to the nearest one. It was unmarked. It was also sealed airtight with a yellow plastic cover. He examined another one across the tube from it. It, too, was unmarked and sealed.

He headed down 2-2-10-10 at a brisk pace, determined to cover some distance, noting that all the side tubes continued to be unmarked and sealed.

He had walked several hundred yards when he saw an unsealed side tube coming up on the left. It was unmarked and somewhat larger than the sealed tubes. He decided to see if he could get his bearings, get some idea of where he might be.

He entered the tube on his hands and knees, but it soon sloped downward and forked. He took the fork to the left. Before long, he could see where the tube ended at a grille plate.

At the grille, McDaniel could see a lecture podium with a blackboard where an old woman was speaking. He could barely see the blackboard and could not see any of the audience. The old woman was saying, "Another aspect of classical Choctaw grammar concerns its complete lack of any equivalent of the punctuation marks of the Germans. We might consider the case of an aborted attempt to create a Choctaw semicolon, which was the work of a North American German missionary in the early nineteenth century, assisted by several helpful Choctaw students at the missionary school."

The old woman turned to the blackboard. She began writing on the board as she spoke. "This Choctaw designation for a semicolon, as rendered by that German missionary, in what we now call Old Missionary Choctaw, was '*koshu ibichilu bakapa okhoata apokfopa atoshba nutakhish achafa*.' Its English translation, for what we know he was trying to say, would be: 'a lop-sided, uncircled, one-whiskered, one-half hog nose.' Its pictograph representation was like this. . ."

McDaniel watched as the old woman wrote on the blackboard:

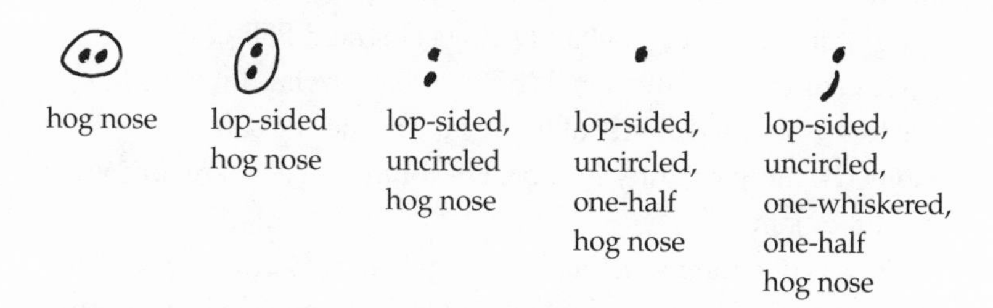

McDaniel backed out of the tube, back to the fork. He tried the right fork.

Looking through the grille plate, he found, to his surprise, that the room was a small office where a man sat at a desk listening to the dress rehearsal of *The Legend of the Little Bitty Bragger*, which was apparently being piped in over an intercom. The grille plate was near the floor level. McDaniel could not see the man's head and shoulders. But he could see that he wore the tunic of a Lighthorseman.

The Head Doctor was hollering, as though from a distance, "Oh, great warrior, we are a miserable people, for we have lost the knowledge of how to find our Sacred Hidden Valley Where Rocks Are Born. If I tell you how to find an old woman who lives far, far away, where the sun sleeps in the sea, who might still be alive, and who might still remember how to find our Sacred Hidden Valley, will you undertake this great quest for us? Will you find our Sacred Hidden Valley?"

McDaniel could picture Little Elroy standing on stage when he heard him shout, "If it's rocks you want, it's rocks I'll get. If they're hidden and sacred that's better yet. It's a great warrior you need, so let's not dally. The whole thing sounds right down my alley. But before I go, there's one thing I must know, and then it is forth I shall sally, but not until you tell me now—what in the hell is a valley?"

McDaniel backed all the way out of the tube. He continued on down 2-2-10-10, surprised to see that no more side tubes entered the tube at all. He had covered another long distance when he encountered something he had not seen before, a narrow passage entering the tube from the right. It was large enough to walk through in an upright position, but just barely. It was marked FFF.

He could not see the details of the tube very far down its length due to the poor lighting, but in the far distance he could see where it joined a more brightly lit tube. He couldn't see where any small side tubes joined it.

He was debating whether to try it when he heard a noise in the distance behind him. He ducked into FFF and peeked back around the corner.

Far down 2-2-10-10, barely visible, he saw movement. He watched for a long time before he was able to make out the shapes of two men walking toward him. They were talking, but they were too far away for him to make out what they were saying. Gradually, he was able to see that they were wearing tool belts.

McDaniel turned and plunged into the dimness of FFF. He walked as fast as he could without running, occasionally looking over his shoulder. It seemed as if it took forever to get to the next tube.

Finally, he was there. It was marked 2-2-10-20. He ducked into it around the corner and peered back into FFF. Far away in the distance he saw the two men leave 2-2-10-10, turn into FFF, and, single file, begin walking toward him.

He eased away from FFF and took off down 2-2-10-20, in the same direction he had been going down 2-2-10-10. He saw that 2-2-10-20 soon had a long sweeping curve, bending to the right. When the tube had nearly curved out of sight of the juncture with FFF, he stopped, crawled into a side tube feetfirst, until only his head was sticking out, and watched for the two men to emerge from FFF.

He had to wait quite some time, but finally they came out of the passage. They turned away from him when they entered 2-2-10-20.

McDaniel watched them until they were out of sight. He crawled out of the side tube and then entered it headfirst. He slithered down to a grille plate to see where he might be. At the grille he could see a huge room filled with long rows of brightly lit greenhouses. Tall stands of corn filled every greenhouse. Somewhere nearby in the huge room, someone was listening to the play rehearsal over the intercom.

The Head Doctor was hollering, "At the Three Forks of the Arkansas, you must pause at the edge of the plains. Before starting across that buffalo range, you must understand that the plains are strange. The people there are many and mean, so you must get through without being seen. To avoid the places they're most likely to roam, you'll have to zig-zag like a drunk staggering home. To get through those buffalo plains in one piece, you must take forks of streams that they use the least. Each watershed forms a separate zone, and each of their streams has long been well known. Their many forks are a map for you to follow a way that will take you through.

You will learn how to fork from stream to stream, following a crazy zig-zagging seam, which will take you across that buffalo range, avoiding those people who are mean and strange. You must master forking to a high degree, and this you will do at the Rivers Three. You will practice your forking at that great place, until you can fork with skill and grace. Oh, great warrior, are you ready to know, the first forking test that will clearly show if you stand any chance of getting through, if forking is something that you can do?"

Little Elroy shouted, "I'll hear your test, then I will show, when I get to that place that I don't know, that you can't zig-zag it too much for me to not get to where I'm supposed to be."

The Head Doctor hollered, "Oh, great warrior, here's your first test, listen closely and do your best. From the Great Forks of the Rivers Three, walk due west to the fifth stream you see. Take that stream downstream until you have learned on which of the Three Forks you have returned. If you did that right, you will clearly see that your return was by Fork Number Three. If forking is something that you can do, there's lots of places we might send you to. But if you mis-forked that simple test, there may be no need to hear the rest. If at the mouth of the Wind Blowing Blue, you see your return was by Fork Number Two, we'll have our doubts about you getting through. Try it one more time to see if you can return by Fork Number Three. But if at the mouth of the Morning Sun, you see your return was by Fork Number One, there's but one thing for you to do then—come home and tell us where all in the hell you have been."

McDaniel backed out of the side tube and headed down 2-2-10-20, going the opposite way the two men had gone. At intervals he tried other side tubes, but the entire area seemed to be an agricultural zone, quiet now, and filled with greenhouses.

Before long, 2-2-10-20 came to an end, by making a sharp turn to the left and emptying him into another arterial tube marked Concourse Connector Two. It had no side tubes. It sloped upward for awhile, curved to the left, sloped back downward, and then curved to the left again. It was still curving to the left when it brought him to an arterial tube marked 3PPP. It didn't look like FFF. It looked the same as MM, stretching away into the distance in both directions in a straight line.

McDaniel paused. He could make no sense out of the designation scheme of the ventilation system. He was so turned around he didn't know which way he was going. He was certain he could retrace his steps back to his room, if he couldn't find a way out of Ishtaboli, but he wasn't sure how much farther he'd be able to go and still be able to do that. He'd have to go back exactly the way he had come. What if he encountered workmen on his way back? What if they were settled in, doing some job, blocking his path?

He stood lost in thought for a moment. Finally, he said to himself, "I am a Lighthorseman. I can go anywhere." And while here, he might as well try a side tube. He turned left into 3PPP and tried several side tubes, finding only darkness and silence at the grille plates.

Finally, quite some distance down 3PPP, after trying seven or eight unmarked side tubes, he came to one somewhat larger than the others, also unmarked. Not long after crawling into it, he came to a fork. He tried the tube to the right. Soon, he could see bright light spilling through a grille plate and could hear, faintly in the distance, an impassioned female voice, but he was still too far away to make out the words. As he moved closer, a loud fan motor somewhere nearby in the tubes suddenly started up, completely drowning out the voice.

At the grille, a very small grille plate, he could see nothing but the back of something that might be a chair. He could hear the woman's voice beneath the noise of the fan but couldn't make out what she was saying. He had begun backing away from the grille, backing out of that fork, when the fan motor clicked off, and the woman's voice came through, loud and strident. "We can blame it on the Beckoning Bitch! 'Send us your weary, your poor, your huddled masses,' she shouts, while holding a torch to light the way! Come—" The fan kicked in again, drowning out the voice.

McDaniel hurried back to where the tube had forked and tried the tube to the left. It was a long tube that gradually opened enough for him to stand up to his full height. He saw bright light spilling through a grille plate. As he approached the grille, he heard the firm, confident voice of Colonel McGee.

The very large grille plate, high on the wall of the room, allowed McDaniel a view of the colonel instructing a room full of elders. Among the audience, McDaniel could see people whom Little Elroy had introduced as the most venerated old men and old women in Okla Hannali, including many members of the Council of Doctors.

The room was like a large theatre in the round, with log walls and a roof covered with brush. It appeared to have a hard-packed dirt floor. The interior looked like the inside of a large, nearly round, brush arbor, with four circular rows of wooden benches rising like stairsteps along the outer wall of the structure.

Colonel McGee stood in a large open expanse in the center of the floor, directly beneath a large circular hole in the roof. The grille plate was at a level that let McDaniel see both above and below the roof of the brush arbor. Suspended well above the circular hole in the roof, out of sight from the audience, was a huge heat lamp, shining directly down on Colonel McGee. The heat from the lamp must have been nearly unbearable. Colonel McGee, wearing only a loin cloth, was sweating profusely. His entire body glistened with sweat, reflecting the bright light from above, giving him the appearance of shimmering, as he constantly turned to face one part of the audience and then another.

The people in the audience, though seated quite some distance from the heat beneath the hole in the roof, were nonetheless all fanning themselves with small hand-held fans as they listened. The scene suggested a speaker being required to stand in the full heat of the Mississippi summer sun, while his audience remained seated in the shade.

Colonel McGee was saying, "But what did he mean when he said, 'First I scare my enemy, then I kill him?'

"I'll tell you what it meant in the gray dawn of an autumn morning in the year 1808, after the Germans had put great pressure on the Choctaws to remove to the West, at the treaty negotiations at Mount

Dexter in 1805. It meant that he divided his three-hundred Choctaw warriors into three groups, holding the third group in reserve under his command.

"Just at dawn, when a large village of the Fast-Dancing People was just coming alive, the first wave charged, filling the air with the sound of one hundred lusty throats . . . *Chahta sai hoke*!"

Having already heard it once that evening, McDaniel was nevertheless ill prepared to hear it as he heard it now. Inadvertently, he had stepped some distance away from the grille before he realized what he was doing.

"The charge caught the village completely by surprise, and the light Choctaw war axes split many skulls before the Fast-Dancing People could marshal to meet the attack. But once they did, they began throwing it back, joyous to see how they so greatly outnumbered their attackers.

"At that critical psychological moment, the second wave launched its attack upon the flank of the Fast-Dancing People. Imagine what went through the minds of those people as they could not help but wonder how many more Choctaws were yet to attack, as they heard for the second time that morning. . ."

McDaniel was prepared for it this time, but still the scream curdled his blood.

"The Fast-Dancing People met the second charge as stoutly as the first. They also got all of their old people, and all of their women and children, moved to the rear, so their warriors could beat back the two-pronged attack.

"Their hearts must have been soaring. They saw that they would repulse the smaller Choctaw forces. Then, from behind them, they heard the voice of Pushmataha and one-hundred others. . ."

McDaniel clamped his hands over his ears as tightly as he could, but still the scream turned his knees to jelly.

"The third Choctaw wave hacked the women and children and the old people to pieces, right before the eyes of the Fast-Dancing warriors. Horrified at what they were seeing, they turned to try to make their way to their helpless loved ones, and as they did, they were hacked down from behind by the Choctaws in the first and second waves.

"The helpless loved ones pushed toward their warriors, trying to flee from the third Choctaw wave, blocking their own warriors from reaching it. In those moments, those Fast-Dancing People knew nothing but terror, and in the next few moments the Choctaw warriors slaughtered them all, every man, woman, and child."

McDaniel turned and hurried out of the side tube, back to 3PPP. When he emerged from the side tube, something beyond his control seized him, and he began to run. He ran and ran and ran.

Finally, he could run no more, but he was determined not to stop again until he came to the end of the tube.

Finally 3PPP ended at a large hatch—a curious hatch, indeed. It would have looked more at home in a submarine.

It opened easily enough, and he stepped through into a huge tube that curved out of sight in each direction. A sign said: Northwest Hanging Wall below, Sector 12 power conduits above.

He had taken a few steps out into the tube, toward the center, when he heard a sound in the distance. The sound was so eerie, so frightening, that he turned to dart back through the hatch. But a recessed trapdoor slammed shut on it. He clawed at the door, which had no handle.

He was still clawing at it when a roaring, howling wind lifted him off his feet and sent him tumbling head over heels down the tube.

CHAPTER 21

The heavy padding of the tube was all that saved him. He tumbled and tumbled and tumbled. The howling and roaring continued for what seemed like forever. Finally, he managed to pull his knees up under his chin and lock his arms around his legs. Tucked up like a ball, he rolled like one, on and on and on.

The wind died away as quickly as it had begun. He found himself sprawled in the tube, not knowing which way was up. He lay with his eyes closed until his head stopped spinning. He heard the inside lid of a side tube spring open, heard it slap back into its recessed holding.

He staggered toward it, wondering how he would ever find his way out of Ishtaboli if he couldn't find his way back to his room. He knew he had failed miserably at trying to figure out the designation schemes for the tubes, knew he could wander around for days until he stumbled upon some tube that he had been in before, some tube that would take him back to his room.

The tube he staggered toward turned out to be the familiar, commodious MM. He could barely contain his joy. He was so relieved that a fit of nervous anxiety washed out of him, leaving him trembling so that he could barely open the hatch.

Inside MM, he took the first side tube he came to, anticipating that it would take him to the Northwest Hanging Wall, a hope that grew as it angled downward before it leveled out again.

Arriving at the grille plate at the end of the tube, he lay staring into the gloom at some sort of vehicle. It was mounted on railroad tracks and looked like a rocket lying on its side. It had an entry hatch on top, and what appeared to be a windshield, and looked capable of great speed.

He heard footsteps. Soon a man appeared, carrying a clipboard. He stopped at the vehicle, raised the hatch, and peered inside. He began writing on the clipboard.

McDaniel heard other footsteps.

"Schedule that one for maintenance."

"The command car?"

"Right. Get Engineering and Development on it as soon as they open. It's got some wires crossed somewhere. The central computer can't shut it down."

"It's entirely manual?"

"It's a loose cannon. Fire it up now and none of the engagement blocks would stop it. It would override the switch signals. The buffers wouldn't even. . ."

The voices trailed off as the men walked away.

McDaniel stared through the grille. Maybe he was staring at his ticket out.

He waited until he had heard nothing for a long time, then he tried pushing against the grille. It wouldn't budge. He crawled backward up the slope of the tube to where it widened enough for him to turn around, and then he crawled backward down the tube to the grille plate.

He placed his feet on each side of the grille and pushed. It popped out.

It seemed to McDaniel that it made a terrible racket clattering around on the ground. But no one came to investigate.

He scrambled out of the tube and replaced the grille. The screws had been forced out of their holes, tearing away the wood that had held them, leaving them nothing to bite into, but the plate did not need the screws to remain firmly in place.

He raised the hatch and climbed into the vehicle. He lowered the hatch and sat staring at the console. There was room for only one person, and that was a tight fit. Gauges, levers, buttons, and dials were spread out before him in a bewildering display. There was no steering wheel, and there were no foot pedals. He could not see through the windshield.

He sat staring at the gauges and dials for a long time. He finally decided the vehicle probably was controlled by the stick that thrust up from the floor between his knees.

He found a button marked START and pushed it. The machine roared to life, and as it did, the windshield came alive.

He sat staring at an electronic display that he guessed to be a map of all of Ishtaboli, or at least all of Okla Hannali. It was a maze of tracks and tunnels and switches. Pinpoints of light filled the display, and, at intervals, flashing lights of various colors competed for his attention.

Above the display a message flashed at him, "Proceed with caution when leaving the maintenance yard."

He studied the display, finding the maintenance yard. He saw a flashing orange dot there, bigger and brighter than the others, which seemed to mark his position. It was along the Northwest Hanging Wall.

The nearest way out seemed to be a direct shot down the curve of the hanging wall to a point marked West Portal.

He was studying the display when the cockpit was suddenly filled with a female voice. "Good evening, Commander. One Switch has no record of your flight plan. Please enter your destination codes."

McDaniel stared at the console and looked up at the display. He looked back and forth between the two. Finally, he took the stick in both hands and pulled it all the way back.

With a thundering roar, the vehicle leaped forward. As it did, the display changed. The map disappeared, reappearing almost instantly, much smaller, at the far left side of the screen. In the center of the windshield, dominating the display, was a large three-dimensional image of the track and tunnel ahead, with objects at the side of the tunnel already beginning to fly by. At the far right was a smaller two-dimensional map showing the layout of switches and tunnels and tracks immediately ahead.

McDaniel was thrown backward in his chair by the thrust of the takeoff. As he roared down the tunnel he saw the image of a man standing in the middle of the tracks waving his arms frantically.

The man was barely able to dive out of the way as McDaniel went flying by.

"Commander, Computer Central shows that your vehicle has been logged for maintenance. Automatic shutdown will follow immediately."

But there was no shutdown.

"Commander, Computer Central shows that your vehicle is defective. Automatic derailment will follow immediately."

But there was no derailment.

The vehicle picked up speed. Objects at the sides of the track appeared and disappeared so swiftly McDaniel could not identify them.

"Commander, the maintenance defect in your vehicle is such that Computer Central cannot engage safety override. Initiate manual shutdown immediately."

McDaniel ignored the voice, concentrating all his attention on the screen.

"Commander, your mission has been tentatively logged as an emergency errand of mercy, possibly a runaway. One Switch is attempting to clear the tracks ahead. Please enter your emergency responder identification authorization codes."

McDaniel watched the objects fly past him on the screen. He watched the flashing orange dot racing along the map, racing along the curve of the hanging wall.

On the display to the right side of the screen he saw a vehicle, which had been coming toward him, turn into a side tunnel. As it did, he saw a red light far ahead turn green.

Out of curiosity, to see what might happen, as the next sidetrack approached, McDaniel jerked the stick to the right.

The succession of things that followed happened in such rapid order, with nanoseconds between them, that later McDaniel was not certain how much of it actually happened and how much he imagined.

He was barely aware that a bright orange light had flooded the cockpit when straps shot around his body from out of nowhere, just as a huge balloon instantly appeared in front of his face, blocking his view of the screen, all barely having time to take place before the vehicle braked so sharply and suddenly, with McDaniel thrust forward so powerfully that, strapped as he was, and with his face buried in the big balloon, only those parts of his body inside his skin could respond.

The feeling of having all of his insides crowded into one small place lasted until he thought he was going to pass out, and then the feeling, and the straps, and the balloon, and the bright orange light were gone as suddenly as they had appeared, replaced by a thrusting of his body to the left as the screen showed his vehicle making a hard, fast turn out of the hanging wall and into the tunnel to the right.

"Yeeeeeee Haaaaa!" yelled McDaniel. What a car! He could go anywhere in this car! Was it not, after all, the command car? And their computers could not control it.

On the screen, far ahead down the track, flashed a bright red light. He found his position on the map.

Dead End Ahead, the sign said. There was one chance to get out before the dead end, and he took it, a turn to the left.

A short distance farther, he took another turn to the left. Soon he was coming up to the Northwest Hanging Wall again, and a sharp turn to the right put him back on it.

With glee he jerked back on the stick, loving the roar of the great thundering machine as it leaped forward. He pulled the stick as far back as he could and held it there.

He ignored the blurred shapes and fleeting images on the three-dimensional screen, ignored the smaller map of the layout of tracks and tunnels in his immediate vicinity, and concentrated solely on the flashing orange dot on the Ishtaboli map as it rocketed down the hanging wall toward the long sweeping curve into the west portal.

In no time at all he felt the machine leaning, fighting to stay on the tracks as it entered the curve.

"Commander, your mission has been officially logged as a runaway. Initiate manual shutdown immediately."

As the flashing orange dot hit the last light on the map, marked West Portal, the maps changed instantly. They all showed, in two and three dimensions, a long, straight track that ended abruptly at a point marked New Construction Zone.

"Commander, collision with rock wall will occur in T-minus twenty seconds. Initiate manual shutdown immediately."

McDaniel watched the walls of the tunnel fly by. He glanced frantically at the maps. There were no sidetracks, no side tunnels, no way out.

He pushed the stick forward, to slow the craft, but nothing happened. The vehicle did not slow.

"Commander, decelerate immediately. Collision will occur in T-minus fifteen seconds."

McDaniel jerked the stick every way he could jerk it, but the vehicle continued flying toward the wall.

"Commander, disengage automatic thrust modulator. Initiate manual shutdown immediately. Collision will occur in T-minus ten seconds."

Frantically, McDaniel searched the console, trying to find the thrust modulator.

"T-minus nine, T-minus eight, T-minus seven..."

He began throwing switches, flipping levers, pushing buttons.

"T-minus six, T-minus five, T-minus four..."

He pushed everything he could see to push. Then he saw a red button off to the side marked STOP.

"T-minus three, T-minus two. . ."

McDaniel hit the stop button.

The release of pressurized air hissed and hissed and hissed. There was a mechanical shuddering in the vehicle, a rocking back and forth, and a distinct feeling of settling downward maybe two or three feet, and then stillness and quiet.

The video display went blank. It was replaced by a message, "Your score 519. Previous high score 286,882 by Little Elroy. If you wish your score recorded, enter your name now."

McDaniel sat staring at the screen. For a long time.

Finally, he raised the hatch and climbed out of the machine. He walked all the way around it and got down on his hands and knees and looked underneath it. When he stepped back several paces, he saw a sign standing above it: Rocket-Powered Roller-Coaster Command Car Ride.

McDaniel stood in the gloom for a long time, staring at the Command Car. He walked in front of it, following the railroad tracks, but they came to an end after about twenty feet.

He looked all around him. In the dimness, he could barely make out a few other objects. He walked to them. They turned out to be amusement park rides, a carousel, a Ferris wheel, a go-cart track. He found a start button for the carousel and pushed it. The carousel lights came on, and music began playing, with toy horses moving up and down. He stood for a long time, watching the carousel go round and round.

After a weary walk, trudging for an immense distance down MM, McDaniel finally arrived at the K-42 junction that led back to his quarters. By then, his mind was numb. All the way down MM, he had tried to make sense out of what was happening to him.

Maybe he was going about things the wrong way. Maybe trying to find a way out of Ishtaboli might be about the dumbest thing he could do. If nobody else had ever stumbled into Ishtaboli, then there were probably reasons for that, reasons that would also make it a high risk, long-odds gamble that someone like him would ever stumble upon some way out.

Little Elroy had no doubt been right. There was probably only one way out of Ishtaboli—pass the Candidate's examination. If they would ever allow him to do that. If he lived long enough to have a chance at doing that.

Thoughts of Elena flooded his mind. He didn't have a life anymore up on the surface. Why would he want to go back there? Maybe he could find a way to make sense out of what was happening to him down here and work his way through it. Maybe that was what he really wanted to do. Maybe a life with Elena would be a life worth living. Maybe that would be something worth fighting for—to have a chance for that kind of life.

He had crawled out of the air tube through the vent into his room and was replacing the useless grille screws when he found himself wondering, idly, why these two grille plates he had removed and fitted back into place had screws they did not need.

He lay down thinking about it. Screws were universally understood to be reversible. They might hold a barrier in place, but they also might remove it. Screws might be viewed as something like a door, and, rhetorically, an invitation. If there had been no screws in the grille plate in his room, would it have occurred to him to try to remove it?

What sort of person puts invitations like that in such a place as this, and to what purpose? And if his trip through the air tubes might have been invited, might it also have been monitored? Might some of the things he had seen and overheard been staged for his benefit?

But how could that be? He likely wouldn't have given the grille plate in his room a second glance if he hadn't been reaching for Elena's panties when the air came on, fluttering them where they'd caught on the lever of the air vent.

Where Little Elroy had tossed them.

Little Elroy.

Surely he hadn't tossed them there intentionally. All the way across the room, and caught them on the lever of the air vent? With only one chance to do that? He had done it with such effortless ease.

But then for the air to come on, just as McDaniel was reaching for the panties, when he'd been alone in the room, would mean that he hadn't really been alone. Someone had to have been watching him, in order to turn the air on at just that moment. Anyone watching then would be watching now, somehow. Maybe a camera hidden in the clock.

Could it all be some kind of game? Some dangerous game?

He remembered being told they'd given him truth serum. Little Elroy had said they'd not gotten much out of him, but what if that wasn't true?What if they knew everything about him?

Little Elroy. Hmmm.

Little Elroy had even provided the tool for removing the screws—the butter knife on the food tray. If Little Elroy might not be trustworthy, then what about Elena? His aunt. Both Natchez. Or Little Ejay? Another Natchez.

Somehow, among all these Choctaws, he'd become dependent on a few Natchez for most of what he knew about the place—or thought he knew. What if some of the things he thought he'd learned weren't true? Was someone trying to mislead him into making a fatal mistake?

McDaniel began compartmentalizing his knowledge, sorting out everything he thought he knew about Ishtaboli—what he'd learned, how he'd learned it, and from whom. He paid particular attention to his own observations, things he had seen or heard that might tend to corroborate something he had been told, while trying to keep track of the things that might lack corroboration. Then, he began creating shifting scenarios based on who and what might be reliable, and who and what might not be. He tried to identify the danger in each scenario and tried to estimate the odds for each scenario's plausibility. It was exhausting, complex thought that kept him awake far into the night.

Just before falling asleep, he found himself wondering if, rather than a game, it might be some kind of test.

CHAPTER 22

McDaniel struggled to awaken from a deep sleep.

"What did you say?" Little Ejay said.

McDaniel fluttered his eyes.

Little Ejay sat on his stomach, elbows on her knees, her chin in her hands, staring intently at McDaniel. She said, "Boy, when you get into that rapid-eye-movement phase, you really get with it."

"What are you doing?" McDaniel said.

"Watching you sleep. You were talking in your sleep. Were you dreaming about me?"

"Of course. Who else would I dream about?"

"I knew it." She tossed her head. "You dumped that slut for me. Did you see me on stage last night?"

"I saw your entrance with the Head Doctor. Did you enjoy the play rehearsal?"

"I'm bored with it. We do that same old thing every year. You didn't see much of it?"

"Only a little bit. Tell me something."

"What?"

"What does *na hollo* mean?"

"You don't know?"

"No."

"It means 'white people.' It's what the Choctaws called them, before they figured out they are Germans."

"Tell me something else," McDaniel said.

"What?"

"I heard a lot of different kids singing last night. One of them was singing about a river in a tree. Do you know what that was about?"

"Sure. You must have heard Little Hop. That's his entry into the boys' songwriting competition. I was on his peer review committee."

"He wrote the song?"

"He wrote it and he sings it. It's his tribute to Rutherford Platt, who wrote *The Great American Forest*. Little Hop's song is a celebration of one of the chapters in that book, 'River of Sap.' You haven't read that book?"

McDaniel shook his head. "Tell me something else. Did you ever hear of a Russian named Maizelles?"

"Sure. He does end-game studies."

"Do you study the Theory of Coordinate Squares?"

"I wouldn't say we study it. There's not much to it. It's hardly more than an application of the Rule of Opposition in King and Pawn endings."

"What is the Rule of Opposition?"

"You don't know?"

"No," McDaniel said. "I never heard of it before."

"It's a basic law of chess," Little Ejay said, "that the two enemy Kings can never stand side by side. There must always be at least one square separating them. In the end game, when the Kings come out to play, there's usually not much material left except Pawns. It then becomes a contest to see who can promote a Pawn to a Queen. For that, the play of the Kings is critical, as a helper, to help the Pawns along. And for that, the determining factor will almost always be who has the opposition, so one King can keep the other King away from the Pawn, as he escorts that Pawn across the board."

McDaniel was thoughtful for a moment. "So it's something that you cannot calculate until the end game?"

"You can calculate it anytime, once the middle game is well under way, for any square on the board. It's often the determining factor for when to try to put together a combination that will force a simplification from the middle game to the end game, by forcing an exchange of the pieces and leaving only the King and some of the Pawns. You look at the board, see what it will look like once all the exchanges have been made, and you calculate who will have the opposition for getting to wherever your King needs to get to, to force a passed Pawn and then to help it get all the way across the board to become a Queen. If it's in your favor, you initiate the combination, force the series of exchanges, play out the end game, and take the win. Or, more likely, after your first few moves to kick off the combination, your opponent will resign."

"Because," McDaniel said, "your opponent can see you'll eventually win?"

"Right," Little Ejay said, tossing her head. "You wouldn't want to be playing anyone who doesn't appreciate what you're doing to them. Watching them squirm is most of the fun."

There came a knock at the door. Little Elroy stepped inside. He looked at Little Ejay, perched on top of McDaniel, and said, "Do I even want to ask what you two are doing?"

"We're talking about chess," Little Ejay said. "He's a complete patzer."

"You never learned the game?" Little Elroy said, in astonishment.

"I learned the moves," McDaniel said, "but that's about all. Why do you study it down here?"

"Lots of reasons," Little Elroy said. "Did you know that Pizarro and his brothers taught the game to Atahualpa, the king of the Incas in Peru, in the 1530s, before they killed him? Then Pizarro's cavalry captain, Soto, brought a set with him into the Choctaw country in the 1540s. The Choctaws found it among the charred Spanish baggage, after the Battle of Moma Bina had burned the town to the ground."

Little Ejay turned quickly to Little Elroy. She said, "You're not supposed to know anything about any of those things. That's Indian history."

"The Head Doctor told me," Little Elroy said. "I know a lot of things I'm not yet supposed to know. I also know that you were supposed to meet your Zero Hour demerit class ten minutes ago."

"Damn!" Little Ejay whirled off the bed and trotted to the door. There she turned to face McDaniel. She reached up beneath her skirt, hooked her thumbs in her panties, pulled them out away from her body a few inches, and released them, snapping the elastic against her hips. She said, "I'd been thinking about leaving without these. But when I do get rid of them, I don't plan on finding it necessary to declare my shame." She disappeared out the door.

"Women," Little Elroy said, watching his sister and shaking his head. He turned to McDaniel. "Where did you go last night? I came by after rehearsal, but you weren't here."

"I took in a few lectures. And I took a ride in the Command Car."

"The Command Car?" Little Elroy said. "You went to the amusement park? What did you score?"

"519."

"519! Did you even get out of the maintenance yard?"

"Yeah," McDaniel said. "But it was a short trip."

"Did anyone give you any trouble?"

"I managed to avoid people pretty much. Is that going to be a problem today?"

"Well, apparently you're in luck on some things. One of them is whether you're even subject to the Lighthorse code of honor. Because your status is without precedent, and you are without peers, that means that you are sort of a walking, precedent-setting, living piece of history. Generations from now, people will look back to your conduct in saying that an A.B.E. should do this, or should not do that. It looks as if there are going to be more A.B.E.s, so the thing is surely going to become more formalized. It will be your example that will form the basis for most of that. Already some of the older boys, the better athletes, are talking about trying out for the team and skipping the exam. There is something intoxicatingly romantic about a man who loves ball play so much that he doesn't care if he is ever allowed to leave. I'll tell you, people are expecting great things from you in the championship game. We are now the betting favorite. Mother of the Sun! Our people are even giving odds against Okla Falaya!

"Can we beat Okla Falaya?" McDaniel said.

"Without you on the team, not even if we poisoned their water bucket. But with you, the people are confident of it. Hardly have they had time to catch their breath after the game, when Elena declares her shame. Elena! When you stomp your foot, the ground trembles. They figure Okla Falaya will never know what hit them."

"Did you say that I might not be subject to the Lighthorse code of honor?"

"Well," Little Elroy said. "Some of that seems to be up to you. But you *are* a Lighthorseman. I think you'd still be expected to take pains at all times to appear indolently resplendent in your leisure, except when some female might bat her eyelashes and say something like, 'I declare, I just don't know *how* I'm going to carry all of these packages all the way back to my quarters.'"

McDaniel was thoughtful for a moment. "You said last night that by today men wouldn't be saying things to me that might cause me to have to defend Elena's honor? Is that right?"

"That's right," Little Elroy said. "They will not insult you now, and no one will say anything really bad about Elena in your presence. The time for that is past. But if Elena is vindicated and you become her suitor, the men will make sport of you. What we're talking about here is the courting ritual for a disgraced suitor. You could have had it all, but you turned her down. She did not suffer the insult lightly. She is taking her lumps now from the public. Then it will be your turn. She will not be allowed to display the slightest interest in you until you have made a complete fool of yourself. The public has a huge appetite for this sort of thing. You will be bombarded by suggestions on what you should do to gain her attention and win her favor. These suggestions will, in fact, be thinly veiled slights about her desirability. They will say, of course you turned her down. Anyone would. If she were desirable, someone would have done thus and so, long ago, to win her favor. And you will be expected to defend her desirability by doing whatever was suggested. But you'll have a bit of a grace period here. For a day or two the public will honor the vindication of her shame. If she is vindicated."

"How will we know if she is vindicated?" McDaniel said.

"Well, her chaperon will have the formal duty of informing you of that. Technically, the vindication is not official until you have been informed of it by the chaperon."

"The chaperon?"

"Yes," Little Elroy said. "But, in reality, you'll probably be the last to know, or the last to be informed. But you will be able to tell by the behavior of the women. If she is judged a slut, every unmarried woman in Ishtaboli will tempt you with her favors. You will be regarded as being even more of a prize catch than you already are. Even married women will make fools of themselves, nudging you with their hips, pampering you, sitting close to you every chance they get, looking moon-eyed at you. It is a game they play. You will have shown yourself to be immune from sluts, and so they will play the slut. But they will only be teasing. The unmarried women, however, will be truly dangerous. A man who has been disgraced by an adjudged slut never remains a bachelor for long. He is presented with too many temptations. He is tormented without rest. For him the only escape is marriage, and the woman who nails him can count it as a great coup."

"And if she is vindicated?" McDaniel said.

"I think you'll be finding out about that for yourself. Now, how about you take a quick shower, and let's go get some chow."

CHAPTER 23

In the serving line at the cafeteria, Little Elroy ordered a huge breakfast of eggs and potatoes, bacon and sausage and ham, biscuits and gravy and coffee, and a big cinnamon roll for desert. When McDaniel saw how good it all looked, stacked high on Elroy's tray, he ordered the same. McDaniel, however, had to wait. The woman who took his order looked him up and down, doing nothing to hide the scowl on her face. "You just wait right there," the woman said as she disappeared into the kitchen.

"Uh oh," Little Elroy said. "I'm going to go on and find us a table."

When the woman finally brought McDaniel his food, he stared at it for a long time before he was able to figure out that the pieces of blackened debris on one of the plates were probably bacon. He could not, with confidence, identify any of the other items, though he spent some time trying to decide which cup held the gravy and which cup held the coffee.

At the table Little Elroy said, "I anticipated this." He gave McDaniel his tray, keeping only the cinnamon roll for himself. He said, "I don't eat much breakfast."

When McDaniel had finished his meal, Little Elroy said, "We'd better be getting to class."

As they approached the area where the classrooms were located, they came upon a group of girls. The girls were whispering and giggling and talking animatedly to one another. Several in the group had been introduced to McDaniel the day before.

When the girls saw McDaniel, the whispering and giggling and talking stopped at once. One by one, they tossed their heads, stuck their noses in the air, and marched, single file, into a classroom.

"Most of those girls are in Elena's dance class," Little Elroy said.

McDaniel tried to fight the feeling, but he felt about two inches tall. He began to understand some of the things Little Elroy had said. He began to see how this sort of thing could operate on a man, how it might eventually wear him down until he didn't know which way to turn. He remembered the bright-eyed excitement the girls had shown when Little Ejay had introduced them. They had been breathless, vibrant, eager. And now. . .

"Has Elena been deeply hurt?" McDaniel said.

"I don't know," Little Elroy said. "Come on. Let's go in and see Colonel McGee."

But Colonel McGee was not in the classroom. Instead, one of his aides was present, a young man who did not introduce himself to McDaniel and the children. He said, "Before your Indian history lessons begin, we want to do some diagnostic testing. These are not tests that you can pass or fail. They have been designed simply to measure your attitudes about certain things. In time, when the Indian history courses have been completed, you'll be given another battery of tests similar to these to measure how much your attitudes have changed. Now, we have quite a bit of testing to do, so we had better get started."

All morning long, McDaniel and the children took one kind of test after another. Some were multiple choice, some were true/false. There was also what seemed to McDaniel a particularly silly ink blot test. None of the tests made much sense to him. There were questions about preferences of colors, and sounds, and odors. There were word association exercises. It was all very subjective. There was nothing even remotely having anything to do with Indian history.

From the beginning McDaniel paid very little attention to the questions. For his answers, he glanced at Little Elroy's test, to his left, and to the boy seated at his right, marking alternately Elroy's answer and then the boy's. It was a boring exercise, and the morning was a long time ending.

Finally, it was done. The aide announced that their first Indian history lesson would be a movie, that they were all to be escorted to a theatre where they would have a special treat for lunch, milk and cookies.

The children filed out of the classroom into the corridor, where they were joined by children from other classrooms. As they entered the theatre, they were each given a glass of milk and a large cookie, and were told, "Eat your cookie, drink your milk."

In the theatre, Little Elroy followed McDaniel about half-way down the rows, and then all the way to the end of an aisle. McDaniel took the seat beside the wall, with Little Elroy to his left. The theatre soon filled up with children. They laughed and talked as the aides moved among them, saying, "Eat your cookie, drink your milk."

McDaniel did not eat his cookie. He sniffed at it, and sniffed at the milk. He took a sip of the milk. It seemed to have a faint aftertaste, something he could not identify, had never tasted before. He crumbled his cookie in his milk and watched it slowly dissolve. At his feet he saw a small grilled drain plate in the floor. When none of the aides were looking and Little Elroy was busy talking to his friends, McDaniel reached down and poured his milk into the drain.

After awhile, the aides began collecting the empty milk glasses. One little girl had spilled her milk. She was led out of the theatre by an aide. Another little boy admitted that he had given his milk to a friend. Both boys were removed from the theatre. A number of children were still munching on their cookies, but the aides didn't seem concerned about the cookies.

By the time all the milk glasses had been collected, the buzz of voices had died away and the children sat in silence. They sat staring at the screen, their hands clasped together in their laps. McDaniel imitated their pose. He glanced at Little Elroy and saw that he was staring at the screen as though in a trance. All the children seemed to be in a trance. When McDaniel looked at the screen, he could see that something was happening there. It was very faint, an interplay of revolving light and shadow, but it held the children mesmerized. As the lights in the theatre gradually grew dimmer and the images on the screen became more distinct, McDaniel began to feel a hypnotic pull. He began breathing more deeply and quickly. He had to fight to pull his eyes away from the screen to take a quick glance at Little Elroy. Little Elroy sat with his mouth wide-open, breathing hard and fast. McDaniel felt as though everything around him was happening in slow motion. He felt very, very sleepy, but when he looked at the screen again some powerful pull held his eyes on it and he felt powerless to do anything but sit and stare at it.

Faintly, a drumbeat sounded in the distance. As it grew louder and louder, a deep baritone voice filled the theatre, booming out the words of a song, in resonant tones, in a language McDaniel recognized as Choctaw, but he could not understand very many of the words. When the voice paused, all the children, as if on cue, rose to their feet, McDaniel rising with them. The boys began singing, imitating the tone of the voice, but failing to match its deepness. Shortly after the boys began singing, the girls joined in, but they sang a different song, a wailing, eerie refrain that set McDaniel's skin to crawling. On and on they sang, the two songs overlapping in such a way that the children were soon swaying back and forth.

The song began to have a hypnotic effect on McDaniel, and it set his pulse to pounding. Images began flashing on the screen. Without effort, he found himself communing with old water, brown and muddy, with old trails trodden deep and dusty by the feet of many generations, with hot summer sweat, with row after row of corn standing tall and proud in bright moonlight, with naked little children running and squealing in headlong delight.

The song ended and the children sat down. Somehow the screen had changed. It was larger than before. It was wider and taller, of that McDaniel was certain. It nearly filled his eyes.

A soothing voice filled the theatre, rhythmic, almost chanting, speaking Choctaw. McDaniel understood hardly a word of it, but he had no trouble comprehending the scenes of ancient village life that flashed before his eyes. A nearly naked people frolicked and cavorted through one long golden summer. The men hunted and the boys played at hunting. The women could barely hoe the corn, so frequent were their outbursts of laughter. They danced and feasted and engaged in great games of ball. The world teemed with wildlife. Deer were everywhere. Great flights of birds all but darkened the sky.

McDaniel was caught by surprise as the voice changed to English, "And then the *na hollo* came." But the change in voice was nothing compared to the changes on the screen.

Suddenly a huge armor-covered war horse came bursting out of the bushes carrying a sword-swinging Spaniard who trampled through the middle of a group of children hacking them to pieces, turning the ground red with blood. The children in the theatre screamed.

With a great, prolonged effort, McDaniel tried to close his eyes. It took all the effort he could muster, but finally he forced them shut. He sat listening to children screaming and the sound of thundering hoofs, the clanging of armor, and the terrible swish of sharp steel.

On and on it continued, the awful noises, the screams of the children. The hoofbeats pounded in his ears. The sound seemed to surround him, to be coming from everywhere at once, so loud, so insistent, he felt as though horses were trampling right on top of him.

He opened his eyes to see a young girl running across a field toward the woods, fleeing from a horseman. She ran as fast as she could run, and it looked as if she might be able to make it to the woods, but the horse was gaining on her. Her face filled the screen, and then the head of the horse, and then the girl, the horse, the girl, the horse, the girl, until finally, when she was nearly to the woods, the horseman leaned forward and with one vicious swing of his sword cut the girl in half.

Scene after scene followed in a rapid succession of terror and carnage that made McDaniel feel physically ill. He couldn't stand it anymore, but on and on it went.

Finally, the awful sounds ceased and the screen slowly faded to black. Gradually, there appeared the same patterns of revolving shadow and light that had begun the presentation, but after awhile they became faint and indistinct once more as the theatre lights came back up.

It was some time before McDaniel was aware that the aides had begun removing the children, starting with the back rows, assisting each child out of the theatre. When McDaniel's turn came, he found that he did need assistance in getting out of his seat, and he willingly allowed himself to be led back to his quarters and placed in bed.

"You should sleep now," said the aide as he left the room.

McDaniel could barely keep his eyes open. He looked at the clock and saw that it was almost 1 P.M. Elena had promised to bring him his medicine at 3:30. Would she be allowed to do that now? He had to find out. But there was no way he could stay awake. He had to sleep, at least for a little while. Blotting out worry about his medicine, he fell asleep wondering what the theatre would have been like if he had drunk all of his milk.

CHAPTER 24

McDaniel paced the floor of his quarters, occasionally feeling the beads of perspiration on his forehead. He looked at the clock on the wall again and again, willing the minute hand to move, and feeling a cold fear every time it did move.

Finally, at precisely 3:30, there came a sharp knock on the door. He opened it at once, started to speak, and then stood frozen in open-mouthed surprise, his hand still on the doorknob.

An old Choctaw woman stood staring him down in the doorway. For all her years, nothing had mellowed the fire in her eyes or the grim tightness in the lines about her mouth. Her hair was pulled back and bobbed in a severe bun, which complemented her demeanor. Her nose, slightly elevated, wrinkled distastefully as she looked McDaniel up and down.

"I am the chaperon," she said, as she stepped through the doorway, backing McDaniel into the room. She looked around the room, clicking her tongue and shaking her head. She said, "This room is not fit for the presence of a young lady. Make that bed."

McDaniel made the bed. As he did, she poked her head in the bathroom, clicked her tongue some more, and closed the bathroom door. She walked to the table, picked up Elena's panties, and fixed McDaniel with a withering stare.

He snatched the panties out of her hand and stuffed them under the mattress. He stood uncomfortably for some time, shifting his weight on his feet.

Finally, the woman cleared her throat, walked to the door, and stepped into the hallway.

Elena entered the room, followed closely by her chaperon. She kept her eyes lowered, not looking at McDaniel, and so did not see his sharp intake of breath. But she must have heard it. He saw a fleeting ripple of pleasure cross her face.

McDaniel barely recognized her. She wore an elegant, full-length, long-sleeved white dress that brushed the floor and buttoned up the front all the way to her chin. The swell of her hips was hidden in the folds of cloth, but the dress revealed the narrow girth of her waist, and, if anything, it accentuated the sharp, uplifting thrust of her breasts. Her hair was done up on the top of her head, revealing a face in full profile so beautiful that McDaniel could do nothing but stare in breathless appreciation. He nearly forgot where he was, but not entirely. His eyes also searched for his medicine. Where was his medicine? Surely she had brought his medicine.

The chaperon cleared her throat.

"Elena," McDaniel said.

"Speak when you are spoken to," the chaperon said, snapping the words at McDaniel. She turned to Elena, "Missy, I will thank you to arrange your face in a more shameful manner. That's better. Now, you have medical business to attend to. So let's not be standing around like a moonstruck cow. Get on with it."

From the folds of her dress, Elena produced a small plastic case. As she loaded a syringe with clear liquid from a small vial, McDaniel could see that her hands were trembling. She steadied herself and glanced furtively at the chaperon.

The chaperon turned her head, pretending to take no notice of what was happening.

Elena stepped to McDaniel and whispered, "By giving you the injection now, that will move your medicine clock ahead a little more than an hour. We'll not be allowed to see each other tomorrow, so you'll have to get your injection at the hospital. You'll need to do that by about 2:30 to avoid getting the shakes." She glanced quickly again at the chaperon, then, for the first time, met McDaniel's eyes. Her face took on a look of grim determination. She said, "Soon, we'll have to deal with this problem."

McDaniel could barely keep from fidgeting. Already, he had begun feeling alternately hot and cold. His brow was wet with sweat.

Elena administered the injection. She replaced the syringe in the kit, replaced the kit in her dress, and stepped away from McDaniel to stand beside the chaperon.

McDaniel felt a wave of relief rushing through his veins. In little more than a moment, he felt calm and peaceful and wonderfully content. Now he could give Elena his full, admiring attention. But when he looked at Elena, there was something in her face that made McDaniel decidedly uneasy. She looked frightened. Staring at the floor, she looked as though she fervently wished she were somewhere else.

The chaperon cleared her throat loudly and looked at Elena. She said, "Missy, is this the man?"

Elena nodded her head, still staring at the floor.

"Speak up, girl. Don't be coy," the chaperon said. "Is this the man?"

"Yes," Elena said, glancing briefly at McDaniel. "He's the one."

The chaperon said, "Uh huh," sounding as though the source of an odor of something long dead had at last been found. She said, "Lighthorseman McDaniel, you have been disgraced. This young lady has disgraced you, and she is now in a state of shame. I must inform you, however, that the community has vindicated her shame, rather than judging her a slut. But the decision of the public need not be your decision. Were she not a Natchez girl, the public surely would have adjudged her a slut, and you may judge her a slut if you choose. Should you judge her a slut, the community will not think highly of having its judgment disregarded, and the community will christen her an Honored Woman, never to have relations with any man again, as a testament to its belief in her virtue. If, however, you do not judge her a slut, you may make application to court her, which she can accept or refuse, as she pleases. You will be the only man ever allowed to be her suitor, whether or not you should be successful in winning her hand. Do you understand the things I have just said?"

"I think so," McDaniel said, feeling some relief that this process seemed to work pretty much the way Little Elroy had explained.

He looked at Elena, his heartbeat quickening. If he could trust Little Elroy, it was much more likely he could trust Elena. He hardly dared imagine her as his wife. He stared at her, mesmerized by her beauty, hoping the chaperon would allow them just a moment of privacy.

But the chaperon wasn't finished. She said, "Very well. Then let's begin." She cleared her throat loudly once more and opened a notebook. "You are now required to hear the common knowledge about her." She began reading. "Lighthorseman McDaniel, it is my duty to inform you that the young lady who has disgraced you is not a virgin. It is my duty to inform you that the young lady who has disgraced you has consorted with more than one man. It is my duty to inform you—"

"Wait a minute," McDaniel said. "I don't need to hear this."

"Yes, you do," the chaperon said. "The community has heard it, and now you must hear it. You must hear it all."

McDaniel heard it all. At first, he was angry at the woman for what she was doing to Elena, but then her words began taking him by surprise. Surprise gave way to shock. Shock gave way to incredulity. On and on the chaperon droned, name after name, detail after detail. Once, Elena flinched visibly, when he had the bad grace to turn his eyes quickly to her. After awhile, he couldn't stand it anymore, but the woman droned on and on. He was numbed by the recital long before it was over.

Finally, the woman stopped reading and looked at him. She said, "Lighthorseman McDaniel, you are required to stand mute at this time. Now begins a period of reflection, during which you will consider all that you have heard. Tomorrow, you must tell me if you can look upon this lady, and think of her, and treat her as a lady worthy of your highest esteem, notwithstanding anything you have heard today. I shall return at this hour tomorrow to hear your decision."

McDaniel was, in fact, speechless, and could do nothing but stand and stare at the two women as they left the room. Elena's shoulders were slumped and her face was drained of color. Her eyes, cast downward, moistened as she went out the door.

CHAPTER 25

McDaniel pulled himself together and tried to put Elena out of his mind. There would be time to think about Elena later, to sort out his feelings, try to come to terms with what he had just heard. But right now there was something he needed to know, and he might not have much time.

Deftly, with a practiced hand, he used the butter knife under his bed to remove the screws from the grille plate that covered the air duct, hiding the screws and the butter knife again under his bed. He removed the grille, placed it within reach, and entered the tube feetfirst, reaching out and pulling the grille into place behind him.

He wriggled backward to K-42, and then crawled quickly down it to MM. He walked at a brisk pace to K-40, crawled into it, and slithered down the second tube. Before he reached the grille plate, he could hear the voice of Pelar.

". . .and you are not responding with your mind anymore, but with your emotions. He is the future of this place."

"Ha!" the Head Doctor said. "He will bring about the end of this place."

"We cannot hide in this hole forever. He is trying to move us forward."

"Forward?" The Head Doctor's voice dripped with sarcasm. "Drug-intensified hatred is a step forward?"

"I'm not happy about that, either. But it will be effective, and it will save time. Since when have you been queasy about teaching the children to hate them?"

"But we don't lie to them! You've seen the lesson plans. You've seen the lies. My God, the Germans are bad enough as it is. There's no need to lie about them. And that's hardly the worst of it. What about us? He's painting us as the sweetest, most angelic creatures who ever lived."

"That's how the Germans portray themselves. Every evil thing they do to us, they justify in the name of their religion and their economic system. Colonel McGee is merely fighting fire with fire."

"But what he intends to do is dangerous! We'll lose everything!"

"We've already lost everything."

"We've not lost this place! But we will, if McGee gets his way. You've seen what he thinks he can get the German slave scientists to produce. All he will need then will be a delivery system. The man is mad. There's too much that can go wrong."

"It might work."

"And what if it does? Have you thought about that? Pelar, what goes through your mind when you hear him say that Choctaws are destined to rule the world?"

"Why not us? Do you want the Germans to rule everything?"

"You know I don't. But this is not the way to stop them. We must reason with them. If we try to pursue a military solution, it will be the end of us. McGee must be stopped before he gets started. Even if he gets no further with this mad scheme than getting it started, at the very least he will have wasted the lives of all these children! How can you approve of that? You've seen what he intends to do with them."

Silence filled the room. It lasted a long time, and when it was broken, Pelar's voice had changed.

"Reason with them?"

"Pelar—"

"You have forgotten your old self, haven't you, Old Man? Where is the angry hatred in your voice? Do you not remember how it inspired us never to give up, never to let the lying bastards off the hook?"

"Please, let's not—"

"No. Let's do. Let's remember, you and I. Who else is left to remember? Where is that angry young man we followed, because we dared not be against him? Can you not see your old self in Colonel McGee?"

"I was never—"

"Do you not recall how Mingo Hoopaii thought you insane? A danger to all of us, and a danger to this place? Have you even forgotten Article IV? Have you even forgotten The Eighty-Three Words?"

"Pelar—"

"I have not heard you speak them for a very long time. Have you forgotten how you shouted them at us day and night? Do you think The Eighty-Three Words do not ring in the ears of Colonel McGee? Who do you think planted them there? I can still hear *your* voice ringing in my ears: 'The Government and people of the United States are hereby obliged to secure to the said Choctaw Nation of Red People the jurisdiction and government of all the persons and property that may be within their limits west, so that no territory or state shall ever have a right to pass laws for the government of the Choctaw Nation of Red People and their descendants; and that no part of the land granted them shall ever be embraced in any territory or state.'"

"Pelar—"

"No. Don't 'Pelar' me. Colonel McGee is a kitten compared to how *you* used to be. He talks of his plans, but you were much more than talk, Old Man. Because of you, and what you have done, we have never given up. But enough of that. My mind is made up. He shall have his chance. Our time is over. Tonight, Old Man, at the meeting of the Council, I shall challenge you to duel."

"Pelar—"

"No. My mind is made up. We shall step aside. We shall step aside together. God, hasn't it been a long, strange trip for us?"

McDaniel had heard enough. He slithered backward out of the tube. When he emerged from K-40, he ran down MM to K-42 and slithered quickly down the tube to his room.

To his surprise, he found Little Ejay asleep in his bed. He shook her awake. She clasped her arms around him, and said, in a sleepy, frightened voice, "I don't like Indian history."

"I know," McDaniel said. "I know."

He left her in his bed and hurried down the hall to the boy's dormitory. He shook Little Elroy awake and said, "Elroy, wake up.

I want to take the Candidate's examination right now. How do I do that?"

"Right now?" said Little Elroy, rubbing the sleep from his eyes.

"Yes," McDaniel said. "Right now."

Little Elroy got out of bed. He said, "Don't you even want to learn Choctaw arithmetic first?"

"No, I want to take the exam right now."

"Okay." Little Elroy shrugged. "Follow me."

McDaniel followed Little Elroy to the Head Doctor's office. There, a surprised attendant scheduled the examination immediately.

"Good luck," Little Elroy said, as the attendant led McDaniel to a back room.

CHAPTER 26

When McDaniel finished the examination, he was escorted into a large room where all of the Okla Hannali Lighthorsemen were gathering. He was taken to the podium and positioned a few feet from a lectern. He was told the proceedings would begin as soon as all the Lighthorsemen had assembled and Colonel McGee had arrived.

It wasn't long before the room was filled with the Okla Hannali Lighthorsemen, and shortly afterward, Colonel McGee entered the room and strode to the lectern on the podium.

"We are here today," Colonel McGee said, "to pass judgment on Lighthorseman McDaniel's Candidate examination. I shall now read the examination. I do not need to remind any of you of the seriousness of the proceedings we are now undertaking. Please listen carefully."

Colonel McGee raised a copy of the examination and began reading: "Instructions: Despite all you may have heard about the legendary Okla Hannali Ishtaboli team of 1743, you are to consider only the following historical recitation for the purposes of this examination.

"Historical recitation: Never in the history of the game of Ishtaboli has there been a team like the Okla Hannali team of the 1730s and early 1740s. The story of how most of its players died during the 1743 season will forever remain a thing of legend. The deaths brought the dynasty to an end, but not before they tried to climb to the pinnacle of the game one last time.

"In the 1742 season, they attained the unimaginable. Never before, and never since, has an Ishtaboli team skunked every single opponent. But, enshrined forever as the most hallowed year on the Field of Honor, that achievement stands as a testament to their athletic prowess, their creative genius, and the precision of their teamwork.

"Their great defensive record, paradoxically, was achieved with offense. Beginning in the 1732 season, they started tinkering with a formation they called the Double T, which soon evolved into the devastating Triple T, and finally emerged as the unstoppable TT Squared formation (TT^2)—with its swinging gate of multiple pitch-back, high-fly floaters, its lateral intercept, toss-back, wing walkers, its floating door of tiptoe, tip-in, picket-post swat slammers, and its algorithmic, multiple-pulsing relay waves of smash-mouth field flatteners.

"When executed properly, nobody could stop it. No other team could duplicate it, some couldn't even diagram it, though they all tried to adopt it. Try as they might, year after year, no other team could execute it, while year after year, Okla Hannali got better and better at it, until, finally, came the Big Stink Season of 1742, when Okla Hannali scored so quickly and devastatingly nearly every time it touched the ball that no opponent managed even a single score against them during the entire season.

"The humiliation of all the Ishtaboli teams during that season was so great, and the desire for revenge so strong, that never has a season been so eagerly anticipated as the 1743 season. And then, on the eve of the opening game, disaster struck.

"A ferocious and prolonged riot in the Okla Hannali slave quarters took the lives of some of the best players on the team. Those players who survived were badly injured. Almost all of them had broken bones. Many had broken ribs, busted shoulders, broken jaws, broken arms, broken legs. Some had ghastly puncture wounds. Some lay near death, in feverish delirium. Others were conscious, but immobilized by their injuries. Many were walking wounded, nursing their broken bones.

"To the astonishment of the Okla Chito Ishtaboli team, the Okla Hannali players took the field, as scheduled, for the opening game, and to the astonishment of everyone, they won the game. But at a great cost. Six of their players, those most gravely wounded in the riot, died during the contest. Three others died within a week. And there began a vicious cycle that lasted throughout the season.

"Every game took its toll. Every week, every injury was aggravated anew. Simple broken bones, which might have healed if left alone, turned to blood poisoning. Men with broken ribs coughed blood until finally they died. Week by week, men who had been immobilized by their injuries recuperated just enough to take the place of the dead, only to aggravate their own unhealed injuries and begin their own dance with death.

"Incredibly, in game after game, week after week, they found a way to win. Gone were the high scores and the lopsided margins of victory. Every game defied belief in the way the razor-thin margin of victory was achieved. In unbearable pain, outmanned, and almost overwhelmed by fate, they had unbelievable good luck in the form of fumbled pitches, over-tossed tip-ins, lateral hand-backing blunders, high-fly foulups, and busted formations by their opponents, many of which defied explanation, while their own scaled-back, undermanned version of the TT Squared formation kept working its magic on the scoreboard.

"To the incredulity of everyone, they found themselves undefeated entering the national championship game, a return grudge match against an Okla Falaya team bitterly determined to avenge the humiliation of the previous season, and equally determined to avoid the humiliation of being defeated by crippled men.

"The national championship game turned out to be not much of a contest. Okla Hannali had used up all its luck in getting to that game. Nine of its dwindling number of players finally succumbed to an agonizing death the week before the game, and six more fell early in the contest. Depleted to a point that it could no longer run the TT Squared formation, or do much but try to slow down the opponent's scoring drives, the team nevertheless covered itself in glory in the closing moments of the game by one last great burst of effort that scored one lone goal to avoid the degradation of getting skunked, to the fury of the entire Okla Falaya team, which did everything it could do to try to prevent that goal from being scored.

"In the end, so devastating were the deaths that it would be thirty years before Okla Hannali would again be able to field a team capable of contending for the title. But to honor those immortal athletes, the TT Squared formation was retired, and to this day no team has been allowed to attempt it, in honor of the memory of what was surely the greatest Ishtaboli dynasty of all time."

Colonel McGee paused. He looked all around the room. He said, "That was the historical recitation. And now I shall read the examination question." He held up another sheet of paper, and, looking at it, said, "Regarding the Okla Hannali Ishtaboli team of 1743, what is the most significant thing that can be said about those athletes?"

Colonel McGee lowered the paper. He looked at McDaniel, and said, "Lighthorseman McDaniel, step forward please."

McDaniel stepped forward to stand beside Colonel McGee at the lectern.

Colonel McGee picked up McDaniel's examination booklet and said, "I shall now read to you Lighthorseman McDaniel's answer." He opened the booklet, glanced at McDaniel's answer, looked all around the room, and shouted, "The bums didn't win the national championship!"

A mighty cheer arose from all the assembled Okla Hannali Lighthorsemen. They surged forward around McDaniel, pounding him on the back, pumping his hand. They pounded one another on the back, buzzing with excitement, their faces all aglow. They stood and cheered and clapped and cheered some more, rocking the room with their voices.

Finally, Colonel McGee called for quiet. He pounded a gavel again and again calling for quiet, until finally the noise began to die down a little. He shouted, "Lighthorseman McDaniel, by the unanimous consent of the Okla Hannali Lighthorsemen, I declare that you have passed the examination!"

The Lighthorsemen exploded again with cheering and clapping, but Colonel McGee raised his arms, asking for quiet. "Furthermore," Colonel McGee said, "Since we are absent our other co-captain, I hereby appoint you a co-captain of this squad. You shall henceforth be known as Captain McDaniel."

Again the Lighthorsemen exploded with cheering and clapping. And then they started shouting, "Speech! Speech! Speech!"

Colonel McGee stepped aside from the lectern, offering it to McDaniel.

McDaniel stepped to the lectern. There was still a light buzzing of excitement in the room as he took a deep breath, and said, "Colonel McGee, in the presence of all these witnesses, I hereby challenge you to a duel!"

A hush fell over the room as the Lighthorsemen stared at McDaniel. After a moment, they turned their eyes to Colonel McGee.

Colonel McGee stepped forward. In a firm, determined voice, he said, "It is a great honor to be challenged to duel by Captain McDaniel. I choose as my second, my good friend Shulushamastubbee. As the one challenged, it is my privilege to choose the weapons. I choose the Okla Hannali war axe. I understand what our heroic teammate, Captain McDaniel, is doing, and I am in awe of the genius of this great plan. He is inspiring us to play the greatest Ishtaboli game of all time. He is challenging us to sacrifice ourselves so we might cease being mere mortals and ascend to a plane of legend, so that this team, every one of us, will be given the opportunity to write a chapter in the history of the game of Ishtaboli that will never be forgotten. I am humbled and honored and thankful that I have lived to be a part of this great day. Therefore, that this great plan might be achieved, and, as the one challenged, it being my privilege to set the date of the duel, I set the date at noon, the day after the national championship game. Who knows, one of us might die in the dark on the Field of Honor. I hope that person might be me, so the greatest Ishtaboli player of all time might live to play for Okla Hannali again. But whatever is to happen, let it happen. Let two condemned men lead our team. Let us be reckless and bold and invincible. Let us smash Okla Falaya and take the title!"

A mighty cheer went up from the Okla Hannali Lighthorsemen. They crowded around McDaniel and Colonel McGee, pounding them on the back, telling them what a great honor it was to play with condemned men.

One shouted, "Can you just *see* the faces of the Okla Falaya Lighthorsemen when they hear the news?"

Another said, "Has it *ever* happened before? Two co-captains playing as condemned men?"

They crowded around McDaniel, each one begging to be appointed his second for the duel, and to reap the honor of swinging the axe.

McDaniel was in a daze, contemplating all that Colonel McGee had said. Finally, he took one of the men aside, put his arm around his shoulder, and said, "Tell me, now that I'm no longer A.B.E, and am free to come and go, if I wanted to go up to the surface, you know, get some fresh air or something, how would I go about doing that?"

"Oh, that's easy," the Lighthorseman said. "Just take the elevator."

"Take the elevator," McDaniel said. "That is so simple. Why didn't I think of that? And where, exactly, might that elevator be located?"

Suddenly there came the sound of a commotion out in the corridor. The man McDaniel had been talking to turned toward the door and said, "What's that?" Another man said, "There's something going on out there."

Before anyone could move, a man burst into the room and shouted, "Lighthorsemen, come quick! Captain Kelley has been found half-dead near the new construction zone!"

The Lighthorsemen surged out the door into the corridor. As soon as they had all gotten through the door, they had to move to both sides of the corridor to allow three men to pass through the middle of them. Two of the men carried a stretcher, while the third man held up an IV bottle.

As the men drew even with McDaniel, he saw Sergeant Kelley lying unconscious on the stretcher. The men stopped to talk to Colonel McGee.

"How is he?" Colonel McGee asked.

"He'll live," said the man holding the IV bottle. "He's badly dehydrated, but I think he'll be *hoke* once we get him to the hospital."

"What happened?"

"He didn't say much before passing out. Just that he was chasing an intruder."

"Clear the new construction zone," Colonel McGee said. "Get all the slaves back in their quarters. Put them in lockdown. Get the trains ready to roll."

"Yes, Sir," the man said.

Colonel McGee turned to the assembled Lighthorsemen and shouted, "All available men assemble at the train stations in ten minutes for a search and destroy mission! Spread the word to all of Ishtaboli!"

Men scurried in all directions, leaving McDaniel and another Lighthorseman to watch the men carry Sergeant Kelley toward the hospital.

The Lighthorseman said, "I sure hope Captain Kelley can regain his strength in time for the game."

"Sergeant Kelley is Captain Kelley?" McDaniel said.

"Yes," the Lighthorseman said.

"But is he a sergeant, or is he a captain?"

"Ah," the Lighthorseman said. "It is a bit confusing, isn't it? On the surface, he is Sergeant Major Kelley, of the United States Army. But down here he is co-captain of our Ishtaboli team."

"Then," McDaniel said, frowning, "why is Colonel McGee called Colonel, when he is also a co-captain of the team?"

"Ah," the Lighthorseman said. "That's because up on the surface, Colonel McGee is Lieutenant Colonel McGee, of the United States Marine Corps Reserve."

The man continued talking, not noticing that, at the mention of the Marine Corps, McDaniel's eyes had narrowed down and darted from side to side before going completely unfocused. His jaw slackened, dropping his mouth open, and when his eyes focused again, his face took on a countenance that the Marines in World War II had called the thousand-yard stare.

The Lighthorseman was surprised when McDaniel turned and walked away from him, zombielike, as though sleepwalking across the corridor. The Lighthorseman shrugged and walked away.

McDaniel, unseeing, walked across the corridor, stopping only inches away from the concrete. Minutes ticked away while his mind was racing, processing information at a dizzying pace. When the answer finally came to him, the muscles in his face sprang back to life. He grinned at the concrete. His eyes slowly focused, and then darted from side to side. He said, "The United States Marine Corps. The sonsabitches herded me down here to see if they could drive me crazy."

Everything made sense now. If the Corps could drive him crazy, they'd be off the hook in dealing with him as a deserter. Nobody would think the less of them for not coming down hard on somebody who was mentally incapacitated. He should have seen that coming, if nothing else, from the things Sergeant Kelley had said to him before they plunged into the whirlpool at the end of the underground river. If he'd been more alert, he might have realized they were already laying the foundation for it.

It explained a lot. Colonel Fay and his Black Berets up on the surface, all Marines, playing their part, and boy had they played it well. McDaniel had fallen for it completely, had let them herd him down here right into the trap.

But something like this would require years of preparation, and a huge expense. They'd have to hire and train actors, including all of those kids, and build this whole place, make it all seem real. And why do it now? Why not years ago? The answer came to McDaniel with sudden, complete conviction. The two-hundredth anniversary of the Marine Corps! That's what this was all about. The sonsabitches were celebrating their Bicentennial Birthday in grand style, getting rid of their #1 biggest embarrassment. And they had spared no expense. McDaniel's eyes misted over in a fit of genuine humility at all the trouble they'd gone to, just for him. But they'd inadvertently let him in on the scheme, and he didn't dare let them know that he knew.

As men began reassembling in the corridor, McDaniel quietly mingled among them. An ordnance crew came by, passing out flashlights and pistols. McDaniel took one of each.

Colonel McGee led the men down the corridor to a door in the wall. They all filed down a stairwell to a subway platform, and from there onto a waiting train. The train took them to another station, where more armed men climbed aboard. The train made quick stops at station after station, until McDaniel had lost track of how many stops they'd made or how many men might have climbed aboard.

Finally, the train stopped in a large dark tunnel. All the men got off and began marching down the tracks in front of the train. Soon the tracks ended and the tunnel was just a long dark hole stretching into the distance, with many side tunnels, all in various stages of construction.

Men dropped off into every side tunnel. Gradually, the number of men moving straight ahead became fewer and fewer. By the time the tunnel played out and became a maze of natural caverns, there weren't many men left with McDaniel, and they kept branching out into different caverns. After awhile, McDaniel was all alone, moving at a determined, steady pace, always upward, and always away from Ishtaboli.

CHAPTER 27

For hour after hour, with flashlight and pistol in hand, McDaniel climbed through the caverns, his mind numb. He didn't understand the world anymore, and he certainly didn't understand the Marine Corps. He didn't like psychological warfare. How was he supposed to fight it? And he didn't understand what it meant.

He just wanted to get away from everything and take a long rest. Then maybe he could sort things out.

But it was hard to make good time through the caves. Sometimes he would be in a fairly large cavern, and he would have at least some idea of what he needed to do to get to the other end of it. But there wasn't always an easy way to get from one end of a cavern to the other. Most of the time he wasn't in any kind of cavern at all, just some narrow, twisting cave that led him first one way, and then another, until he didn't know which way he was trying to go. Sometimes he had to crawl on his belly. Often he found himself having to choose between different ways to go. Several times he found himself in blind alleys and had to backtrack to find some other way.

He saw nothing that he recognized from when he had descended through the caves the first time. He saw no tracks anywhere, no evidence that anyone had ever been there before. The dust of centuries lay undisturbed everywhere he looked.

He got thirsty long before he got hungry. But he found no water, and he had no food. Gradually, the lack of water and the hours of intense effort began to take their toll. He found it harder and harder to go on. He consciously slowed his pace to conserve his energy, so that at least he might keep covering ground without having to stop and sleep. Sleep was no antidote to not having water. He would continue dehydrating while he slept. He had to keep pushing onward and upward until he got to the surface. He had to do that before he could allow himself to fall asleep.

He plodded onward, wishing he had taken a big, long, cool drink of water before entering the caves. The lack of water was making him feel hot. His skin felt on fire. If only he could douse his face and arms with a bucket of cool, cool water. The thought made McDaniel shiver. He suddenly felt cold. Within a few moments his teeth began to chatter.

His eyes began to sting. He stood batting his eyes, trying to figure out what was wrong, until finally he realized that sweat was running into his eyes. He put down the flashlight and felt of his forehead. It was covered with sweat. "Oh, no," he said to himself. "I've got the shakes. It's the medicine."

There was nothing he could do about it. Grimly, he picked up the flashlight and went on. He forced himself to go forward, forced himself to put one foot in front of the other. He would kick this thing. He would fight it and conquer it. He would harness the power of it and use it to propel him onward.

He didn't know when he stopped, didn't know if it had been the uncontrollable chattering of his teeth and the shivering of his body that had forced him to lie down and try to warm himself by rolling in the dirt, or whether it might have been the unbearable ovenlike heat enveloping him that caused him to look for a cool rock to lie beside, and he didn't know how long he had been stopped, but he knew when he rose to his feet and said, "I want my medicine."

He turned and started back down. He was furious that his medicine was not immediately at hand, that it wasn't even remotely close at hand. What could he possibly have been thinking to leave without his medicine?

He stomped through the caves, angry at every obstruction, at every dead end. It seemed as though he had hardly gotten started when he looked down and saw that he was no longer on his back-trail. When he shined the flashlight on the ground in front of him, he could see nothing but undisturbed dust. When he shined the flashlight behind him, he could see his tracks clearly. In a rage, he threw the flashlight against the rocks as hard as he could throw it. It shattered, plunging his world into darkness. He raised his pistol and fired round after round into the dark, yelling and cussing at the top of his voice, causing brief, bright explosions of light with every shot. Then he threw the empty gun as far as he could throw it and went stomping after it into the dark.

He screamed at the dark, daring it to come and get him, daring anything in his path to try and stop him.

Gradually, his initial rage spent itself, and he became a cold, calculating blur in the darkness, moving deliberately and steadily downward, any way he could find.

It was then that he saw the distant beam of a flashlight. Stealthily, he moved toward it. It was stupid to have smashed his flashlight, he now realized. But there was one he could have.

He gradually became aware that he was in a large cavern and that whoever was holding the flashlight was at the far end of it, and up above. When he reached the end of the cavern, he stood at the bottom of a long, steeply sloping incline of sand. At the top of the incline was the beam of light.

McDaniel had climbed most of the way up the incline before the man holding the flashlight saw him. He shined the light on McDaniel, and said, "Hello. I'm a reporter for the *Daily Oklahoman*. Can you tell me anything about why the U.S. Army is in the McGee Valley?"

McDaniel grabbed the flashlight out of the man's hand, shoved him to the ground, turned, and headed back down the incline.

The man yelled, "Hey!" But McDaniel kept going. The man yelled again and again until McDaniel was finally so far away he couldn't hear him anymore.

For hour after hour McDaniel stomped through the caverns, raging at them, yelling at them, cursing at them. At one point he found himself waist-deep in water without having any idea how he had gotten there. He drank and drank and drank until he was saturated, but it did nothing to ease the awful craving in his veins.

For a time, he must have gone mad-dog insane. When he snapped out of it long enough to be aware of his condition, he was surprised to find himself in total darkness. He didn't have the flashlight anymore, and he had no idea what he might have done with it.

At one point he found himself screaming "Elena! Elena!" but only his own voice echoed back to greet him.

He was crawling on his belly through the dark when a great, quiet calm descended upon him. He stopped. It was so soothing and peaceful. He lay breathing in quiet contentment, at peace with the world.

He rested for a few minutes, and then he turned and started trying to make his way upward out of the caves. He had no idea how many hours he crawled, and clawed, and worked his way upward. Every time that exhaustion overtook him, he managed to rest a few minutes and then continue on, until finally, he could go no farther. He tried to force himself to get up, but it was no use. All he could manage to do was roll over on his back and stare into the darkness that had defeated him. He tried to force himself to stay awake, but he couldn't stay awake. He gave up then. He closed his eyes and fell asleep, not hearing the distant rumble of thunder, not feeling the wind stir the air, not feeling the soft, gentle rain falling on his face.

PART 3

The Secret of Bugaboo Canyon

CHAPTER 28

McDaniel was still lying on his back, sound asleep, the sun hitting him full in the face, when he was startled awake by the roar of an Army helicopter hovering above him. Before he could move, soldiers came slithering down ropes from the chopper and restrained him while the chopper landed. He was ushered aboard for a fast, low-level flight to the Katie Lake lodge.

As soon as the chopper landed, McDaniel was hurried across the compound to the main room of the old lodge. The scene had changed greatly during the time he had been gone, not the room itself but the people in the room.

It was filled, wall to wall, with generals of the United States Army. Wearing regular Army uniforms, they occupied every chair, stood in every available space. McDaniel could see no one who was not a two- or three- or four-star general. Some of them were talking on telephones, others were clustered in groups of five or six, holding intense conversations, their faces drawn taut with anxiety. Extreme fatigue showed on every face. Hollow eyes were underlined with deep, dark smudges of exhaustion. Few had found time to shave or change clothes during what must have been several straight days. If they had slept at all, they had clearly slept in their clothes. Their uniforms were wrinkled, stained with coffee. The combined odor of their unwashed bodies was nearly overwhelming, but they seemed not to be aware of it. Cigar smoke hung so heavily that the room appeared to be enveloped in fog.

McDaniel himself looked like some kind of cave man, nearly naked, scratched and bruised, his hair in wild disarray. The nearest generals gawked at him, and as more and more generals caught sight of him, the room grew ever more quiet.

One general moved slightly, and McDaniel saw Colonel Abbot Fay seated in the middle of the room, with a four-star general hulking over him, shaking his finger in the colonel's face. Colonel Fay caught sight of McDaniel.

"There he is!" Colonel Fay shouted, jumping to his feet. "That's the man I've been telling you about. That's my best man, just back from that reconnaissance. Thank God you got back in time. Come here, Son. Come here."

A path opened between McDaniel and Colonel Fay as the generals stepped aside. McDaniel squared his shoulders and marched across the room to stand in front of Colonel Fay.

He gave the colonel a smart salute and said, "Lance Corporal McDaniel reporting, Sir."

The four-star general said, "Lance Corporal?" and looked quizzically at Colonel Fay.

Colonel Fay swallowed hard. He smiled nervously at the general. He said, "He sometimes thinks he's still in the Marine Corps. He's a little bit mental." Colonel Fay raised his hand and patted the air in front of him, saying, "But it's okay. The man's got a super genius IQ. We'll just have to overlook anything a little bit strange because, well, a man with his rare abilities doesn't come without a certain price, but it's worth it to have him on our team. You'll see."

Colonel Fay squared his shoulders and said, "Private McDaniel, make your report."

McDaniel looked from general to general, all around the room, then looked at the eager but nervous face of Colonel Fay.

"Sir," McDaniel said. "I got a little bit sidetracked because I thought I'd stumbled into a secret, subterranean civilization of Indians, and they got me hooked on some kind of dope that wrung me out pretty good. I mean, it almost caused me to get married. They're right below us, Sir. A huge underground city. Lordy mercy, they've got subways and trains and theatres and schools and hospitals and women like you wouldn't believe. And their religion is ball play, Sir. Well, games theory, actually, but the ball players practically run the place. They spend all their time playing games, and studying games, and singing and dancing and carrying on like Columbus had never been born. But they were about to turn militant, Sir, pose a threat to the security of the United States. So I figured out a way to stop that. But then Sergeant Kelley showed up, from your staff, and he's one of them, Sir. He's the one who chased me down there after he killed Major Jameson. And I swear, when he killed Major Jameson, I thought he was an alien invader from outer space, because he can do this thing with his eyes that makes them glow in the dark. Anyway, it turns out he wasn't an alien invader at all, and they weren't even Indians down there. They were United States Marines. I figured out that they set this whole thing up to see if they could drive me crazy. Probably hired actors and whatnot to make it all seem real. I'll bet it's all part of the celebration for the two-hundredth anniversary of the Marine Corps. I should have seen that coming years ago. You guys are all Marines, too, aren't you? You guys have been planning this thing for years and years, haven't you? Ever since you started that psychological warfare stuff. That's what this is all about, isn't it? You didn't think I'd figure it out, did you?"

Again, McDaniel looked from general to general all around the room, but nobody said a word.

Colonel Fay sat down heavily in his chair, his face frozen in the half-smile of a man plummeting toward the earth who has just pulled the ripcord on his parachute and watched somebody's laundry come fluttering out.

The four-star general stepped forward, impatient, his hands on his hips. He fixed Colonel Fay with a withering stare and pointed his finger in his face. He said, "So this babbling idiot is your best man, huh? *This* is how you run your outfit? This is how *you* got us into this mess?"

Colonel Fay swallowed hard again. He gave McDaniel a pleading look. He said, "Son, you're my last hope. Don't do this to me now. Please, for the sake of the memory of your dear old daddy, did you talk to anyone who was not a secret Marine, or an underground Indian, or an alien invader?"

"Oh, sure," McDaniel said. "There was that reporter from the *Daily Oklahoman*. He was down there in the caves somewhere."

Half the generals spoke at once. "A *reporter*! From the *Daily Oklahoman*!" They were all on their feet, half of them already heading for the door.

The four-star general shouted, "I want every man for an immediate search of those caves. Get that reporter!"

The general turned to Colonel Fay and put his finger in his face again. "Everyone but you. This is it, Colonel. There's no more time. You stay here and think of something to tell the president. And it had better be good, or you'll be dialing long distance to hire somebody to try to find your ass!"

The generals flooded out the door, yelling orders, gathering up all the men. McDaniel stood quietly, watching Colonel Fay, seeing the colonel's eyes go unfocused as he stared into some interior distance. His face was so fallen that he might have been asleep.

All around the building, men were piling into jeeps and trucks and roaring away. Helicopters took off one after another until all of them were gone. Gradually, the noise died down until there was only silence. When it had been quiet and still for a long time, McDaniel began easing slowly toward the door. He inched across the floor, a half-step at a time, watching the colonel's face, until he could finally turn and reach for the doorknob.

CHAPTER 29

"That was brilliant, Son," the colonel said. "Simply brilliant."

McDaniel froze, his hand on the doorknob.

"Damn, that was quick thinking." Colonel Fay slapped his knee and stood up. "Whew, you had me going there for a minute."

Colonel Fay walked to McDaniel and put his arm around his shoulder. "There's no way I thought I'd ever have another moment alone to try to solve this problem, but you've gotten rid of all of them, and you've bought me some time. They told me you were a genius, but I guess I had to see it in action to believe it. Son, I should have confided in you from the very beginning. If anybody can figure this thing out, it's you. Now, together, we're going to figure out what to do."

"You guys are not Marines?" McDaniel said.

"Son, I'm sorry to disappoint you about that. Does it really matter anymore?"

McDaniel's brow wrinkled, and he began chewing his lower lip. He said, "Oh boy, oh boy, oh boy. I might have myself a real big Indian problem."

"Son," Colonel Fay said, "whatever kind of problem you've got, I'll make it my problem, and then it won't be a problem anymore. I guarantee it. Now, can you pull yourself together and help me figure out what to do?"

"What to do about what, Sir?"

"What to do about the president. He's breathing down our necks and we can't put him off any longer." The colonel looked McDaniel straight in the eye and heaved a big sigh. He said, "Son, I have lost the United States Army's secret military oil reserve."

"Lost it? How?"

"It's those goddamn Texans!" Colonel Fay said. "They infiltrated my staff with a cartographer, and he has tinkered with all of my maps."

"Those were Texans who were shooting at me, when your men first brought me here to the lodge. I heard them yelling at one another."

"That's right," Colonel Fay said. "Apparently their man, Denton, has double-crossed them, too. They're out for blood. They're camped down at the south end of the valley. So far we've been able to keep them out of this while we try to find Denton, but there's no more time for that. We might have to strike a deal with them somehow. I might need you to be my emissary."

"What's it all about?"

"Did you ever hear of the Teapot Dome scandal," Colonel Fay said, "in the early 1920s, during President Harding's administration?"

McDaniel shook his head.

"Big oil strike," Colonel Fay said, "up in Wyoming, early this century. The U.S. Congress set it aside as a military oil reserve. That didn't work. Goddamn Texans bribed government officials, even got a cabinet member sent to prison. They drilled slant-hole into the oil from adjacent land, draining it off. That convinced the next president, Calvin Coolidge, that no oil was safe as a military reserve if anybody knew about it.

"Then along comes a hotshot in the U.S. Geological Survey, testing some new kind of seismic device, and he stumbles upon a huge oil field, somewhere here in the United States. It turns out he had gone to school with Coolidge, knew him real well, and knew his concern about creating a workable military oil reserve. The two of them became the only people who knew its location, a secret they carried to their graves.

"Coolidge took a big map of the United States and picked 379 remote locations, scattered all across the continent, one of which was the location of the reserve. He gave that map to the Army and told them to make detailed separate maps for each one of those 379 sites, with special encoded information on the maps. Then he had the key to the code drawn up in such a way that the piece of paper could be cut in half in a zig-zag pattern and the code key would be revealed only when the pieces of paper were fitted together. He put half the code in a White House safe and gave the other half to the Army."

"And you lost the code?" McDaniel said.

"I wish it were that simple. We've got both pieces of the code key. But the encoding on the maps has been changed, rendering the key worthless."

"There's no other way to find the reserve?" McDaniel said.

"Yes. There's one other way. Coolidge had benchmarks implanted at each location. All of them show a sea gull, from below, in the last stage of flight before landing. Three hundred and seventy-eight of them are ordinary sea gulls, and the other one is the Great Salt Lake (this is "the place") subspecies. Coolidge figured it would take an ornithologist to tell the difference, and a Mormon to figure out the significance. But the bench mark locations were part of the encoding on the maps. We can't find the bench marks. We've got the entire United States Army looking for them, at all of those 379 sites." Colonel Fay looked at his watch. "As of half an hour ago we've found fourteen of them, all the wrong kind. They're hard to find."

"Can't you just tell the president what happened?" McDaniel said.

The colonel rolled his eyes. "The presidential election is riding on this. Haven't you seen the polls?"

McDaniel shook his head. "I don't even know who is president right now."

The colonel stared at McDaniel in disbelief. "His name is Gerald Ford, and he's about to get buried in a landslide by Jimmy Carter, the governor of Georgia. President Ford has decided to reveal to the nation that we have this secret military oil reserve, and, because of the dire national emergency created by the Arab oil embargo, that he is going to throw the reserve open to immediate domestic oil production. Industry officials will confirm to the American people that they can soon expect the price of gasoline to drop to about twenty cents a gallon, and that news will trounce Jimmy Carter in the election. Son, the key words here are 'dire national emergency.' You have to understand how Coolidge set this thing up. His greatest fear was that some day a Texan might become president, so he gave the Army explicit, written instructions about how each future president was to be dealt with. Each new president was to be informed of the existence of the reserve, but told sternly that its location could not be revealed except in time of war or dire national emergency. President Roosevelt didn't have to tap into the reserve during World War II because of the discovery of the East Texas Pool in the 1930s, and the construction of the Big Inch and the Little Inch pipelines from it to the East Coast. Everything was fine until Lyndon Johnson, a Texan, became president."

McDaniel said, "I served in Vietnam under his command."

"Yeah, well, if only you'd known."

"Known what?" McDaniel said.

"That when he took office, and I informed him of the existence of the oil reserve, and he demanded to know its location, and I refused to tell him, he sat back in his chair and said, 'So you have to have a war, do you?'

"We thought he couldn't possibly be serious. When he looked around the map and picked Vietnam, we didn't think the American people would ever go for that. It made no sense at all. But he dug in his heels, and the Army dug in its heels, and it became a nightmare.

"Every time he demanded that we tell him the location of the reserve, and we refused, he responded by pouring more troops into Vietnam. The Army, of course, was outraged, and we responded by thinking up ways to bungle the war, to make him look bad, but he responded by turning to the Air Force and starting a bombing campaign. The whole thing just kept escalating and escalating. God, the Russians and the Chinese must have been out of their minds trying to figure out what in the hell was going on. We couldn't even tell the Air Force, or the Navy, or the Marines what was happening.

"The Army tried everything we could think of to try to turn American public opinion against Johnson. We transported reporters into every pocket of the war, let them see exactly what was happening, the things we dreamed up to make us look bad, things that somebody would have to see to believe, and that got the war on the network news every night. We tried to bait the environmentalists by using Agent Orange. We planted agitators on college campuses to stir up the students. We swallowed our pride and tried to appear as bungling in our management of the war as possible. Believe me, that wasn't easy for proud men to do, but we got creative about it, especially in dreaming up ways to lower the morale of the troops. We knew that disheartened returning troops could be some of our strongest allies. Eventually, we were able to overwhelm Johnson with it all, to threaten his chances of reelection, and it nearly brought the nation to a standstill, but all we got for our effort was a showdown with Johnson that still makes me tremble to think about.

"The showdown came during the winter of 1968, after the Tet Offensive. We thought we had him on the ropes, but he called us into his office and gave us an ultimatum. Tell him the location of the oil reserve within three days, or he would use nuclear weapons in Vietnam, would drop one on Hanoi.

"That could have started World War III, but we didn't dare think he might be bluffing, not after the hell he had already put us through. When we got back to the Pentagon, the generals locked me in a closet and said I would stay there until I thought of a way to get us out of that mess. Son, I came up with one hell of a gamble. I told the generals, look, we know that the reserve is somewhere in the lower forty-eight states because that's where all of the 379 sites are located, but Johnson doesn't know that. It's the middle of winter. Why not tell him the reserve is way up in Alaska, way up on the North Slope of Alaska? It'll be months before his oil cronies can get in there to begin checking it out. If we can stall him until November, maybe he'll get defeated in the election. That's what we did, but to make it look like we were playing it straight with him, we demanded that as soon as he'd confirmed the location of the oil reserve, he'd give up the presidency. He agreed."

Colonel Fay shook his head. "Never underestimate Texans. Within weeks they confirmed to Johnson that they had indeed found a huge oil field on the North Slope. We couldn't believe our good luck, and true to his word, Johnson went on TV and stunned the nation by announcing that he would not seek reelection and wouldn't even accept renomination.

"The whole thing left us so shaken, we didn't even tell President Nixon about the secret reserve. Now they're blaming me for telling President Ford about it. I convinced the generals that we had to start telling the presidents about it again, that if Congress ever found out about the reserve, and found out that we weren't telling the presidents about it, we'd all go to jail."

The colonel had been talking nonstop, but now he paused and looked at McDaniel closely. He said, "Son, the history of this whole thing is a no-win situation for everyone. If the story ever came out, it would tear the nation apart. You can see, can't you, that this is something that can never come to light?"

What McDaniel could see, plain as day, was a dangerously deranged man who was apparently still wielding some kind of awesome power within the United States Army. Whatever Colonel Fay was involved in, the stress had pushed him over the edge, into a world of fantasy. If the colonel actually believed the things he had just said, then he might be truly dangerous. McDaniel wasted not a moment debating what his responsibility might be. Fate had revealed to him a threat to the security of the nation. He would just have to be careful how he dealt with this psycho. He said, "Sir, I can see the problem clearly, and I am prepared to bring to the task whatever might be required to get the job done."

The colonel's face brightened. He said, "When this is over, I'll see that you are commissioned an officer in the United States Army. You'll have a top job on my staff. I don't know what we'll be doing, but it won't be this. I am finally going to get rid of this oil reserve, one way or another."

"How long have you been in charge of it?" McDaniel said.

"Since 1945, since shortly after the war ended. God, I thought I was on my way. I thought I would be a brigadier general in no time, and would retire with at least two stars, maybe three or four. I was the youngest colonel in the United States Army, but that's what got me into this mess. I didn't know that when Coolidge set up the secret reserve, he specified that the caretaker should be a colonel, so that he would be inconspicuous within the Army. He also specified that it be a young colonel, so that he might hold the job for a long time, and that would cut down on the number of people involved. There have been only two of us. The first one held the position from the midtwenties, when it was created, until he retired at the end of the war. If I'd known that the job offered no possibility of promotion, I wouldn't have taken it. Son, I've had this job for thirty-one years. All I want to do is get rid of it so I can be promoted to general, and then retire as a general."

The colonel's face took on a strained look. He said, "I deserve being a general. I've had to contend with nothing but generals for thirty-one years. They come and go, but I'm always here. They retire and start living the good life, but I'm always stuck with this same damn job. And no matter how good a job I do at it, there is nothing I can do to work my way up even one grade higher in rank."

The colonel's eyes had taken on a dangerous look. It frightened McDaniel enough that he tried to change the subject. "Sir," he said, "are all those 379 sites in a place pretty much like this one, a remote valley like the McGee Valley?"

"At one time most of them were. Now a lot of them are buried underwater."

"Underwater?"

"Yes. You see, I had to figure out some way to discourage oil exploration near these sites. And I had a great tool for doing that, the U.S. Army Corps of Engineers. It was easy to maneuver congressmen into seeking appropriations for dams because they are big projects for their districts. We hired lobbyists to do that, without anyone involved having any idea why we would want it done or that the Army was behind it. Hell, most of the big dams that have been built since World War II have been built specifically to put as many of these sites as I could get underwater. I've already got the wheels in motion to put the McGee Valley underwater. Lake Powell, I invented that. I've buried half the Missouri River Valley underwater. The Snake River, the Arkansas, the Brazos. You name it, and

I've put a dam on it. That has greatly reduced my work. Once I get a site underwater, all I have to worry about is oil exploration around its periphery."

"What do you do about that?" McDaniel said.

"I drill a dry hole, or at least a fake dry hole," Colonel Fay said. "Nothing will throw cold water on a Texan faster than a dry hole. I've drilled thousands of them. I've formed more oil exploration companies than anyone in the world. I've formed hundreds of them, and every last one of them has gone broke. When I first came up with the idea, I thought it was the perfect answer to the problem. Just form fake companies to go out and drill fake dry holes. At first we drilled them right on the sites. Then we drilled them in ever widening patterns all around the sites. I just didn't see what the consequence would be."

"What do you mean?" McDaniel said.

"What I mean is," Colonel Fay said, looking a little nervous, "I guess I didn't look at the big picture. My God, Son, we drilled so many fake dry holes during the '50s and '60s that the American oil exploration industry just gave up on trying to find oil in the United States. All anybody was drilling over here were dry holes. They didn't know they were my fake dry holes. They all went overseas. I thought that was good at first, because if they're not drilling for oil over here, they're not posing a threat to the reserve. But this Arab oil embargo has revealed to everyone how critically dependent we've become on foreign oil. If the Congress ever finds out what I've been doing, they'll say that I am single-handedly responsible for us becoming dependent on foreign oil." The colonel shuddered. "Son, can you see how complicated this mess has become? If it ever goes public, I'll be the scapegoat. I'll either get court-martialed or go to prison, or both. I'll never make general. I'll never get to retire as a general. I just want to relax and be a general. I've been a colonel for thirty-one years! I want to be a general!"

"Oh, yes," McDaniel said, "you will be a general."

"How?"

"I've got it all figured out," McDaniel said. "Just come right over here and sit down and let me explain it to you."

McDaniel walked the colonel back to the chair in the middle of the room. The colonel sat down, watching McDaniel's face eagerly. He said, "How will we do it?"

"President Ford doesn't know any details about the oil reserve, right? He doesn't know about the 379 locations, or the Army maps, or anything, right?"

"That's right," Colonel Fay said.

"He doesn't know that the East Texas Pool, the one discovered in the 1930s, is not one of the sites, right?"

"That's right," Colonel Fay said.

"Then you can tell President Ford that when you put the two halves of the code key together, it turned out to be the East Texas Pool."

"That's right! I could do that!"

"That was before you took over guarding the reserve. You can tell him that the secret didn't even last more than a decade before the Texans found out about it and got the oil."

"By God, this might work!" Colonel Fay said. "But what do we do about the real goddamn Texans. They're camped downriver. They won't buy this crap, and if we don't get them appeased somehow they're going to end up getting this whole thing blown wide open."

"You make a deal with them," McDaniel said. "You let them have the oil reserve, if they can find it. You're going to have to give it up, anyway. The president will think it's already gone, so the Army will have to act like it's gone. You tell the Texans that the Army has decided that the country needs it to be put into commercial production, but the Army can't find it, thanks to the Texans. They're the ones who've lost it. Let them track down Denton or do whatever they have to do to find it. That's their problem. It's not your problem anymore."

"Not my problem anymore," Colonel Fay said, with a wistful, dreamy look on his face. "Oh, Son, you are a genius. Now, you've got to go get the Texans and bring them here. I need you to be my emissary on this. The generals will be back here before long, and I want to have this thing set up when they get back. You can do that for me, can't you? I'm counting on you, Son."

"You can count on me to do the right thing," McDaniel said. "And when it's over, they'll promote you to general. You'll be General Fay."

"General Fay," said the colonel. "General Fay." His eyes glazed over, and he stared into some far, far distance.

"And there'll be no need to retire," McDaniel said, crouching down beside the colonel's chair, face to face with him. "You can enjoy being a general for awhile. I'll bet the Army will be so grateful to you for solving this problem that they'll make you an inspector general. Just think, at Army bases all over the country, at one base after another, men will get up at 4:30 in the morning to stand all day in the hot sun for an inspection that doesn't even begin until the middle of the afternoon. And all because General Fay is coming. General Fay. General Fay. General Fay."

McDaniel waved his hand in front of the colonel's face, but the colonel, mouth open, eyes wide, had fallen into a catatonic trance.

McDaniel stood up, but he could barely walk. He shook with nervous tension, with the certain knowledge that at this moment he was taking his life into his own hands, that Colonel Abbot Fay was not a man to be crossed.

On unsteady legs, McDaniel made his way to a far corner of the room. He got down on his knees and clasped his hands together in front of his face. He lifted his eyes toward the heavens and said, "Dear God in Heaven, this is your humble servant, P. P. McDaniel, speaking. Lord, I don't know much, but one thing I do know, even if there is nothing more at stake than my mortal life. . ." McDaniel pointed at Colonel Abbot Fay and said, "*That* son of a bitch is crazy!"

CHAPTER 30

McDaniel left the main lodge and hurried to the next building, looking for a telephone, praying that he could do what had to be done before Colonel Fay recovered his composure. The next building looked a lot like the main lodge, only smaller. Once inside the door, McDaniel saw that it, too, had a large plate-glass window on the far wall. Cigar smoke still clouded that room, too, like a thick gray mist. On a long table in the middle of the room was a row of telephones.

McDaniel grabbed the first phone, dialed the operator and got her to ring the sheriff's office. Sheriff Grady answered the phone.

Hurriedly, McDaniel explained that he was at Katie Lake Lodge, all alone with a dangerously insane Army colonel who needed to be put away, and that it had to be done quickly before the colonel's men returned to the lodge.

McDaniel knew it would be a waste of breath to try telling the sheriff any of the things the colonel had said, so he told him that something awful was about to happen to a newspaper reporter, and that probably a whole lot of Texans were going to get killed, all because this colonel had gone psycho. But Sheriff Grady didn't seem concerned.

"Now, McDaniel," the sheriff said. "I'm sure the Army knows what it's doing. That's supposed to be a top-secret operation going on up there, some kind of training maneuvers. They'll be gone in a few days, and then everything will be back to normal."

McDaniel pleaded with the sheriff, trying to convince him of the grave threat to the security of the nation if this colonel were not dealt with immediately, but the more he pleaded, the more he heard only patient, calm reassurance from the sheriff.

"But you don't understand!" McDaniel said. "They're shooting at civilians up here!"

"Now, McDaniel," the sheriff said, "you're just upset because somebody has come busting into your backyard, and you don't like it."

"Oh no," McDaniel said. "I'm not upset about that. That's not what this is about. I'm not acting for myself. In fact, I stand to lose a lot by doing what I'm doing. It's costing me something to get this guy taken care of. This colonel has promised to make me a commissioned officer in the United States Army."

There was a long pause on the other end of the line. The sheriff said, "You stay right there. I better come check this out."

Relief washed over McDaniel as he hung up the phone. He began pacing back and forth across the room. Endlessly, he paced back and forth, as time ticked away, until it occurred to him that as soon as this problem with the colonel had been taken care of, he was going to have to get far away from there, find someplace to go, and that he could be doing something about that right now.

He grabbed the telephone. From the operator he got the number for Billy's Gas 'em Up, in Whitewater, Colorado. But before he could dial the number, he heard the sound of vehicles squealing to a stop in front of the building.

A moment later, Sheriff Grady came through the door.

"He's in there!" McDaniel said, pointing to the main lodge. "But be careful. He's a dangerous man."

The sheriff nodded and pulled his gun. Behind the sheriff, McDaniel could see two ambulance attendants, dressed all in white. One of them carried a strait jacket. The sheriff and the two attendants hurried toward the main lodge.

Quickly, McDaniel dialed Billy's Gas 'em Up. He soon had his old buddy on the phone.

"Billy, listen," McDaniel said. "I've not got much time. I'm in a real complex situation, and I've sort of worn out my welcome down here. If I hitchhike up to your place, can you set me up with a grubstake and take me up to the Kannah Creek Valley? I think I can disappear pretty good up there."

"Well, sure, Injun," Billy said. "I'll get you set up somewhere. But nobody can get anywhere near Kannah Creek. The Army's got it blocked off."

"The Army!"

"Yeah, the United States Army," Billy said. "I'll tell you what, you'd have to see it to believe it. We got this colonel up here, says he comes from Fitzsimmons Army Hospital over in Denver, got what looks to be a whole battalion of WAC nurses, running around with shovels, digging holes all over the place, acting like somebody's about to start World War III."

McDaniel dropped the phone. He froze, staring at the door. From the thundering roar coming out of the main lodge, he knew that Colonel Abbot Fay had snapped out of his trance.

McDaniel was still frozen, staring at the door, when Colonel Fay came bursting through it, followed by Sheriff Grady and the two ambulance attendants.

The colonel pointed at McDaniel. "That man is a traitor to the United States of America. Shoot him!"

Sheriff Grady wasn't about to shoot anybody, though he still had his gun out. He said, "Now Colonel, let's calm down and see if we can't get to the bottom of this."

Colonel Fay grabbed the gun out of Sheriff Grady's hand. He said, "I said shoot the son of a bitch! And that's just what I mean." The colonel pointed the gun at McDaniel. Confined within the lodge, the shots sounded like a cannon going off, one explosion after another in rapid succession.

McDaniel hit the plate-glass window with bullets flying all around him. They shattered the glass a split second before he leaped through the window frame.

Sheriff Grady grabbed the gun and twisted it out of the colonel's hand, as the ambulance attendants wrestled the colonel to the floor and into the strait jacket.

Thrashing wildly on the floor, Colonel Fay gathered a big lungful of air. His voice boomed. "You can't run away from me, McDaniel!

There's not a hole deep enough where you can hide! I'll track you down if it's the last thing I ever do! Do you hear me, McDaniel?"

Colonel Abbot Fay was not wasting his breath. Dodging rocks and bushes and trees, streaking through the woods at an ever accelerating pace, Patrick Pushmataha McDaniel heard every word the colonel said.